SEERS AND SIBYLS

SEERS AND SIBYLS

An Anthology Edited by
MJ Pankey

Edited and formatted by MJ Pankey
www.museandquill.com

Cover illustration and design by Elizabeth Leggett.
www.archwayportico.com

First Edition: September 2023

ISBN (paperback): 978-1-957537-77-1
ISBN (ebook): 978-1-957537-76-4
Library of Congress Control Number: 2023944633

BRIGIDS GATE PRESS
Bucyrus, Kansas
www.brigidsgatepress.com

Printed in the United States of America

INTRODUCTION

By S.D. Vassallo

"The beast shall emerge from the depths and plunder and ravage this land until the fields are barren and the people are scattered and nothing lives within. Desolate will the land be, and desolate it will stay, until the coming of he whose hand is marked with seven stars. Then shall there be battle, and the sons of the line of Arvek will vanquish the beast and restore the land to its former glory."
—from SONGS OF THE TWILIGHT KING, author unknown

Who doesn't love a prophecy? Folklore, mythology, fairytales, and literature in general are full of seers, prophets, and oracles who pronounce their tidings of the future.

- The Oracle of Delphi foretold the Trojan War, prophesied that Laius' son would grow up to kill his father and marry his mother, the death of Alexander the Great, and gave many other visions of the future to those who asked.
- The Book of Revelation is full of prophecies concerning the so-called End Times.
- Norse Mythology contains the tale of Ragnarok, which will bring the end of the world and the beginning of a new one.
- Nostradamus wrote down many prophecies, and his predictions are still hotly debated today.
- In The Lord of the Rings by J.R.R. Tolkien, the Witch-King of Angmar is told that he will not die at the hand of any man.

And so on.

Prophecies capture and hold our attention, and make us wonder exactly what those visions mean, and how they will come to pass. Often, there's a heavy dose of irony involved. Laius, upon hearing the words of the Oracle, sent his son away to be killed. The shepherd who took his son away could not bear to do the deed and gave the boy to be adopted. Of course, years later, the son, Oedipus, returned and brought about his father's death and married his mother, fulfilling the prophecy. If Laius had never heard the prophecy, likely his son would have grown up under his tutelage and in time, would have received the throne from his father and then would have found and married his true love, and not his mother.

Prophecies. Tricky things indeed.

Those who speak forth prophecies are sometimes revered and honored, like the Oracle of Delphi. At other times, they are feared and hated, and scorned for the words they speak. Cassandra, anyone?

Loved or hated, though, the words of those seers occupy our thoughts, and fuel many a passionate argument. Nostradamus has been dead for almost 470 years, and we still discuss and argue about his prophecies. The Book of Revelation was written close to 2,000 years ago, and every sect of Christianity still talks about the prophecies therein and what they mean.

Hmm… the debates will continue until the day without a dawn, when the herald bearing a ruby crown shall sound his horn, and all the kingdoms of the world shall fall; all the old prophecies shall be forgotten, and a new tale shall be told.

There. How's that for a vision of the future?

This anthology of stories that you are about to read is full of tales of seers, oracles, prophets, and sibyls. We hope you enjoy them, and may they entertain you with their tales of those who utter their visions of the future.

S.D. Vassallo
From the vast prairies and big skies of the Midwest
13 August 2023

FOREWORD

Every culture around the world has a history of belief in the supernatural, a mythology that shaped their current existence in some way, and may continue to shape their present and future. In our modern world, this realm is often dominated by Anglo-European influence: Greek and Norse mythology especially. These will always hold a dear place in my heart, and when Brigids Gate approached me to edit Seers and Sibyls, I had thought these well-known pantheons would be almost exclusive to these pages. But as submissions rolled in, I was in awe of all the forgotten voices that cried out from every corner of the world, desperate for their stories to be told too: those of India, of Israel, Nigeria, China, and the Choctaw in North America.

Within these pages, one will find thrilling reimaginings of renowned legends, those of Cassandra, Pythia; new stories pulled from the world of Norse and Celtic culture; and some tales inspired by historical legends, such as the founding of Britain and the turmoil of middle-Egypt during the reign of Akhenaten. But I hope one will also encounter the *unfamiliar* within—new threads of intrigue and mystery and be as amazed and delighted as I was to discover them for the first time.

The diversity in this volume is not all-inclusive. To capture all the voices of the world would be an impossible venture and encompass such a vast number of pages that no one book could ever hold them. But I hope this small sampling will provide readers a roadmap to new adventures, to new worlds and discoveries of peoples and pantheons that exist, past and present, on the planet we all share, and unify humankind in common curiosity to explore the unknown without fear or judgment.

MJ Pankey
13 June 2023

EDITOR'S NOTE

The stories in this anthology contain adult themes and explicit content, some of higher severity and intensity than others, which I feel may be triggering to some readers (myself included). A detailed list of triggers is provided on page 277 under Content Warnings, but to make this anthology as accessible as possible for *all* readers, **the stories with more severe or intense content are marked with (CW) in the Contents**. I hope this designation allows readers more freedom and confidence to explore this exquisite volume of tales without fear or apprehension, so each story may be enjoyed to its fullest.

CONTENTS

SEERS AND SIBYLS

THE ORACLE OF PLUM HARBOR

A Tale from North America

By David Marino

PLUM HARBOR HAS A population of 15,612 people.

Grace Morgan knows every single one.

In the mornings, she can be found on her porch on Second Street, doing the new crossword puzzle in the *Plum Harbor Courier*. At lunch, you can find her at the local diner, *The Brave Sheep*, where she eats one of her seven meals on a fixed weekly schedule. In the afternoon, you can find her back at home, inside, watching old episodes of *Murder, She Wrote* or *Columbo*, depending on her mood. At night, she sits down for a meal in her kitchen, always making enough to share.

Her only deviation from this schedule is during the holidays, where Grace takes a break to make her Christmas lasagna and have her three boys, their three wives, and her seven grandkids over to exchange gifts, or when the high school teams in basketball or football have a home game. Then you can find Grace shouting "Go Pumas!" in her scarlet sweater, waving a big flag.

And, with the exception of holidays, Grace is almost always accompanied by someone else from Plum Harbor's population of 15,612. That's why her schedule is so well known throughout town. If the townsfolk need to see her, the Oracle of Plum Harbor, it's only polite to work around her schedule.

It is not uncommon on a day like today, November 22nd, to find a small line outside Grace's enclosed porch. Right now, Grace is sitting in her rocking chair, the heat blasting full force, a pen in her hand, trying to solve 9 across (seven letters, to limit or reduce). Next to her is Katie Smears, a sophomore field hockey player who came by to ask if her relationship with chess team captain Gregory Felt will last.

Ah, Katie, Katie, Katie. Grace spins her mental rolodex, organized by ethnicity, down to the eighth, then last name, then generation, then sex, to identify a person. Once she does, she pulls out their card in her mind, and there it is, their entire future. In Katie's case, this includes Grace herself informing Katie that Gregory will not be the man she marries. Katie will call Grace a liar, then three weeks later, Gregory will break up with Katie for Allison, that Italian slut. Katie will spend the month of December weeping, then will rebound with lower-classman Reginald Sutton. They will date for two years, four months, and six days, after which Katie will break up with him before going to college on the path to dentistry.

Then, like a good citizen of their fair town, Katie will return to Plum Harbor and get a job with her aunt, the current town dentist. One year after that, Reginald Sutton will sit in her chair, not knowing Katie is going to be working there. They will reminisce about old times, then go on a date to *Sam's Bar*, a dour place whose existence Grace tolerates because it facilitates meetings like this. Katie and Reginald will live happily ever after on Lakeview Drive until they both die of smoke inhalation in their seventies.

Grace only answers Katie's initial question, as, unless asked, most people do not want to be informed of their deaths. Katie calls Grace a liar, as predicted, then huffs and puffs out the door, letting the cold air in. Grace's hand shivers as she writes in *Stunted* into 9 across. Hmm, that gives her a T for 5 down.

Next comes a frequent visitor of hers, Fred Clauson. A father of three, Fred is very worried that his middle daughter, Gretel, isn't going to do well on her math test today. That Fred named his seventeen-year-old daughter Gretel is unfortunate, such a deviant name, outside the ordinary. But Grace didn't receive her oracle powers until two years ago and thus couldn't whisper into Fred's ear that she should have a more ordinary name, like Katherine or Jill.

But yes, young Gretel will fail today's math test with a 45, tied to her inability to factor polynomials. And no matter how many times Grace has told Fred that Gretel's failures in high school will have little impact on her successful career reporting for the *Plum Harbor Courier*, Fred still worries.

Grace never worries. It's easy not to worry when you know everyone's future, generations down the line. Grace even knows her own future. Five more years and two months as Oracle, then, two weeks before her death from pneumonia, she'll pass her powers onto Carol Shackling, just as Roberta Evanson passed her powers onto Grace shortly after her husband died from esophageal cancer. Plum Harbor always has an oracle, and that's why Plum Harbor has flourished so well. It's a role Grace is more than happy to step into. Such wonderful celebrations and festivals, a main street lined with flowers in the spring, a steady birthrate. Yes, Plum Harbor is flourishing, and all without needing anything from outside the town. Without needing anything from the people Grace cannot see.

On her crossword, 5 down is *Fester*, such a vulgar word. She thinks about having a talk with Tony down at the courier about the crossword's answers, but a quick scan through her rolodex indicates Tony will not listen to her complaints, so Grace sighs and reaches out for a sip of her iced tea.

She drops her drink, the glass's fall softened by the carpet. Because in the special section of her rolodex, where all the most important citizens of Plum Harbor's future lie, under English (5/8ths), all signs of Bridget Long, Marching Band Drum Major, just disappeared.

***

As Grace drives her Oldsmobile Cutlass to Plum Harbor High School, she grips the brown leather steering wheel tight. What could have happened to Bridget? Bridget is integral. Married to her high school sweetheart Chad Ryans next fall at nineteen, pregnant by twenty, child at twenty-one, cashier at the grocery store at twenty-two, deli slicer operator at twenty-four, grocery store manager at thirty-five, but more important than all of that is her role as the head of the PTA at forty. She'll be pretty and charming, and thus can sway parents away from teaching any of that new history they'll try to force down Plum Harbor's throats. It's silly, is what it is. When did it become bad to have settled the west? There is nothing wrong with watching *Gunsmoke*, and Grace is simply too old to hear counter arguments. Leave those for younger people, people like Bridget, who will help keep Plum Harbor secure long after Grace is gone.

That's what the young people never understand. Grace is building things to last, like the beautiful lakefront jetty her husband had helped fund. Sure, three kids will drown in the lake because of that jetty in the next twenty years, but so many other romantic dates and new generations will be conceived in those canoes, figuratively and literally, that it is worth the sacrifice.

Grace pulls into a spot in the school's parking lot, enters the hallways just as the fourth period bell rings. She knows the way to Principal Kelly's office by heart, frequently needing to scare a student straight about their future or, on occasion, to see which possible teachers would be the best fits for the community, to prevent them from bringing in deviant ideas. All the students politely step aside of Grace's ambling walk, more than a few looking up from their blasted smartphones to wish her a good morning. See, that's one difference between Plum Harbor and the rest of the country. Here, children know to respect their elders.

A simple wave gets Grace past Principal Kelly's secretary, and a single knock plus an "It's Grace," gets her through his door. She sits across from the principal in a stiff chair. Great for forcing students upright, not as kind on her back and knees. Grace sees her own upcoming knee surgery next year and isn't looking forward to it.

"We need to talk about Bridget Long," Grace says. "Be a dear and bring her here, would you?"

Principal Kelly makes the command, then also orders his secretary to get Grace a cup of tea. An old tip from Roberta after Grace took over oracle duties. People see the teacup and assume, correctly, that the person holding it has wisdom. Having a teacup in her hands always bends the future a little more…correct. Grace shoos away Principal Kelly after once again assuring him his daughter will come back to Plum Harbor from that faraway city school unscathed. Let the children fly away. There's nothing wrong with them seeing a bit of the world if it teaches them where they belong is right back at home.

There's a knock on the door. "Come in, dear," Grace says. Now, to be careful. Futures are on the line here, Bridget's and Plum Harbor's both. Once Bridget's card comes back, white and shining, then all will be well. Grace just has to make sure that happens.

Bridget enters, more metal than girl. Jesus, what is with the children these days and piercings? The lord's own son got pierced thrice with nails, and any hussy treats that as a record to break! And the shredded sweatshirt Bridget sports, spots of her pale skin visible around the shoulders and above her waist. It is a good thing Bridget will clean up and get rid of that horrible black dye she puts in her hair, ruining what should be pretty and blonde.

If Grace can get her back on track, that is. "Sit, please," Grace says, and Bridget does, playing with one of the chains dangling from her earlobe. "Do you know who I am?"

"Everyone knows who you are, Mrs. Morgan," Bridget says. "Is something wrong with my future?"

Yes, but Grace can't tell her that. Not yet. There's always a risk with the truth. "Do you have any new interests, Bridget?" Grace asks. Let her ponder that, let her reveal where this newfound wanderlust comes from. If Bridget has disappeared completely from Grace's Rolodex, it means she's planning on leaving and not returning.

Bridget shrugs, unable or unwilling to meet Grace's eye, fiddling with something in her pocket.

"You used to be such a nice girl," Grace says. "Someone who would never do such a thing."

"Is the raven tattoo I got that bad?" Bridget asks. "Or is this about Chad?"

"Not Chad," Grace says, because, while it takes some effort, she can still pull Bridget's previous future, even if the index card in her rolodex yellows, the ink on it fading fast. "Perhaps something else. Some activity with Chad, or with your friends." There's no chance this one isn't on drugs. Marijuana, most likely. The state has gone mad with all this legalization legislation. Prohibition is the only thing that works for something mind altering like that.

Bridget shrugs, too much shoulder visible. How could the marching band possibly take her seriously? "Everyone does it, Mrs. Morgan. I can get you some, if you want?" She pulls out a metal lighter from a pocket in her jeans. "Can even set you up with some…apparatus?"

Grace smiles, takes a sip of tea, shakes her head. Perhaps it would be good for Grace's hip, but best not to take the risk. At least Bridget is generous in her debauchery. "You must promise me you'll quit that stuff," Grace says. "It's the best way to get you back on track. If you don't, well…"

They sit in silence for a time, Grace letting the implication hang in the air. Always better to let the girl's imagination do the thinking for her. Especially with one so active.

Bridget sighs. "Okay, I'll stop. If weed's gonna send me to hell or whatever." She puts away her lighter. "Anything else?"

Hmm. Bridget's card is still missing. Her smoking habit isn't the cause of her problem.

"You've not been honest with me, Bridget," Grace says. "You've been planning something else, haven't you?"

Another quick shrug. "I mean, I'm going to Spain for Thanksgiving tomorrow. Is that what you mean?"

"And who gave you that idea?" Grace asks. What type of parents would allow their daughter to take such risks? Who knows what European men or worse, women, might do to their young girl?

"My aunt called yesterday. From California?" Bridget scratches her neck, looks away, too guilty to even look Grace in the eye. "She was going to go by herself but thought it would be more fun for me to come along. Plus my parents said I could go because I did well in classes this semester."

"Spain, is that all?" Grace puts her teacup on her plate. "Well, you simply must not go. You know what they say about the Spanish, after all."

"I…don't?" Bridget picks at one of the holes in her jeans, looks up at Grace. "Why can't I go?"

Ah, a tricky one, Bridget is. "I don't think your life will go the way you or God would want if you visit Spain."

"But like…why, though?"

"Must you make me say it?" Grace doesn't like being vulgar. Not if she doesn't have to be. The world outside Plum Harbor is a brutal place, and any kindness she can spare her people's ears, she will.

"Yes. I think you have to tell me why, Mrs. Morgan." Bridget leans forward, arms on her knees. Such a masculine pose. Who is teaching these youths today? She'll need to have a talk with the principal about acceptable body language, about resetting the dress code to something appropriate.

"Fine." Grace sighs, takes a sip of her earl grey. Her fingers shake as she brings it to her throat. "In Spain, you'll go to a bar. You're eighteen, right? You'll get a beer, something local, and a pretty boy with bright eyes will compliment your hair. The two of you will conversate, he'll touch your arm, you'll like it, and you'll say yes to the second beer he offers, which you will gulp down eagerly. Not knowing that it contains a knockout drug. Your vision will shrink, you'll get woozy, and your pretty boy will tell the whole bar he'll make sure you make it back to your hotel. Instead, he'll take you back to his apartment, where he'll strip you naked and rape you. Later that night, he'll invite some friends over to do the same, and you'll wake up sobbing, hurt in ways you've never imagined, violated, wishing you had never gone across the sea to that devil's place."

Bridget's eyes moisten. She lets out a sniffle. Grace does not like having to tell the young people how the world is. But someone has to if their parents will not, if this blasted school will not.

"Now," Grace says, "I assume all of this Spain nonsense is finished?"

And before Bridget nods, her card is back in the rolodex, pristine. PTA president and, oh, that's new. A nice, new capstone to Bridget's life. At age eighty-six, far after Grace's death, far after Bridget has shed her piercings and had her tattoos laser removed, she'll become Plum Harbor's twenty-third Oracle.

Grace stands, puts her hand on Bridget's shoulder, and starts to walk out.

"Which city?" Bridget says as that rolodex card starts to yellow in Grace's head, starts to fade away.

"What?" Grace says, clutching the doorknob.

"Which city does that happen in?" Bridget asks from behind her.

"No one makes me sit back down, young lady," Grace says. "I believe I've made myself perfectly clear."

"No, you haven't." Bridget stands, a wisp of a thing, all skin and bone and eating disorder. "Which city does that happen in?"

"Madrid," Grace says, fingers shaking. "It happens in Madrid."

"Huh," Bridget taps her chin. "I wasn't planning on going to Madrid? Okay. Definitely won't go to Madrid."

What? Who does this child think she is? What right does she have to disobey? Lord, give Grace the patience to deal with the young ones.

"You see, honey," Grace turns slowly, so as to not disrupt her hip. "It'll happen everywhere you go. You don't understand how dangerous the world is out there."

"So, like, Seville, Valencia, Barcelona, Lisbon," Bridget says. "Everywhere I go in Spain, I'm going to get raped?"

"Well, no, sweetie, of course not. In Seville and that second one, merely a horrid car crash. In Barcelona, stabbed in an alley, and Lisbon, well. You don't want to know what happens if you go to Lisbon. What the Spanish will do to you there…"

That will shut her up. That will get this rebellious child back on track and get her card to solidify.

Bridget squints. "Lisbon's in Portugal, Mrs. Morgan," Bridget says, right as her rolodex card disappears again. "Goodbye."

***

Grace holds her breath the whole drive home. People need her. This town needs her. And without Bridget in place, without a secure future…

When she gets back to her home, she locks the door, ignoring the bratty middle schoolers who want to know how they did on their social studies tests. She sits in her recliner and thinks, picking children at random.

Benjamin Smith, seven-eighths German, currently seventeen. His rolodex card yellowing, two years at the local community college, two more years at a state university, then out of her sight.

Paula Giordano, half Estonian, currently fifteen, rolodex a complete blank.

Kayla Schifter, half Jewish, currently sixteen, does stay. She joins her father's construction company, and they build so many houses, absolutely ruining the charm of main street and the pastoral serenity of Twelfth Street. And the houses are cheap too, affordable so new riff-raff can come into town, new names waiting to jump into Grace's rolodex. Bridget can stop this. Grace is still going to die in five years, two months, and fourteen days, but someone has to fight for this town. Someone has to hold this world together against the insanity of the outside, against the cesspit America is becoming.

And the problem is there's no way for Grace to know how to get Bridget back on track. She'll know when it has worked, when everything clicks back in the rolodex and Bridget's card comes up pristine and laminated in Grace's mind.

SEERS AND SIBYLS – *North America*

So Grace reaches over to her rotary phone and calls the police.

***

Two hours later, Bridget is brought before Grace on the porch. Officer Williams orders her out of the police car. Grace had been specific. No cuffs, just scare her a bit. Just to show off Grace's power. A phone call from Grace, the right whispered prophecy, and she can make anyone do what she wants. Anyone.

"Sit, dearie," Grace says, and Bridget obeys, the gaps in her ripped jeans not nearly covering enough for the cold. "Would you like some banana bread?"

"No," Bridget grumbles. "Can't believe you had me arrested! Marijuana isn't even illegal anymore."

She's right, of course. Another travesty the governor enacted, another example of the forces Grace must shore Plum Harbor against. "It is illegal to use under twenty-one, Bridget. Now, my efforts to scare you straight have failed, so let me try something else. Let me tell you how special you are."

Bridget pushes her jet black bangs behind her ears. "If this going to be about how God made my body a temple, let me just say—"

Grace lets out a single laugh. "Not quite. Oracles can see their own death, you know. But they can also see past it. Do you know how Oracles get their powers?"

A typical teen shrug. Grace's own children had been no different.

"In the woods," Grace says. "There is a plum tree. Different than all the others. This one grows a single, large fruit marked with red leaves. And whoever eats that fruit, who bites through its red shell for its sweet flesh, making sure every bit of juice goes down her throat, gets to See."

Bridget's blue eyes widen. "The future."

"Yes," Grace says. "Only for Plum Harbor. And there can only be one Oracle at a time, the fruit only grows right before the previous

10

Oracle is about to die. So, nine oracles from now, at the age of eighty-six, you'll become the Oracle of Plum Harbor. But you'll be crucial here for years before that. You'll protect this town from so much. New development from outsiders, from crime and gang violence, all before you even become like me. I have seen your future, Bridget, and it is bright and important, and it is here. You can have it all if you simply don't go to Spain."

In her mind's eye, Grace rifles through her rolodex, lingering on the place where Bridget Long's card should re-appear. That brilliant white card starts to materialize again, faded memory replaced with a crisp, clear image, like when Grace puts on her glasses while reading the *Courier*.

Bridget pulls her lighter from her pocket, flicking the lid back and forth, back and forth. She rubs her eyes, saying "I have to think about it," before she steps off the porch. Grace shouts for her to wait, Bridget's parents should be called to pick her up, but the teenager is already walking home, yelling "I have to think about it!" as she walks away.

The card in Grace's rolodex yellows once again.

***

Later that night, Grace is washing her dishes at the sink, scrubbing off the remnants of her tuna casserole from the pan. Sure, she could use the dishwasher, but she just can't trust the modern appliances. They don't get all the crust and grime out like steel wool and elbow grease can.

It's when she puts the pan in her drying rack that she smells the smoke, feels the heat. Where is it coming from? She looks around, checks the stove, nothing. The toaster, nothing. The microwave, nothing. She can see clearly, her house is fine, her alarm light a steady green, her smoke detectors silent. But there's a fire. Somewhere, something is burning. Burning down Plum Harbor. Burning down the town she's put her life into. Burning down all her hard work!

One of her rolodex cards burns away.

No. No no no. Another card scorched. Another. The fire isn't here, it's in the woods, in a tree that will one day grow a single plum that her successor will eat.

Except when she checks the cards she still has, all their futures end. Right now.

Every rolodex card, every vision she had so carefully organized and catalogued catches fire, a red burning curve that sweeps across every guaranteed future. She holds onto the memories of as many she can, all her favorite futures. Katie Smears, Gretel Clauson, her sons and daughters and grandsons and granddaughters.

Every single one up in smoke.

As Grace goes back to her sink, scrubbing dishes long since clean, she knows two things before everyone else. That they will find ashes, all the magic up in smoke. And that fucking Bridget Long is on a flight to Spain right now.

*****

The next day, after a lovely Thanksgiving with turkey and gravy and stuffing, just like it all should be, Fred Clauson returns to Grace's porch, just like he always has. This time, he's worried about Gretel's chemistry test. He rambles about how she has to calculate moles, which, Grace knows enough to know is some math thing. Gretel will do poorly on this test because Gretel is a fool. And Grace will once again remind Fred Clauson that everything with his daughter will work out. That she'll be the star reporter for the *Plum Harbor Courier* once she graduates high school.

This is despite Grace now having no idea at all what the future will hold. But people still come, and she'll still tell them their futures. Stability is her duty to provide. So what if her stability is a lie? Grace has a job to do for the next five years, two months, and thirteen days.

DAVID MARINO

After that, Plum Harbor can go to the dogs.

13

TIRESIAS' LIFE

A Tale from Ancient Greece

By Beth O'Brien

MY LIFE IS DECIDED by others,
changed and changed back,
on the whim of a will
that is not my own,

but I say nothing.

I navigate the world
reading the lines of my skin
like an experimental map
I was never meant to decipher
but must still follow.

(Power would rather that sense
eludes those it controls)

My life settles their debate
then starts one anew,
blinded by the anger of a god
who is not used to hearing "no".
Balanced by the guilt of a god
who is only too used to it.

They decide my fate and how I must feel,
never thinking that my life
was always that—

mine.

BEARER OF THE GODS

A Tale from the World

By Victoria Brun

THREE WEEKS AFTER TERRA decided that she no longer believed in the gods, she was chosen to be the Bearer of the Gods for the upcoming Rain Walk.

There was no dramatic moment, no epiphany, no tragedy that caused her to lose her faith. Instead, her faith seeped away, dying like a chokenut tree struck by blight. Leaf by leaf. Branch by branch. Until the trunk cracked. The tree remained standing, but no one would argue that there was any life left in it.

Blight could spread, hopping from tree to tree. It could take out a whole grove, a whole orchard.

That, she thought, is why nonbelievers were so feared. If caught, they would be culled like a sick tree. Cut down before the blight could spread. That is why she could speak no doubts. Ask no questions. That is why she continued to attend daily prayer, paid her weekly tithe of grain, said all the right words in every ritual and prayer, and curled her fingers into all the right signs—all exactly as she did before.

The only change was in her heart, where she felt nothing but a dull anger. During prayer, she listened to the voices around her and wondered whether they were all just going through the motions, or whether they still had faith. Were they liars, hypocrites, or fools?

And this decision by the priests, this decision to have *her* become Bearer of the Gods, only strengthened her belief—her certainty—that there were no gods. Otherwise, why would the priests choose her, a secret non-believer, for this task?

Being chosen was an honor, she was told. But that didn't stop her mother from crying that night, once the ceremony and celebrations were over.

It was a grand celebration, with music, songs, and dancing—although Terra didn't dance. She only sat, watched, forced a smile for those wishing her well, and made the sign of thanks to those who praised her.

People from the surrounding villages attended as well. Even people from distant Ziana came, including their famous priest Kierar. Terra had never seen him before and was horrified to discover that he was as scarred as the rumors said.

He approached her at the celebration, making the sign for peace. She mimicked the gesture and tried not to stare at the scars ruining his face. Two years ago, pagan bandits had sacked Ziana, beaten him, and mockingly carved the sign of the goddess Yu into his face. People said the gods saved his life. Terra thought if the gods truly cared for him, they could have intervened a little earlier.

"Are you well, sister?" he asked as he stood in front of her, leaning heavily on his staff for support.

She was caught off guard by the inquiry, not expecting to be addressed. None of the other priests had spoken to her. She was a symbol now, a living statue—not a person who had feelings and exchanged pleasantries.

"Yes, I am well," she said stiffly.

"I hope you know, sister," he said, his voice barely audible over the choir and the drums, "that just because you have been chosen does not mean you do not have a choice."

She frowned, having no idea what he meant. She wasn't able to ask either, as one of the other priests stepped forward and ushered him away. With a feeling of unease, she turned her attention back to the festivities happening around her.

It was a lavish celebration. The only thing missing was festival food and drink. Both were limited, seeing as it had not rained in several moons, and the fields were turning to kindling. Only the priests feasted as it was part of their rituals. She was supposed to fast in preparation. She had no appetite anyway.

"I should have arranged your marriage earlier," her mother whispered once they were back home and alone. Her father was not there, having gone north seeking work a moon prior. She stroked Terra's hair. "Oh, forgive me, child."

"Why?" Terra snapped, a sudden flood of anger pouring out from an unknown well. "Why apologize? You think the gods and goddesses will not protect me?" It was the closest she'd ever come to asking whether her mother believed.

"No," her mother said, her face contorted in horror. She grabbed Terra's shoulder. "No, child, no. Of course not. I know you are beloved by the gods, and they will protect you.

This speech would have been more convincing had her mother not immediately started sobbing at its conclusion.

Terra supposed this meant that her mother must not believe. If her mother truly believed, she would not cry. However, her anger seeped away as her mother clung to her. It was replaced with fear. It crept down her spine and pooled in her stomach like ice.

She did not sleep that night. She lay awake. A moon ago, she would have prayed, but now she had nothing to do but stare at the dark ceiling.

Her mother rose before the sun and fixed honey cakes for breakfast, but Terra couldn't eat them despite her mother's begging. She knew that she would need the sustenance, but her stomach couldn't handle it, as full as ice as it was.

Her mother walked with her to the temple in solemn silence. The air was crisp, and Terra pulled her cloak tighter around herself, although she knew the cold was a good thing. If anything would save her, it would be the cold.

The priests greeted her with wine still on their breath. Their full faces were carefully painted white with the signs of their chosen god or goddess in red. They were garbed in long tunics of fine orange linen embroidered with the signs of the gods in red thread. They were garbed, she thought, in hypocrisy.

She noted Kierar among them. He stood out as the only one who hadn't painted his face, strangely forsaking this opportunity to hide his scars. But if the signs were all that mattered, she supposed he had no need for paint. He made a sign of peace to her, but she pretended not to see it. She was worried he would speak to her again. She was nervous enough without his baffling words.

The temple maids gave her a new dress, one with white beads weaved into the sleeves and red embroidery down the front. She had never worn anything so beautiful before. She hoped she didn't die in it. The maids painted her face with the sign of Mu.

All too soon, she found herself standing outside the temple. Multiple villages worth of people crowded the square, watching her, desperately hoping she succeeded—not, she thought darkly, because they necessarily thought it would bring the rains, but because if she failed their daughter or their sister might be chosen next.

Drums beat steadily as a large copper bowl was placed in front of her by a nervous temple servant who promptly fled. Terra's heart raced as she peered down into the bowl.

A cowled rattlesnake lay coiled at the bottom. It had a black head and dark saddle pattern running down across its keeled scales. It was only about three feet long, but it had a thick body, and one bite from it would kill a large man before the sun set. At the moment, the snake was still, unmoving. She hoped it was dead, but she knew it was just cold. As the sun rose, the serpent would slither to life.

She raised her eyes to the top of the Aster Mountain, to the point where she must carry the snake. It was a trek of at least two hours. Once there, the priests would invoke the goddess Mu, goddess of life and of rain, and ask for her to bring the rains to the parched earth.

The snake was a demonstration of faith, a test. If the goddess kept the serpent from striking her, the Bearer of the Gods, it meant she was worthy, and the goddess would grant the community's request.

The holy stories said the goddess Mu was once bitten by a cowled rattlesnake. The venom did not kill her, but it stole her immortality, and she became the first human, seeding the human race. Thus, the cowled rattlesnake was said to represent the difference between gods and humans.

It was never explained how a single woman started the human race. Or how a snake bit a goddess. No one ever asked, at least within Terra's hearing. To question it was to be a heretic—a tree with blight. There was, at least, an elaborate tale that explained how Mu regained her godhood, although depending on who was telling it, the story varied.

The priests started chanting, and she picked up the bowl as gently as she could, keeping her fingers well below the vessel's rim. The snake within did not stir. After a moment of hesitation, she raised the bowl high and placed it on her head, mimicking the painting on the temple wall and how the last Bearer carried her bowl in Terra's vague memories.

Terra had seen a Rain Walk only once before. It had been when she was too young to understand, perhaps three or four—but she knew the stories. It had started on a warm day, and the first Bearer had been bitten within minutes. Afterward, the Bearer had put the snake back in the bowl and tried to keep walking, insisting it had been a dry bite, but she did not make it up the mountain. The snake was caught, and a new girl was chosen, and the walk was performed again the next day. Eventually, the fifth Bearer of the Gods, a woman named Kunna, made it, and she was revered for her piety. She married well and later died in childbirth.

The bowl was not heavy, yet it was also the heaviest thing Tera had ever carried. Her heart pounded as she rested it on her head. The fact that the snake was now out of sight doused her with a mix of relief and greater terror.

And then she walked, following the priest. The priests moved slowly. Painfully slowly. Although the oldest and feeblest among them, including Kierar, went by the road in a cart drawn by donkeys.

Terra wanted to run up the mountain, but she walked with slow, careful steps. The drummers walked behind, keeping a steady, ominous beat. Behind them walked the congregation, talking, praying, singing. She was sure her mother was among them, but she did not dare turn to look.

She kept imagining that she felt the snake slithering out of the bowl, over her head, and down her neck, but it was merely her imagination playing a cruel trick on her. The snake stayed in the bowl, barely moving.

She silently prayed that it was dead before she remembered she didn't believe in prayer anymore, but then she figured that she had nothing to lose and finished her prayer. Strangely, this brought her some comfort, or at least distraction.

She studied the priests in front of her, their well-fed bodies struggling over the terrain, and some of her fear twisted into anger. Anger at the priests and their fake gods and all the fools who believed in them. Anger at herself for playing along, although she knew she couldn't have refused.

Still, she imagined herself flinging the snake away. What would they do if she threw the bowl at one of the priests? She could say the gods compelled her to do that—whispered in her ears that she must throw the snake. If they believe their nonsense stories, surely, they could believe that.

But she did not throw the snake.

Instead, she kept walking. It was easier to conform, less scary, somehow, to carry the snake than throw it.

Her arms ached from being over her head for so long. Her fingers went numb. They tingled. She became scared that she might drop the bowl. The path also became more onerous with roots and rocks impeding her way.

But worst of all was the sun. The sun crept out, peering down at her between gaps in the canopy, and sweat trickled down her neck.

The snake stirred in the bowl. She could feel it shifting around, and it was not her imagination this time. She listened for the sound of its rattle, straining to hear over the drums, but she heard nothing.

She found herself praying again, begging every god and goddess to save her.

She heard someone gasp behind her, and she was certain the snake was sliding down toward her neck, but she kept walking, and the weight of the snake stayed in the bowl.

She prayed and walked. Prayed and walked. It felt like she walked for days.

Her back and neck burned. Her fingers felt swollen. Her shoulders seared, but she didn't change position. She moved nothing but her legs and willed the snake to do the same.

She neared the top. She couldn't see it, but she could tell that the slope had changed, that she was close. She saw some of the priests who had ridden ahead in the cart standing along the side of the trail, waiting for her. She was close.

She felt a flicker of hope, tinged with desperation, and then she felt the snake move. She felt it slide over the rim of the bowl. Looking down, she could see its shadow, its long head extending from her own as it stretched away from the bowl.

Her heart pounded, but she kept walking, her eyes fixed on that terrifying shadow. The snake's shadow dipped down, merging with that of her own. Terror flooded her veins like venom. Something touched her shoulder. She didn't look at it. She kept her eyes on her shadow, which now showed no snake, and she kept walking. One foot, then the other. She felt it slide onto her shoulder and then down her front. She froze as it dropped to the ground in front of her.

The serpent coiled at her feet, its body wound tight, and its head raised and facing her, ready to strike.

She froze. She didn't know what to do. She could only stare. She couldn't move. She couldn't even lower the bowl from her head. She couldn't breathe.

There was a clamor behind her, yelling, although she couldn't make out the words. The pounding blood in her ears distorted all sounds.

Distantly, she was aware that the priests had stopped and turned to face her.

"You must put it back in the bowl," one called to her, his deep voice cutting through the noise.

"Back in the bowl," she repeated as she stared at the snake coiled within striking distance of her foot. She dared not move. It buzzed its tail, and its namesake rattling sound cut through the air. She couldn't move.

She was so focused on the snake that she didn't even notice one of the priests approaching her until he was nearly at her side. It was Kierar, stepping forward with a pronounced limp and leaning heavily on his stick. When he reached her, he slowly lowered himself until he was kneeling beside the snake.

The snake twisted toward him, but to Terra's shock, it didn't strike as he reached out and gently scooped one hand under its belly. He lifted the snake into the air. The snake hung there, as if too shocked by the event to strike.

"If you'd lower your bowl, sister," he said, his voice strained.

Overcoming her shock, she lowered the bowl, and he deposited the snake into it.

"Thank you," she said, or tried to. She wasn't sure the words made it past her trembling lips.

He smiled at her, which pulled at his scars, and, using his stick, he leveraged himself back to his feet with obvious difficulty.

She took that as her cue to go. She didn't put the bowl back on her head. Instead, she held it at arm's length and walked as fast as she could. The priests, when she caught up to them with the outstretched bowl, picked up their pace. It seemed they had no wish to be close to the snake.

The snake peered over the rim at her, its tongue flicking, and her breath caught, but it did not leave the bowl. It stayed within and beat its rattle against the side, causing a loud, metallic din.

Finally, she reached the stone altar. She placed the bowl on the edge and staggered back as cheers erupted around her.

She had no recollection of what happened at the following ceremony. She knew the priests petitioned for the intervention of the goddess Mu, and her hands automatically made all the right signs, and her lips chanted along with the familiar words, but her mind was not there.

When the ceremony finally ended, they walked back down the mountain with the priests leading again, striding forward like soldiers returning from a victory. She walked behind, carrying the bowl, but not the snake. The snake had been sacrificed on the altar—and she felt strangely sad about that. It hadn't bitten her after all. It seemed unfair to kill it.

She noticed that Kierar didn't join the old priests in the cart, but instead walked back down. He quickly fell behind the others, limping as he was, and they did not slow for him. She caught up to him and slowed her pace to match his.

He smiled at her and made the sign for peace. She returned the sign.

They walked in silence for several minutes, although it was far from silent. Behind them, the villagers were celebrating, and their collective voices became a din of noise, but they remained several paces behind Terra, respectful of the customs. Even her mother hung back, although Terra had spotted her in the crowd crying tears of joy.

Finally, Kierar spoke. "I used to capture snakes—not the venomous ones, the harmless ones, mind you—often during my boyhood. I learned that if I do not show fear or act like a predator, most will not bite."

Her eyes widened, and she stared at him. The implication of this comment sounded almost blasphemous. "Was it not your faith in the gods that saved you?" she asked.

"I believe in the gods, sister," he said, as if he could read her underlying thoughts. "I know they are there. But do I believe they bend to the whims of mortals and stop serpents from biting when we command them to? No. I do not."

"But," she whispered, unable to turn her thoughts into words as she struggled with this comment. It seemed to shatter through all her beliefs. She had never considered this before. She had thought there were either gods who behaved as the stories said or there were none at all. This new possibility made her feel unsteady.

"Have I upset you?" he asked. "It was not my intent."

"No, you haven't upset me," she said. "I…" she trailed off.

"I ask that you forgive my brazenness," he said. "I've discovered that having the sign of a goddess carved into my face has given me some liberties to speak in a way that others may not—although not enough to talk anyone out of these… activities." He waved a hand vaguely at the trail before them.

"I see," was all she said. She felt the sudden urge to tell him she did not believe in the gods at all, but she lacked the courage. She held her tongue and turned his words over in her head, trying to make sense of them.

He halted abruptly as they came upon a particularly steep stretch of trail. He studied it for a moment before continuing, carefully placing his stick before taking each step. She realized how easily and almost carelessly she moved down the trail in contrast. She barely glanced at the path, confident her legs and feet could handle the rocks and roots. She didn't even recall coming up this steep section when carrying the snake. They walked in silence for some time as she worked up the courage to ask another question.

Finally, she asked, "But what of the rain? If you do not believe the gods would save me from the snake, do you not believe it will rain?"

"I know it will rain, sister."

Terra frowned. "How?"

"How? Because it rains. That is what the sky does. It has not rained in moons, true, but that has happened before, and it always rains eventually."

"But it might not rain soon," Terra said.

He inclined his head. "It's possible," he said. "But it will rain."

This didn't make much sense to Terra. "But people are suffering. Why do the gods not do something?"

"Ah, but they have. If the wealthy opened their coffers and storehouses and gave them to the poor, would there be enough for everyone?"

Terra blinked. "I suppose."

"Then the drought is not the problem. The problem is human greed. The gods give us all we need, but it is up to us to do right with their gifts."

"But," she started, but then again fell short. He was a priest. She shouldn't question him, even if he was odd. Besides, she had so many questions pushing to escape her lips she was scared to voice any, afraid they would all come tumbling out.

"Yes?" he prompted.

"You've made me more confused than ever," she admitted. She still didn't believe in his gods, but she no longer had the certainty of disbelief either. She recalled how praying had brought her some comfort when she carried the snake. She missed her certainty.

His eyes shimmered with amusement. "Although I imagine that is frustrating, I believe that is a good thing. We're all on our own journeys of faith, sister. If you want to know where yours leads, you'll have to walk it with open eyes."

A drop of water landed on her thumb. Startled, she stared at it for a moment before she looked up and saw that between the leaves the sky had darkened to a gray overcast. As lost in their conversation as she had been, she hadn't noticed the sun slipping away and the winds changing.

And then it started to rain.

BLOOD, TEARS, RAIN

A Tale from Medieval India

By Rose Strickman

IT WAS THE THIRD year of the drought.

The wind lifted veils of dust through the empty, lifeless corridors of the forest. The trees were dry as matchwood, tindery branches snapping at the slightest movement. Herds of desiccated antelope slipped silently through the brush, searching in vain for water. The monkeys' shouts echoed no longer through the trees. Tigers panted and grew thin in the unrelenting heat, and birds fell silent. Even the insects died away in the dusty aridity.

And the lake, once a great blue jewel at the edge of the forest, now gave up its long-held secret. The dry winds siphoned dust into the muddy puddle at the bottom of the lakebed, but nothing could hide the macabre discovery.

"They're skeletons," whispered Nila, standing with Jahan at the lake's edge. "Great long skeletons at the bottom of the lake, all covered with mud…people's skeletons…but they're snakes too."

"Naga," said Jahan. He didn't look at the lakebed or the skeletons within it. But even if he had, he would have seen nothing. His clouded brown eyes, blind from birth, stared into the distance. "They're Naga."

Naga. The same word was being repeated around the edge of the lakebed, among all the gaunt, ragged, dust-caked people who had trailed out of the village to the dried-up lake. *Naga.* Gods of rain and storm, rivers and lakes. Half-human, half-serpent, all divine.

"They can't be," Nila said. "Naga are gods. They don't die."

"Maybe not," said Jahan. "But they can wither away over time. As these have."

Nila did not ask him how he knew. She had lived with Jahan's insight all her life and had learned to trust it, however irrational or unfounded it might seem. "So…those skeletons are still *alive?*" Her flesh crawled.

"In a sense," said Jahan after a pause.

Nila shuddered and looked away. Other villagers were making their way down the sloping lakebed, approaching the muddy puddle and the skeletons lying within it. One young man had reached the first skeleton and was tugging the skull out of the mud. "Maybe we shouldn't be disturbing them then. Maybe we should leave them alone."

"It won't do any harm to take them out," said Jahan unexpectedly. "And I'd like to touch them for myself."

"We can't let *you* touch them, Blind Jahan!" Padma, the headman's daughter and Jahan's cousin, looked over from her knot of friends, eyes bright with spite. "Who knows what would happen if a witch like you touched one of the divine serpents?" Her friends laughed nastily.

"Leave him alone." It slipped out before Nila could stop it.

"Oh!" Padma sneered, and her friends tittered. "Are you in *love*, Nila? Going to marry the blind orphan? Well, why not? No one *else* will have you!"

The other girls all burst into jeering laughs. Nila's face burned, but her mouth stayed steady, a grim line, and no tears pricked her eyes. Of course not; Nila didn't cry. She'd never cried, not once in all her life. Not when her parents died, not when her brother left her, not when she'd had to go work as a maidservant in the headman's house. *Nila's eyes are as dry as drought,* villagers said, and it was by now an established truth.

The girls had already forgotten Nila and Jahan, returning to their speculations. "It's a sign," said one excitedly, scanning the hard, bare blue sky. "The Naga will bring the rain back!"

All around the lakeshore, others were echoing these sentiments, pointing out the long serpentine tails of the skeletons and peering in hope at the empty sky, the blazing-white sun. Nila wanted to point out the logical fallacy of this—if living Naga really did have power over rain and water, surely their bare *skeletons* meant the exact opposite—

but she knew no one would listen, especially not Padma or her friends.

So Nila and Jahan remained silent and watched as the villagers extracted the skeletons from the mud and hauled them painstakingly up the slope, sliding and jostling on hastily-rigged litters. There were a few heart-stopping slips on the way up, but each skeleton was still intact when they reached the top of the slope, straightened out for viewing as the villagers crowded near. Nila couldn't see much, peering over others' shoulders, but what she saw brought an unexpected shudder. There was something horrible and unnatural about seeing human torsos, skulls and arms, with no hips or legs, instead transitioning smoothly into long tails, lined with rows of ribs. And… "Are those *fangs*?" They gleamed, curving and translucent in the skulls' human jaws.

"That's right," cackled old Parvati, grinning toothlessly and bent almost double over her cane. "There's nothing more deadly than Naga venom!"

Shivering, Nila turned away. "Jahan—" She broke off, seeing how still Jahan had become, his head cocked, as though listening for something. "Jahan?"

"They're coming." His voice came out flat and calm.

"Who's coming?"

Jahan smiled, blind eyes blank on the distance. "People who will be most interested in what our lake has produced. Rumors are already flying."

Nila scanned the horizon. There was nothing but dust plains and dried-out woods on the other side of barren rice paddies. Still, she fought back another shiver and looked away.

Everyone else was so hopeful, their spirits raised by their amazing discovery. Why, then, did Nila feel nothing but foreboding?

***

It was five days before the Raja's entourage arrived.

29

SEERS AND SIBYLS – *Medieval India*

Nila, sweeping the wide veranda of the headman's house, was among the first to see them, the glint of their armor and the fluttering of their flags approaching across the wavering, dusty distance. She paused, squinting into the heat-haze as they materialized further into view; men with swords, mounted on horses with tasseled bridles, other men carrying banners, gold glowing, steel shining, a great canopy held over a man who rode a black horse, his turban gleaming with gold.

Nila dropped her broom and ran. The household was already in an uproar, the women running about shrieking. The headman, Aravind, hastily pulled on his embroidered red *kurta* while splashing precious water in his face and simultaneously trying to trim his beard and straighten his best turban. In the midst of the chaos, Nila found Jahan, sitting ignored as always.

"Jahan! The Raja is coming!"

"I know." Jahan alone was still, cane in his lap, face calm. "Help me up, Nila."

Nila pulled him to his feet, and they made their way out into the village street, where the villagers were already assembling, men adjusting turbans and women patting down saris, everyone trying frantically to clear away any trash and pen up the animals. This visit hadn't been announced, and no one was prepared. Nila spotted Padma smoothing back her hair, inspecting her reflection in a polished cooking pan, and fought the urge to laugh. Did Padma really think the Raja would spare any thought for one skinny village girl on a surprise visit, at such a time?

The Raja's party thundered into the village in flashes of gold and clouds of dust, and everyone fell to their knees, even Aravind. "Hail, Raja Aadesh!"

Raja Aadesh, gold turban gleaming, pulled his horse to a halt, foam dangling from its mouth, flanks shining with sweat. The blood-red jewel in his aigrette winked as he looked down on Aravind. "Rise," he commanded, and the villagers climbed to their feet. "Fear not," Aadesh continued in his deep, calm voice. "I come in peace to verify rumors of your discovery in the dried-out lake."

Aravind bowed deeply. "The Naga skeletons, Raja?"

"The same." Aadesh dismounted, swinging easily to the ground. "I have brought my priest, Darpan, to inspect them and determine what they portend."

A skinny man, with the white robe and the wild beard of a priest, stepped forward, bowing and nodding. "I will enact rituals of divination over the bones," he said in a scratchy old-bird voice. "I will determine the Nagas' will, to end this accursed drought!"

Nila rolled her eyes, but an excited cheer ran through the rest of the village, a shower of applause. Aravind bowed again. "Then please follow me, Raja, Your Holiness. I will show you where the skeletons lie."

He turned and led Aadesh and Darpan, with a contingent of royal guards, out of the village. The other villagers followed at a distance, Jahan holding onto Nila's arm and tapping his way forward with his cane.

The skeletons had been laid in neat rows under a rough canopy of thorny dried branches not far from the lake. Fragments of sunlight and shadow played over the white bones. Aravind led the Raja and his priest among the Naga. Nila, Jahan still clinging to her arm, hung back with the crowd. Despite herself, a spark of desperate hope lit in her breast as she watched Aadesh and Darpan inspect the skeletons, occasionally kneeling down for a closer look.

At last, Aadesh called a halt. He turned to Darpan. "Well?"

Darpan reached into a canteen slung around his waist. Singing out a chant, he cast a few drops of bright, clear water onto a nearby ribcage.

Everyone cried out. Nila reeled back, heart pounding.

"What?" Jahan clutched her arm. "What just happened?"

"Darpan…the priest, he…he chanted and threw water on a skeleton and it…it moved!" Nila wanted to deny the evidence of her own eyes, but there was no doubt about it; when the water touched them, the ribs *twitched*. "You were right, Jahan…they're still alive!"

SEERS AND SIBYLS – *Medieval India*

"The signs are clear!" Darpan scratched out. "These are truly skeletons of the divine serpents!"

The villagers and even the soldiers all started cheering again, the soldiers shaking their swords. Aravind looked like he wanted to fall to his knees again, but Aadesh simply said, "Good." He stared at Darpan with hard black eyes. "Is there any chance they can bring back the rain?"

"A very good chance, my Raja!" Darpan bobbed around, looking more like a mad stork than ever. "Let me spend the night here with their remains. I will pray to the gods, I will enact divination—and I will discover what is needed to bring the Naga back to life and restore the rain!"

At this the villagers all burst out cheering yet again—all except Jahan, who remained still and silent, sightless eyes unreadable, and Nila, who clung to him and watched while the priest preened, there among the bones of gods.

***

"Why are you so unhappy, Nila?" Jahan knelt beside Nila where she crouched, cleaning supper dishes in the yard. Overhead, the stars shone bright in the empty sky.

"I am not unhappy." Nila gritted her teeth as she scrubbed sand across another bowl. She hated cleaning the dishes this way—first scraping off all the crumbs and stains, then rubbing sand across the utensils, bloodying her fingers and tearing her nails—but there was simply not enough water for proper washing.

"So it would seem," said Jahan, sounding amused. "Come on, what's the matter? The end of the drought may be near."

Nila stopped scrubbing and looked at him hard, although he couldn't see her. "Do you really believe that pretentious old priest?" she demanded in a harsh whisper. She would not have dared speak so to anyone else. The village was even now buzzing with hope and speculation while Darpan spent the night out with the skeletons. So many people had snuck out to spy on the priest, meditating and chanting by his fire, that the Raja had posted guards to keep spectators away and give Darpan some peace.

"He knew how to test that they were real Naga skeletons, didn't he?" said Jahan. "You can't deny his expertise just because you don't like him."

"Yeah, well…" Nila scrubbed at the bowl again, her movements sharp with anger. "Where are the gods as the land dries up and famine looms? Where was that priest when my parents died? Who cast rituals of meditation and divination when my brother ran off, leaving me alone?" Her voice rose in an agonized note. She reined it back in with a sharp breath, surprised by her own anger.

Jahan was silent a moment. "My parents are dead too, Nila," he said quietly. "And at least you've got eyes."

Nila took a deep breath. "I know. I'm sorry. It's just…" She shook her head. "Why do people have to suffer so? Why do we always have to lose so much? Why does no one we love stay with us?" Her voice ached with pain, and she knew that if she'd been anyone else, anyone but Nila the Dry-Eyed, she would have been weeping by now.

Jahan laid a hand on her shoulder, warm and comforting. "Maybe better times are coming, Nila. Let's hear what the priest has to say in the morning."

***

When the sun crested the horizon, orange and fiery over the blighted land, all the villagers and the Raja's entourage gathered at the skeletons.

Darpan, still in meditation position, finished his final prayers before climbing stiffly to his feet. He turned to face the crowd and bowed to Aadesh. "My Raja," he said. "The gods have given me the answer to our dilemma."

An excited murmur rose, all the villagers shifting, and even Nila half-stepped forward. Jahan, however, stayed still, leaning on his cane.

"What?" Raja Aadesh's voice trembled with urgency and excitement. "What is it?"

"The Naga skeletons hold the key to our salvation." Darpan gestured at the skeletons, lying quiescent in the dust. "But not in their current form. They must be wetted with the lifeblood of one who has lived in darkness all his life, and then with the tears of one who has lost all light."

Another murmur rose at this, more confused and uneasy. "What does that mean?" Aadesh frowned.

Darpan shook his head. "That is all the answer the gods gave me, my Raja."

"Darkness," Aravind murmured now. "One who has lived in darkness…" Then, with a slow, sick finality, he turned to face his family. To face Jahan.

An icy sweat broke out on Nila's face, on her hands, as all eyes turned to the boy who stood so still beside her. She clutched his arm. A scream tried to tear itself from her throat, but no sound emerged.

"My cousin's son was born blind." Aravind's voice was regretful, but cold with intent. "He has lived in darkness all his life and never seen the light."

"Yes." Darpan's eyes lit as he took in Jahan. "Yes, he is the one."

"NO!"

Even Nila was surprised at the scream that ripped from her. She clutched Jahan, threw her arms around him. The world blurred and swirled around her as she held him tight. "No, no, you can't do this—"

The Raja gave orders she couldn't make out through her ongoing shrieks, and hands seized Nila, dragging her back kicking and screaming. She fought against the grip of the soldiers, trying to break away, to reach Jahan, even as more of the Raja's soldiers surrounded him and led him away, glaring sunlight reflecting on their swords. Nila screamed at the light, at the pain, at the horror. She screamed and screamed and screamed.

But not once did Jahan scream while he was marched away.

***

Nila looked up from her blank, despairing reverie when the shed door opened. She blinked and winced against the flood of light.

"I brought dinner," Padma said in a small voice.

Nila took the bowl of millet and cup of water without a word. She felt like something was broken deep inside her. After Jahan had been taken away, the soldiers had handed her over to Aravind, who had dragged her back to his compound, still screaming hysterically, to lock her in one of the storage sheds in the yard. Nila had pounded on the walls, yelling, until her voice gave out and she fell to the ground. Her eyes burned, but still she shed no tears. Still dry as the drought, even now. All day she'd been left there, sinking deeper into helpless misery, while the noise of the household went on outside and she fancied she could hear the rest of the village making ready for the ceremony of blood, tears, and bone—and Jahan's murder.

Now Padma stood in the doorway, watching Nila shovel millet into her starving mouth. "You…you really love him, don't you?" Nila had never heard Padma sound so soft, so tentative.

"Yes," said Nila. There was no point denying it now, not even to Padma, not even to herself. "What's it to you?" She was past caring whether she was rude.

Padma looked away, worrying her lip between her teeth. "They say they're going to do it tonight," she said quietly. "It's the full moon tonight. When it rises, they'll…they'll cut his throat and let his blood spill on the skeletons."

"And what about the other half?" Nila demanded with a hard laugh. "The tears of one who has lost all light? Have they thought of that?"

Padma's eyes sought Nila's pleadingly. "They're desperate, Nila. We're all desperate."

"So you're just going to let them kill your cousin? Butcher him like a goat?" Nila's voice rose in agony. She reined it in with another angry laugh. "Well, of course you are. You never cared for Jahan—you never cared for anyone but yourself—you spent all your time bullying him!"

"I bullied him," Padma agreed. "I did it because I could, because I always got away with it. I was a mean, small person. But that doesn't mean I don't care for him." She looked at Nila pleadingly again. "If it brings back the rain—"

"Why are you begging forgiveness from *me*? I'm just the maidservant." Nila waved her hand around the hot, stuffy shed. "An imprisoned maidservant now. Why don't you go off and dance with your friends and hope your cousin's murder brings back the water?"

A long silence passed. Padma stood in the doorway, hands clenching and unclenching.

"I'll open the door after dark." Her voice was so quiet Nila could barely hear her. "They've got Jahan locked in the old rice barn at the edge of town."

Nila looked up, blinking. Hope, fragile and disbelieving, crystalized within her. "Padma..."

"I don't want Jahan to die." Padma stared hard at the ground. "I'll unlock the door. It's up to you to get to the barn afterward."

"There'll be guards—"

"They're not watching the back door, the women's entrance. I've already checked." Padma gave Nila a miserable smile. "Get Jahan out, Nila. And then go far away from here."

"Thank you." Nila's voice was a tight-squeezed whisper. "Thank you, Padma."

"Just don't get caught." Padma took back the empty millet bowl and water cup and stepped back outside. The door closed and the bolt locked, leaving Nila in shadow again, heart thudding, mouth drier than the lakebed.

***

The day crawled by, a small eternity. Finally, as the light waned and darkness filled the shed, the door creaked open once more.

Nila, roused from a fitful half-sleep, launched to her feet, heart pounding. Padma stepped in, a barely discernable shadow in the night. "Here," breathed Padma, shoving a basket into Nila's hands. "For your journey."

"Thank you, Padma," Nila said as she stepped outside into the dim starlight.

"Like I said, don't get caught." Briefly, Padma's hand squeezed Nila's arm. "I'm sorry, Nila." Her voice was barely audible.

"For what?"

"For everything. Good luck, Nila." Padma slipped away.

Nila waited until Padma ghosted away back into the house. Then she darted across the starlit yard to the old wooden gate.

The gate gave a creak as she opened it. She flinched, expecting pursuers to come pouring out of the house, but no one roused. She slipped out through the gate and into the village street, keeping to the shadows, a shadow herself.

She knew exactly where the barn was; she and the other women had hulled rice there in happier years, following better harvests. Nila ghosted through the village, along its border. The Raja and his entourage had set up camp near the barn. The camp was mostly dark, but a few fires stayed lit, men laughing. Merry at the prospect of Jahan's death. Nila's jaw clenched and she hurried on.

The moon was cresting the sky, soaring up from behind the forest, when she reached the barn. Just as Padma had said, the soldiers hadn't bothered to watch the women's entrance, hidden at the back of the building. Moving as quietly as she could, Nila pulled back the bolt and slipped inside.

"Jahan...?" Her whisper echoed in the empty building. "Jahan, where are you?"

A stir came. "Nila…?"

Nila's heart lit. She hurried forward, to the dim shape that stirred, moaning, from the floor. "Jahan, are you all right?"

"Nila, what are you doing here?" His fingers ran over her face, verifying her identity. "If they catch you, they'll kill you."

"You think I care?" Nila's voice broke. "I'm getting you out of here."

Jahan paused. "Nila—"

"Don't tell me you believe that evil nonsense about your blood bringing back the rain!"

"Nila, please, listen, it won't make any difference—"

"It will to me!" Nila let out a dry, tearless sob. "You're all I have left, Jahan. Everyone else I've loved—*everyone*—has either died or abandoned me. There's no one in my world but you now. And I can't—I *won't*—let them take you from me! Not without fighting. You're all I love, and all that's important to me."

A moment's silence passed. Nila's breath was jagged in her chest, her very heart hurting.

"All right," said Jahan in a small voice. "Let's go."

Nila embraced him. "Thank you," she whispered. "Follow me. Be quiet." She pulled him up, and together they made their way to the women's door.

Nila peered outside, but no one was there, just the dried-out rice paddies, shadowed and abandoned under the moon. She took Jahan's hand, guiding him outside. She wondered frantically what to do. They could sneak across the rice paddies, but they were dreadfully exposed. To the west lay the Raja's camp. East then, to the forest, beyond the lake and the Naga skeletons.

"Follow me." She tugged Jahan along, their footsteps swift and silent through the night.

Nila's heart pounded. She was certain that at any moment an arrow would fly into them, or a watchman's shout rise. But the night was still and silent, only the stars and moon to bear witness, as the fugitives scurried along the village's edge toward the Naga skeletons and the relative safety of the forests beyond.

"How did you get me out, Nila?" Jahan whispered.

"Padma told me they left the women's entrance unguarded." Nila worked her way around a pothole. "Careful here."

"Padma?" Jahan sounded surprised. "How did she have the courage?"

"I guess she cared more for you than we thought." The branch canopy set up over the skeletons loomed, flickering in the fires lit by the watchmen. "Quiet now—"

"*Now, men!*"

The night blazed into bloody, lurid light as torches flared around them and village men and Raja's soldiers alike ran forward, swords drawn, arrows trained. The Raja himself was there, Darpan standing beside him, eyes burning.

Padma was there too, Nila saw through the haze of shock, standing beside her father. Her face was wet with tears. "I'm sorry, Nila," she sobbed. "They made me—"

"Jahan, run!" Nila seized Jahan and sprinted forward, but the arrows were already zinging around them while Darpan screamed, "No, don't kill the girl—!"

There came a wet *thunk*. Jahan choked and staggered beside Nila. She caught him in her arms, eyes stuck to the arrow sticking grotesquely out of his back. She stumbled, and they fell forward into the shadow of the thorn canopy, Naga bones clattering under their bodies.

Jahan, face pale with agony, gave a weak, wavery smile. "I...told you..." he panted. "Would make...no difference..."

"Jahan! Jahan!" Nila clutched at him, screaming, scattering Naga bones. "No, *no!*"

But already the Raja was striding forward, knife in hand—Nila tried to lunge at him, but she was tangled up in the bones and her reach fell short as Aadesh drew back Jahan's head and slashed across his throat.

Blood spilled out of the gruesome gash, spraying over Nila, staining her sari, filling her hands when she tried frantically to staunch the wound. The blood splashed across her lap, over the bones, and all the Naga skeletons quivered and trembled, knocking against one another in a dry, unholy chorus in the torchlight.

Nila watched the life fade from Jahan's blind eyes, felt his body go limp with death. A vast chasm opened in her heart, in her soul. She threw back her head and screamed, wild and inhuman as a jackal, as the very last light in her world was sucked into darkness.

Around her, the bones increased their tempo, clattering more and more urgently.

Nila's scream went on and on, born from the emptiness that had been her heart, while she cradled Jahan's lifeless body in her arms. Her eyes burned, filling with water—with *tears*. Of course, of course; her tears were what they wanted, these traitors, these murderers, who had seen her love for Jahan and set a trap for them both, to ensure his death and to shock tears from Nila's infamous, drought-dry eyes. She tried to hold her newborn tears back—she would not give them what they wanted—but there was no way to stop the tears, a hot salt tide. They spilled out of her eyes and fell to the vibrating bones.

Light blossomed, searing. It sheathed first the skeleton nearest Nila and then spread, enveloping each Naga in turn, until every skeleton lay cocooned in white light. Far away, thunder rumbled. The onlookers cried out.

A searing pain ran through Nila, and she almost dropped Jahan. She writhed on the ground, agony lancing through her. Her legs were fusing together, black scales emerging, muscular tail sprawling long. Of course, she realized as the transformation roared through her like a fiery flood; she too had been touched by the blood and tears, surrounded by Naga bones, under a gathering storm. Then she bent backward, screaming, all thought lost under the slamming wave of

Naga magic.

Her tail pushed against the earth, powerful and strong. Blood oozed into her mouth as fangs thrust out, long and translucent, filled with venom. Her new golden, slit-pupiled eyes pierced the darkness with ease, her new senses stretching out, seeking, sensing…water. Water all around her, water in every part of the world, from the saltiness of her tears and Jahan's blood to the moisture trapped inside the watching mortals' bodies to the vapor of the clouds now gathering overhead. Around her, the other Naga writhed to life, black-scaled tails slapping from side to side, arms flailing. Golden eyes opened and hands reached up to feel now-unfamiliar faces, while overhead the storm clouds massed, lightning cracked out and the first of the rain hissed down.

The water washed over Nila like an elixir, filling her with strength, with power, even in the depths of her wretchedness and grief. She looked wildly at the mortals. Some raised their arms and faces to the rain, rejoicing, but most stood and gazed at the newborn Naga in awe and terror.

Darpan lurched to his skinny knees. "I was right!" he cried, rain plastering his hair and robe to his emaciated frame. "Blood and tears!" He bowed, forehead to the soaking ground. "I greet you, O great Naga!" Behind him, Aadesh and Aravind both followed suit, and the other mortals bowed, a wave of genuflection.

Nila stared at the abased men. In her arms, Jahan lay limp and cold.

Her tail was strong, her fangs were sharp. Once Nila lunged, twice, thrice. Hot blood exploded into her mouth, fangs piercing mortal flesh. Aadesh, Aravind, and Darpan all slumped to the ground, mouths wide with surprise, eyes already glazed with death.

"No!" Padma lunged to her feet and staggered forward through the pounding rain, hair plastered to her scalp, reaching for her father's body. "Papa—!"

Nila hissed at her and she flinched back, eyes widening as she beheld, in the near-incessant flashes of lightning, what Nila had become. Nila, enveloped in the buzzing energy of the storm, tail coiling in the sodden mud, smiled into Padma's eyes.

"Go!" she cried, and another slam of thunder rolled. "Go, before I bite you too, you traitorous weakling!" She raised her voice, shouting at the stunned mortals. "*All of you!*"

Padma squeaked and bolted away, slipping through the mud as fast as she could. The villagers and soldiers all followed, glancing back over their shoulders in terror. They disappeared through the curtains of rain, the jagged flashes of lightning.

A hand fell on Nila's shoulder, and she turned to face one of her new kin. "Come, sister," the Naga woman said. "The water calls us home."

Jahan's head lolled back on Nila's arm, rain washing into the open wound. Nila clenched him. "I won't leave him!"

"Bring him, and we will lay him to rest beneath the water," her new sister said. "And we will honor always his sacrifice and yours that returned life to this land."

"I don't *want* to return life to this land!" Nila's voice rose in anguish, her dead love in her arms. "They don't deserve it! They're murderers, murderers—"

"And you have had your revenge." The other Naga spoke gently. "Now come away, sister, and join us in our realm, the heart of all the world's waters."

Nila took one last look at the earth: the night, the storm, the dead bodies lying in the mud. Then, still cradling Jahan, she turned away and followed the other Naga, letting the water carry them home.

THAT WHICH YIELDS

A Tale from the Ancient Hebrew

By Zachary Rosenberg

ALL THE TOWN PITIED Sarah when she lost her first husband, though after the seventh, they grew suspicious.

Sarah did not look up from her wools and linens as Tobias came to call upon her. In all Ectabana or even Judea, he was the only one who dared risk her home at night. Mordecai had been dead several months and Sarah was pleased for Tobias's company. He had arrived years ago from Nineveh, known and loved by all in the village for his strength and righteousness.

She'd known he'd come. She'd dreamed of it, just as she dreamed of the other nightly visitors whose arrival was as dreaded as it was constant.

"Sarah." Tobias's deep voice was a shepherd's, lulling a lamb to security. Sarah did her best not to stare at his handsome face, his muscled frame. She kept to her linens, a proper seamstress, demure and gentle as was expected of her. Her black hair was bound beneath a shawl, proof she had expected his visit. "Are you well?"

"Night is falling." Her voice was soft and forlorn, for both knew what came with the advent of the moon. A shiver ran through Sarah as she gazed out the window, the sun's dying embers bringing a bouquet of fire to dance across the river's waters. She thought to her dreams of Tobias and what the night held; gifts from Hashem, Tobias had said. "They're coming."

"Then I will stay at your side, as I have for so many nights," Tobias murmured. He did not ask for an invitation. He never did. She should have been grateful, but Sarah could only curb an ember of resentment within her chest. Such ill feeling was sinful, she thought. He was her friend, her protector. If her dreams of prophecy were to be believed, he was her destiny.

She would marry Tobias if he asked. If he were brave enough to risk the fury of nightly suitors kept at bay by the sacred wards of her home. Tobias stood silent and strong, the proper protector. Sarah told herself it was the way of things, telling herself not to mind it. She failed, hiding her frown.

Would he allow her to dance at the riverbank? Would he allow her hidden scrolls, kept just under her bed? With each marriage, she had feared her freedoms were at an end. As much as she desired a marriage pact, part of her was relieved to still know her own private pleasures.

Night came, and the reflection of the moon was blotted out as something passed overhead, the flutter of thick wings reaching Sarah's ears. She focused on her sewing, not caring now that to have a man here with her, an unwed woman, was improper. She heard Tobias tense, bracing himself next to her as he had before.

Despite herself, Sarah looked through her window, the chill breeze bringing bumps upon her skin. She stared there, seeing the demon, the *Sheydim*, standing by the riverbed.

He was beautiful as temptation. Skin the shade of resplendent moonlight, his short hair curling shadows to frame an agonizingly lovely face. His eyes were serpent-gold, his smile sharp as sin and twice as inviting. Black wings flexed from his shoulders, powerful as the cords of muscle through his body. He looked exactly as he did in her vivid prophecies, those warning gifts from the Almighty.

She always saw the demons in her mind, just before Tobias arrived, smiling and proud. Ready to defend her from these creatures' depredations.

Sarah stared deep into those slitted eyes, heated beneath her shawl in spite of the cold night air. A woman slid from the night to stand beside the *Sheydim* male. Taloned fingers ran upon his shoulders, her wine-dark lips curving upward into a mirror of her mate's smile. She wore a thin shift, her black hair whipping behind her in defiance of all the modesty expected of the women of Judea. Her eyes were pools of blood, hotter than the sudden burning inside Sarah's skin. Even sleep was no escape from them; only when Tobias entered her dreams did the image of them stop.

"Begone and trouble her no more, demons." Tobias had the voice of a hero, bold as brass as he wielded his faith as a weapon. He looked at her like she was his and his alone. "Have you not cost her enough? You cannot touch one who yields before the Lord!"

The male looked into Sarah's eyes, and she knew him, though she feared to speak his name. Ashmedai of the *Sheydim*, next to his consort, Lilith the Defiant. She was good, she was devout, Sarah told herself. She did not stare, not at the bare torso of Ashmedai and not the promise of a beautiful body that Lilith's pale shift highlighted. Their beauty struck a chord in her, just as their unwanted attention made her long to shout for their departure.

But Tobias braved the demons while Sarah was silent, for it was commanded unto women to yield in devotion and submission. In Ectaba, it was whispered Sarah was tainted, that she drew demons to her. Tobias never seemed to mind, full of a righteous fire as the demon before him grimaced. They could go no further, not with her home warded. Their lips moved, but Sarah could hear no words; their poison could not penetrate a godly home, Tobias had told her.

"This is the final night!" Tobias called. "I will marry her and break your power forever. No more of her husbands shall you slay!"

Ashmedai rocked back as though offended, a scoff upon his pale lips. Sarah realized she had been offered her proposal. She looked into Tobias's face, seeing his smile, his eyes shining even as the demons thundered outside. "If you will have me, Sarah."

"Tobias," she said, "they killed all the others. All my husbands. Benyamin, Elijah and his brother Simon, to Mordecai the butcher. I am tainted. All in Ectabana know it." The *Sheydim* had first come nights after Benyamin's death, but the priests had blessed her home just in time to ward them off.

"I love you even so. They broke the wards on your husbands'

homes each wedding night, but they have never broken yours." Tobias said, though his words brought Sarah little comfort. He put a hand over his chest, the same spot where Mordecai's heart had been ripped from him upon their wedding day, Sarah finding him in the marriage bed after terrible visions of bloodshed. It was odd that such wards had failed, but the *Sheydim* were clever, and it was not Sarah's place to question.

"I will marry you, Sarah. We will exorcize them for good and all. Ectabana shall know peace. You will have nothing to concern you again, save being my wife. You've told me of your dreams before; it was a sign from God Himself. I will chase them away for good and all. You and I are meant to be."

Sarah could think of no reason to refuse, even when her gaze lingered again upon Ashmedai and Lilith with a silent look of defiance and feelings she could not name.

***

After several years of dead husbands, Sarah was relieved to be marrying Tobias. She feared for his life. He was strong, godly, and she felt bound to accept him now, even though she had grown to enjoy solitary, quiet mornings.

They had not spoken since that night, Sarah remaining indoors when the moon rose, for the *Sheydim* had no power during the day. Villagers of Ectabana whispered when they thought she could not hear that Tobias would join the other seven in death.

She thought she might even miss the demons. The thought welled up unbidden. She dismissed it swiftly. People whispered about her and the secret things she saw. Prophets were men. Divine revelation was not for the like of Sarah.

They met with the Priests to inform them of their union, the holy men agreeing to the proposed exorcism. Priest Elyahu asked Sarah if she was ready for marriage again. Sarah nodded, examining one of

Tobias's strong hands. She longed to grasp another, to feel flesh against her own, to-

"Yield for him, your husband, as all women must?" the Priest asked. Twin emotions dueled within Sarah; a sudden resentment meeting the notion of excitement. She nodded once, modestly as ever. "I will," she said.

"When they are banished, your visions will be at an end. Hashem is good to warn you of their foul approach."

Sarah repressed a shudder that was not quite disgust. "Then I'll be rid of Ashmedai and Lilith?"

"Speak not their names!" The Priest snapped, glancing about fearfully. "Even words have power!" The priest scowled, before his shoulders sagged as if in relief. "We cannot expect women to know this," he muttered.

No, Sarah thought. For women were not given involved in the law, save to follow it. Women played no part in shaping it, nor in interpreting it. They were merely expected to yield to it. She looked at Tobias, at his bold eyes. "Fear not," murmured her betrothed. "I must prepare with the Priests. Remain inside tonight, Sarah. Once this is done, there will be nothing but you and I. All you must do-"

Was yield unto their commands. She walked home alone, knowing she should feel happy. But all she felt was the bitter taste of the unripened fruit of submission they offered.

In a strange way, she admired the honesty of the demons. They simply embraced what they themselves were.

***

"Sarah." The voice was the sinuous murmur of shadow.

Sarah realized she was hearing Ashmedai's voice for the first time, trying to ignore it and focus on her sewing. She must ignore it, though the sweet sound of him aroused a heat beneath her skin. Secretly, she had hoped they would come again, if only that she might refuse them,

prove to herself she had the power to do so.

"Sarah!" The voice was desperate now, anguished.

Her hand tightened on a sheet, and she set it aside, rising and walking to the window in a quiet defiance. Outside was Ashmedai, still barred from her home. "Can you cease? I am trying to work." Her voice was prim, clipped as a collected flower. "Every night, you bring your unwelcome company to my doorstep and my dreams, you and Lilith both!" She stared at the demon, golden eyes blinking rapidly in his handsome face.

"You can hear me now!" His voice was a joyous purr. "You said my name! My voice can carry over even the wards!"

"What makes you think I want to hear anything you have to say? Do you think I will step out and be yours? Ridiculous. I am getting married soon, and I demand you not kill this one! Trouble me no more."

"I only wish to talk to you," Ashmedai said at last. He was crouching low, a feral posture with his gaze lingering on Sarah. Not as prey, but with respect. "A moment outside your wards. That is all. I shan't harm you, I swear by *Hashem*."

"A demon's vow?"

"We are creatures of the natural order," Ashmedai protested. He drew himself up to his full height. "Did the Creator not make us, just as He made you a Prophetess?"

That word. Sarah paused, hearing acknowledgment in ways she'd never realized from the men of Ectabana. "Is that what I am?"

"You are as much his creature as we! I am Ashmedai, Lord of Lust. We yield before that order, before our natures. But that which yields is not weak."

Sarah collected herself, turning from the window, contemplating going back to her sewing and the future of domesticity that awaited her. Her wedding night was ahead, a night beneath Tobias as his new wife. A life of servitude, meek boredom she was supposed to want. Without dancing and reading.

The prospect of disobedience lit a new flame in her. Before she realized it, she stepped from the window to the door. She pushed it open and walked into the cool night. Ashmedai stared at her, even more beautiful standing so close. "Sarah," he murmured that name with more devotion than any Judean had ever breathed into their prayers. He reached out a hand and Sarah slapped it away.

"I gave no such permission." Her voice was colder than the night breeze about them. "*Sheydim* or no, you shall respect my wishes."

Ashmedai did the last thing Sarah expected.

He bowed before her. "Forgive me. I shall never touch you without permission, Sarah," he said, "I have watched you a long while, since the day you danced and sang by the riverbank by a setting sun. I heard you laugh as you read scrolls, even though they were forbidden. Lilith and I watched you, saw the spirit of fire within. I wanted to speak to you."

"And for that, you killed my husbands?" Sarah could not believe her ears. "You wished to possess me? Did you think I would love you after that?"

"Did you love them?" The voice was a tender song, Lilith emerging from the night to join her mate.

"No. I barely knew most of them. Our marriages were arranged," Sarah admitted. "But they did nothing to deserve their blood upon your hands. Nor such terrible deaths." She recalled her visions, the haunting bloodshed, with Tobias always there to chase away the images of the demons.

"Surely not," Ashmedai agreed. "For our hands are clean of this sin. We have tried to tell you, but the wards dampened our words until you invited us by speaking our names. We were trying to protect you, *warn* you. We did not harm them.

"Your betrothed did."

Sarah felt a great weight collide with her very soul. She took a step back, staring mutely at the two, as though it must be a lie. "Tobias would not. He's always been there to protect me when they were slain, before…"

Before the *Sheydim* could arrive. Always shepherding her back to her house just in time. Always around in time to hear her shout when she found the bodies. "No," Sarah whispered. "If you call me a prophet, Hashem gave me visions of you. Of those deaths, each time…"

The demons, always appearing before her eyes. Tobias following the blood, chasing them away. She lifted a hand to her head, the realization setting in.

"He has watched you for years as we have, but in his eyes you are a possession," Lilith murmured. She stepped closer to Sarah, her eyes imploring. "The men of Ectabana expect you to bow before *their* desires and smother your own. They long for the pliable, the submissive. But yours was a fire that would not easily be quenched. That man coveted you, a true prophet, so he murdered your first husband with magic most foul. Then the others, until no suitors remained, so you would lean only upon him."

The betrayal shot through Sarah, a bolt of anguish that lanced through her heart. Her mouth opened, a hand flying to her chest. "I do not believe you." She shook her head, strands of hair escaping their perfect binding from her shawl. "I cannot!"

"Sarah, you know his measure deep within. And you have known mine from the second you first saw me. I am Lust, but I am freedom as well," Ashmedai urged. He kept his hands from her, though Sarah found herself looking at those strong arms, gazing back at his beautiful face. "I swear by *Hashem* that my words are true. Think to your visions, find your own truth!"

She saw the truth in Ashmedai's eyes. Deep within her soul, she knew it. She thought of her dreams, Ashmedai and Lilith ever silent. Sarah closed her eyes, trying to conjure the visions before her, summoning her dreams with all her willpower.

And she saw. Tobias, but his warm, godly smile was lustful and covetous. His hands were drenched with blood. Ashmedai and Lilith's serpentine gazes were full of concern, trepidation, calling silent warnings she'd never been able to hear.

Sarah stepped back and she screamed, a sound of fury and release, bound emotions suddenly unleashed. She howled at the night, before the demons, tears pouring from her eyes as she realized not what she had lost, but what had been nearly unjustly thrust upon her.

"I rebelled from my role once," Lilith said to Sarah, a smile on her face. By the moonlight, the demon's beautiful face was kind. "So can you. Choose your role, Sarah."

"Why this for me?" Deep within her heart, Sarah realized the lingering gaze she cast on them had never been fear.

"Sarah, you already know." Lilith's smile was warm. "We love you."

The words were a key that unlocked the shackles Sarah was bound by. She saw their faces in her mind, her dreams replaying before her eyes. Lust, coupled with beautiful emotion, want, warmth.

She hurled caution away, broke from the role the Priests and Tobias would have forced on her, that they chained the women of Judea with. She took Lilith's face in hand and kissed her like a storm, a tempest that threatened to swallow the demon. She drank in Lilith's wine-dark lips, naming that feeling within her at last.

Desire.

"I said not to touch me without permission. I grant it. I *want* it." She kissed Ashmedai with the same fervor, a furious heat. "If a woman's passion is blasphemy to these men, then help me blaspheme.

"*Show* me."

The Lord of Lust did not need to be told twice. He gathered Sarah into his arms, enveloping her with his wings. His kiss was rough, heated, his tongue guiding its way between her lips and lacing itself with her own. Sarah slid her hands into his black hair, pressing herself to his strong body.

She broke the kiss and turned, seeing Lilith before her. At the next kiss, she brought her hands to Lilith's shift, undoing the fastenings to let it slip from the demoness's body. Sarah delighted in the sight, the tantalizing promise fulfilled.

Their hands were upon her, their lips meeting her own, her neck, her shoulders. Sarah's body erupted with fire, the heat burning beneath her legs. She cast aside the shawl so her hair might tumble free, no longer bound in chaste submission. She undid her clothes, joy reaching a crest as she stared into Ashmedai's eyes.

"I submit only as I choose. If I wish to stop, you *will* heed me."

He gave her a word, one that he vowed would be that signal. They guided her to lay upon the soft grass near the river.

She gave herself over to every feeling she had been taught to deny out of wedlock, embraced the beautiful carnality. If women had no part in writing the laws, then Sarah refused to be bound by them.

Sarah let them pleasure her, the heat overtaking her. Sacred bonds of pleasure in marriage were just as sacred outside it.

"That which yields," Lilith murmured into her ear.

"Is not weak," Sarah finished. She answered passion for passion, giving and taking in equal measure. She let them show her, an ardent and eager student. Her lips brushed Lilith's again, hands in the Sheydim's hair as she pulled her close. She shrugged away the bonds of society, letting them fall away from her like loosened shackles.

They were *hers*. Hers, as she was theirs. She felt the demons give themselves to her, yielding before her, knowing it was their will and their strength. And in that heat of passion, she felt no shame, no remorse, nor any hesitation.

Within the pleasure, there was naught but triumph.

***

Sarah slept a while and dreamt again. But this time, in her vision, she saw what she must do.

"Will I bear Ashmedai's child?" Sarah asked after awakening, her head pillowed upon Lilith's shoulder.

"Do you wish to?" Was Lilith's only reply. Sarah shook her head. "No. Not yet at least."

"Then you shan't," Ashmedai vowed. "For the body, like consent, is inviolate, sacred." After the rough passions, they had bathed in the river and then lay holding one another, curled together in shows of tender affection within Sarah's bed.

"You two share alike so easily," Sarah said as she traced a finger over Lilith's thigh.

"And why should we not? We have been together for so long that pleasure is like love; best when shared. You may. If you choose to."

"First," Sarah said, "I have business yet unfinished."

Sarah left the *Sheydim*, walking into Ectabana. Her heart pounding, she made her way to Tobias's home with the first rays of the sun peeking across the horizon.

She walked with purpose and strength, no longer demure. She strode with poise and confidence through the village and murmurs spread like wildfire.

They saw her, one after the other. Men and women, to see Sarah with her loosened hair, a cloak set about her. She called Tobias's name before his house. He emerged, puzzlement writ on his face.

"I know." She said those words with all the finality of a descending blade. Her eyes were dark crescents of fury, her gaze fixed upon him. "I know everything. I've seen it."

He might have denied it, but she saw the flickers in his eyes. His mouth opened slightly, the lie ready to issue forth, but Sarah dismissed his mendacity with a flick of her wrist. "Do not bother. Tell me why."

"They were not good enough," he said softly. "None of them were."

"That was not for you to decide."

"I would see you *exalted*. Our children—"

Sarah raised her voice. "My story is not yours to write! I am Sarah, a Prophetess of Hashem. I bring a message of freedom. My submission, my body, my soul, are my own, to be given to those whom

I would choose. That is the right of all women, all Jews, all human beings."

Tobias's face darkened, his teeth clenching. "You speak madness. This means nothing, you have agreed, and the law says you are mine."

"Do not think the law is your shield before me. You would have bent my life to your own through your sorceries. You sought to force my hand. Now you have forced my wrath."

"You cannot deny me!" Tobias said furiously. He took a step forth but halted. Sarah's smile grew, for she felt them at her side, standing beneath the morning sun. Tobias stepped forth, eyes gleaming with anger. "The *Sheydim* have no power beneath the sun!"

"You are gravely mistaken," Sarah spat, "as to whom you ought fear, Tobias."

Sarah felt the *Sheydim* lend their power to her. Their power, her strength tore through Tobias's defenses. He fell to his knees, trying to intone a desperate prayer, though even the Lord seemed to have deserted him. He collapsed, his eyes wide as Sarah stalked towards him, imperious in her victory.

Pitiless in her wrath. The people of Ectabana waited, mortified as she set her hand to Tobias's chest. "I have banished your power, as I banish your hold. People of Ectabana, this man is a murderer, confessed before you all. Judge him as you will, for his life is nothing to me." She stepped from him, leaving Tobias to fall upon the ground, gibbering in loss and terror.

"I will return." She looked into the faces of the women, the young and old alike. The men murmured in fear, but Sarah extended her hand.

"There are laws of men that seek to crush us beneath them. We may yet worship as we will, for if the Almighty made all things, he made lust for us to enjoy as well. All women who wish to may follow me, for *choice* is what we must prize."

And with that proclamation, she walked from the quivering form of Tobias, joining Ashmedai and Lilith once again. Sarah kissed them both, unashamed before the sight of heaven, men, and demons alike.

She laughed joyously, peering across Ectabana as young women emerged from their homes with unbound hair.

"Must we do as you do?" One asked haltingly, tentatively. "Are any unwelcome?"

"No," Sarah said. "Whatever bodies you were born with, whatever your desires. Choice is all I ask. Yield only to what you would." She smiled at them, hands linked with Ashmedai and Lilith's in their union. Their smiles were dedications, warm as sun rays. Just as she had glimpsed from above. It was on her now to make it reality, to discover her truth and to share it.

Call her witch, call her monster, Sarah thought. She was strong. She was joyful.

She was free.

THE SECRETS WE SEEK

A Tale from the World

By Erin L. Swann

WHERE LIGHT BLEEDS THROUGH cracks in rotted wood, in the shadow where the willow weeps, near a bank salted with the tears of a river. There you will find the cache."

The woman before me narrowed her eyes, a skeptic from her angular brow to her smartly shod feet.

Her companion leaned forward with each piece of the riddle I spoke. He licked his lips, cracked with grief reflected in his red-rimmed eyes. "Does that mean the old fishing shack? That's where Ma hid it?"

I bowed my head.

The woman beside him was not convinced, face shriveling like a plum laid out to prune. "Can you be less cryptic?"

I ignored the woman; the man came to me for an answer, and I had no interest in his tagalong. The phrasing wasn't my own, I only repeated what I heard.

Words unspoken, silently passing through the lips of the dying with their final breath. Whispers carried on the wind, voices hidden beneath groaning wood planks and behind poor plaster jobs. Some secrets were as light as gosling down, caught in a summer breeze. Others were murky, like the bottom of Miller's Pond, where the catfish liked to cool their bellies.

I'm uncertain what higher power gifted me with the ability to hear them, or why they deemed me worthy. I only know that from an early age, I felt compelled to pass on the knowledge given to me.

My hand, powdered in its usual dusting of glitter, stretched out to rest on the man's fist, which was clenched in a tight ball around my velvet tablecloth. "I suggest self-reflection. Retrace the steps of your childhood. I sensed the heavy weight of nostalgia; the location is tied to a tradition."

The crystal in my hand sighed, the information within winking out. Secrets could only exist for as long as they remain concealed.

The woman continued to grumble as her companion slipped payment into a clouded gray vase by my door and murmured a few broken words of thanks. They left as so many of my patrons do, dubious and heartened at once. I couldn't look at the vase with my compensation. It always made me feel dirty. Instead, I allowed myself a small moment to cradle the empty crystal.

Witches had to eat, but my favorite patrons were often the ones who couldn't pay, finding their way to my doorstep without knowing why. They were just like me, seeking something deeper than a lost inheritance or a distant noble lineage, more valuable than ancient treasure.

We were lost, looking for answers we aren't always certain we wanted.

Perhaps that was what drew secrets to me like orphaned children seeking a home, a keeper. Someone to watch over them long after their significance had passed. I gathered them as I used to gather wildflowers with my eldest sister, Klea, though my obsession with collecting these unspoken words was something I couldn't explain. The more I found, the more I wanted. And the less everything else mattered. Possessing the answers to someone else's riddle wasn't just empowering, it was intoxicating.

And while I disliked giving secrets up to mere treasure hunters, I was their custodian. Who was I to question who they revealed themselves to?

I placed the newly emptied prism in a glass bowl filled with water formed from melted ice. It would need time before it could house another secret.

After readying my basket of primed crystals by the door, I donned the filmy shawl of autumn hues hanging beside it. My mother had woven it for me before she disappeared back into the woods when I was young. Dryads were flighty, and I still pitied my father for falling in love with her. Just as I pitied my sisters for the hole she left in our lives as well. We were scattered like windblown leaves now, looking for answers we couldn't find, determined to seek them anyway.

I heard a rattling whisper dangling from a cypress tree on the edge of the woods behind my cabin. My fingers fished in my basket for a prism as I listened, barely breathing, to the murmurations snaked around a prickly pinecone.

Borne of a torrid love affair, shunned by enraged elders, a life spent in exile. Concealed at the edge of the world where cold, violet stone cuts the sky, you will find her there.

After I left the cypress tree, I checked other likely places. The fox den held a trembling voice shuddering in the shadows.

He is not real. They must not know.

Some secrets felt more like fugitives searching for a safe place to hide. I discovered another splashing in a well ringed by oaks, and one got blown into my headscarf with a nasty gust of wind as I turned back to the cabin.

Four newly infused crystals nestled in my basket when I returned home. By late afternoon, I suspended them like stars from rafters in my cabin with the rest of my collection. And much like expired stars still sending their light to Earth, the owners of those whispers no longer existed. Only the secrets remained. The purr of their gentle legato kept me company during my self-inflicted solitude. One cannot hear whispers when surrounded by the crescendo of life.

I touched my apron pocket, feeling the crunch of paper from my eldest sister's letter. I didn't need to read it again to remember what it said.

Chel,

Father's not doing well. I've written to the others. Please come home soon. We miss you. What good are answers if you have no one left to share them with?

I promise to cook something special.

Klea

But tearing myself away was not as simple as that. Secrets called, seekers came. They needed me to unite them, to give them answers, closure. Surely, I was chosen for that purpose. And what was more, I might miss an answer I never knew I needed. When did I have time to go home?

I hung the apron with the missive over a knob in the kitchen and went to draw a bath. Klea might be frustrated, but we were sisters. I knew she still loved me the same.

***

"Hello? Is anyone home?"

A seeker. I could hear her friend's giggles pecking my soft wood walls before I rounded the corridor to the front parlor.

"This place is creepy."

"Shut up. We don't have to stay here long."

"She's probably going to ask for your blood or a lock of your hair."

"Shut up."

I hoped I didn't have a secret for this one; I already didn't want to give it. Still, I donned my shawl for comfort and breezed through the threshold. My larder was growing empty.

The girls hovering in my doorway were dressed like women, with full skirts or starched trousers, but their dewy skin and wicked grins spoke to cruel naivety. They froze when they saw me, but only for a moment. The girl at the front, dark hair done up in an elaborate crown of braids, raised her chin while her two friends whispered behind her back.

"Are you the witch that can speak to the dead?" she asked.

I suppressed a sigh; it was a common misconception. "I collect secrets that the dead have taken with them. Is it a secret you seek?"

"Why else would I be here?" The girl's sour tone was a touch too tart, and I could hear the uneasy warble behind it, even if her friends didn't. I could also hear something else. One crystal above calling louder. Something in my twinkling sky belonged to her.

"Your name?"

"Nora."

"Have a seat, Nora." I gestured to the velvet-clothed table.

"How gaudy," one of her friends muttered.

"If my tastes aren't to your liking, wait outside." When the two friends hesitated, I lowered my tone. "That wasn't a request."

The girls scurried out and Nora chuckled softly, but I saw her finger tapping a nervous rhythm against my table. I unfolded my stepladder and climbed up to fetch the whispering crystal.

"Can't your kind fly or something?"

I smiled at her ignorance. "I just don't like to show off. What is this secret you hope to find?"

"I need to know what the code is."

The moment my fingers brushed against the crystal, it buzzed with electricity, desperate to speak to me.

A safe with no combination, containing nothing, for I have nothing left. I gave everything to her in life. Let her think better of me than I deserve.

That tugged at my heart. The secret was to *keep* the secret from her. I gazed down at the girl in women's clothes.

Nora puckered her lip. "Well?"

I took a breath, stepping off my ladder and sitting down beside her. If I couldn't give her the truth, what lie would best serve her? "Your father left you a puzzle to solve. When you find your worth, you will find the answer you seek."

"Find my worth," she said, eyes studying the tablecloth. "What does that mean?"

"That is an answer I cannot give. It's the journey we are all on. Your father was a wise man."

She nodded, eyes misting with private thoughts as she glanced at the door.

I couldn't help myself. "Finding our worth only through others can deter self-discovery." I reached out to rest a hand on hers. "Reach deep. The answers are in you."

My lies reached her, face softening in the absence of her friend's judgement. I felt sick as I watched her leave, dropping money in my jar. I had falsified that truth and felt my magic diminished by it. The secret in my palm hummed in appreciation, but it numbed my skin.

I felt dirtier for taking her money.

***

Another letter found me the following week, accompanied by a teal tin of fresh shortbread biscuits. Klea's words were less gentle this time.

There are plenty in need of answers, in need of guidance. They were there before you took up this practice and they will be here long after we're dust in the wind. Stop trying to heal the world, Chel. It won't make you whole.

I understood her words, but they couldn't reach me. While I loved my sister dearly, my work here was far too important to abandon. I was close to something, something important, and I didn't want to miss it. An inner voice, some higher power, insisted I stay.

After I dressed for bed, the curtain of wooden beads clattered at the front of my cottage.

I had locked my doors at sundown.

A true seeker had come to call.

With quiet excitement under my skin, I slipped down from the loft and into my back parlor. Nora's visit had shaken me, and I was desperate to provide an answer that truly mattered. To make up for my deception, however well-intended.

The curtains clattered again, and I slowed, donning my shawl.

If the seeker had come after dark, it was by magic or mischief. Had they stepped through an enchanted mirror or had they picked my lock, bent on stealing what they couldn't take?

I searched through the towers of stacked books left around my sitting room. The tomes stretched from floor to ceiling, filled with musty words—some wiser than others.

At first, I thought my guest was hiding, but then a sigh brushed my ears, dark hair peeking above my kitchen counter. The tangled bramble of locks reminded me of my youngest sister's hair. She wasn't fond of brushes.

But the girl in my kitchen wasn't Fauna. Paper crinkled, and I tugged the shawl around my foamy nightgown before stepping around the counter. "A mouse in my kitchen?" I asked.

The girl spun, a feral gleam in her eyes reminiscent of the stray cat I startled in my strawberry patch last week. The young waif had two biscuits stuffed partly in her mouth, cheeks hollow with hunger. Her eyes enlarged, but not nearly as much as they should have, considering her situation.

Her hands held Klea's teal tin. After a moment, the girl resumed chewing, stuffing the ends of the biscuits past her lips. I stared, wondering at her gall, when I heard a prism screaming her name.

Not whispering. Screaming.

The girl continued to study me as she backed around the counter with the tin still clutched in her fingers. "These are good," she said in a cookie-muffled voice.

I struggled between listening to the prism and figuring out what to say to this midnight thief.

"They're usually better when you're *invited* to eat them."

The girl cocked her head at me. "Really? I doubt that."

"I suppose you'll never know." The side door to the kitchen was slightly ajar and a few hairpins littered the threshold, some broken.

"Got any milk?"

I drew myself up, lips in a grim line. "Do you have any manners?"

She grinned, crumbs stuck to her cracked lips. "Can't afford 'em."

I couldn't help seeing my younger wild sister in her. Maybe she could sense my weakness. "I have a little goat's milk in the icebox. But I want something in exchange."

"Don't have anythin'." She stopped chewing, scruffy eyebrows rising. "You the kind of witch that eats people?"

"No. Too much work," I said with a wry smile. "I want your name."

"Oh. Mara. What's yours?"

"Chel."

The prism continued to tug at me, and my curiosity was too great to it ignore any longer. I fetched the step ladder after giving Mara a bit of milk and strawberries, insisting she eat something aside from biscuits.

I could hear the moans before I even touched the crystal, and it made my heart still. It was from the girl's mother. I remembered collecting this secret a few years ago, nestled in the nest of a robin beside speckled blue eggs. It had only been a fragmented whisper then. As I listened now, a burning grew behind my eyes, my throat swelling. But my heart swelled as well.

This poor kid had no one left, but the secret her mother wanted to give to her daughter would change her life.

"You okay, old lady?" Mara asked, eyes narrowed, milk mustaching her top lip.

My legs had frozen on the top step of my ladder, hand wrapped around the prism. I studied the girl with new eyes and joy in my heart. This was why I lived so far out, isolating myself from the world and even my family. Because I could change lives, bring others not only peace, but changes of fortune. This was my higher purpose.

I eased off the ladder, cradling the crystal, eyes clinging to Mara. The girl hunched over, suspicion growing in her eyes.

"Do you know what I do, Mara?" I asked softly, trying to contain my emotions.

"Yeah, Johnny told me you talk to dead people."

It didn't even bother me to hear it this time; I was too excited to give this secret to her. "Well, Mara, there's someone who has something they wish to tell you."

Mara snorted and tossed back the rest of the milk. "Don't have any more money than I did earlier."

"This one is free." I didn't care about the money. Not when something this important needed to be passed on.

The girl's face scrunched. "Oh yeah? Who's it from?"

"Your mother."

Mara's change was instant. Hesitant to hostile, like an alley cat against a wall. She shuffled back to the door, ready to escape into the night. "Tell her to go away. I won't want to talk to her."

My eyebrows rose; that was not the reaction I expected. "She's not here, Mara. She just left something behind. Something you need to know."

The girl relaxed a little, but kept her hand on my doorknob. "Don't care what she has to say."

I crept from the sitting room to the counter leading to my kitchen, worried I might spook her. "I think once you hear it, you'll change your mind."

Mara shook her head. "If she couldn't say it to my face, I don't want to know."

"She wanted you to know," I implored, needing to release this secret as if it were my own.

"No." Mara calmed the more she refused me. "If she wanted to tell me, she would have bothered to stick around instead of leaving to start a new life."

Not the best mother, to be sure. While Mara's bitterness was understandable if she was abandoned, this secret could alter everything for her. "Are you certain? It will change your life, Mara. For the better. She wants that for you."

"Good. At least I get to ignore *her* this time." Mara's smile was so cold.

I didn't know what else to say. Her lack of curiosity, her lack of care, cut me deep in a way I didn't fully understand. "Maybe she had her reasons." Why was I defending this woman I didn't know? I knew nothing about the situation; perhaps the mother didn't deserve to be heard.

It was Mara's indifference I couldn't stomach.

"Maybe she did, but she can't expect me to care now." Mara turned the door handle. "She made a choice for me. Now I'm making one for myself."

Before I could push her any further, the waif slunk out of my kitchen door, blending into the night. I tightened my fist around the prism and felt it crack. The secret escaped with a hiss, wailing for her daughter.

I couldn't bring myself to recapture it. It was hard not to chase after Mara, to beg and plead. To take this life-changing secret. But why?

Mara had made her choice, and she seemed perfectly content with it.

Could I say the same for my own choices?

My writing desk called from the shadowed corner of my sitting room, buried beneath books and spent crystals. For the first time in ages, I paced over to it with purpose. The prism sky above tinkled, but my attention remained on the desk, hands clearing it of clutter. I tugged a wrinkled paper out from beneath a stack of tomes.

Klea,

I could use a home-cooked meal. I'll bring the strawberries.

Mara's expression of disgust burned in my brain. Would my sisters make that same expression about me one day? When I passed on, who would treasure the secrets I left behind?

No duty to a higher power compelled me more than that fear.

Whispers pulled at me as I wrote, but I ignored them. Those secrets weren't going anywhere. They would continue to seek me just as I would continue to preserve them, searching for my own. But deep down, I knew the secrets I sought would never hang from my rafters.

More often than not, we hide the deepest secrets we seek within ourselves.

IN HINDSIGHT

A Tale from Ancient Greece

By Nico Penaranda

YOU WERE A BAD brother.
Always thinking of everything
you could do. Did you ever dwell
on the things you did?

Once, no one held
the weight of the sky.
You changed that.

They paint us in opposing lights,
and why would you disagree?
You like being called the clever one,
but we are not so different.

You make—I make more.
Only we should decide
what are mistakes.

All we do
is all we can.
Steal what you must.
I'll form the rest.

-Epimetheus, Titan God of Afterthought

THE WAGER

A Tale from the Choctaw Nation

By A. L. Munson

READ 'EM AND WEEP, SUCKAS!" Darius said as he spread his cards out in front of him. Another royal flush.

"Goddammit!" Melvin chucked his cards onto the table. "Man, that's the fifth hand in a row that you've won. You hiding an extra deck up those sleeves?"

"Right, like I need to cheat to beat y'all's sorry asses." Darius raked in the cash at the center of the table and caught the sour expression on Cedric's face. "You're murdering me with that look, C."

"I'm not mad."

"Could've fooled me, 'cause you look fucking pissed," Melvin replied, grinning with amusement.

"I'm *not* mad. And I'll tell you why. Because you—motherfucking card sharp over here—and Angelique have a baby on the way. So I know you're gonna spend every penny of that money on diapers and baby food and shit. Say goodbye to your paycheck for the next eighteen years, fool!"

"You sound a little vindictive for someone who's not mad." Darius tried not to laugh, but after several hours of joking around and more than a few beers, he'd become too slap-happy to control himself.

He waved to the bartender. "Another round on me!"

"No, not for me," Cedric said as he stood up from the table. "I'm out."

"What, you don't want to contribute more to my kid's college fund?"

"It's late, man. And Tonette's gonna kill me when she finds out how much money I lost. If you don't hear from me again, maybe send someone to check under our floorboards for a dead body."

"Alright, man. See you around."

Cedric left the bar, and Darius turned to Melvin. "You heading out too?"

"Shit, I ain't got a wife. I can stay."

"Just you and me, one-on-one? Sounds like someone wants to go home broke."

"I'm up for a nice game of poker if you gentlemen don't mind," said a voice from just behind Darius.

He turned to find a man in a wide-brimmed hat and a long, grey overcoat standing just over his shoulder.

"You may want to rethink that," Melvin said to the stranger. "Darius has been cleaning us out all night."

"On a lucky streak, are you?"

"You could say it's luck," Darius replied in a faux boastful tone, "but I say it's skill. Know what I mean?"

The man didn't respond. The shadow of his hat brim obscured his face, making it impossible to read his expression.

Darius's smile faded. "Uh, but if you want to join in, you can."

"Thank you," the stranger said and took his seat. "What's your usual ante?"

"A dollar, man. We ain't rich," Melvin replied.

"Very well." The man removed a wallet from his pocket and placed a dollar in the center of the table.

Darius caught a glimpse inside the wallet as he and Melvin anted up. He counted only two more singles. The stranger wouldn't last long in this game.

Melvin dealt the cards and then looked at his hand. "Oh, I'm gonna kick your ass this time, D!"

"We'll see about that." Darius picked up his cards—a straight flush. "Sorry, Mel. I don't think this is your night."

The stranger tossed his last two dollars into the pot. "Raise."

"You sure you want to do that?"

"*Raise*," he repeated in an almost threatening tone.

"Alright then." Darius placed a five-dollar bill in the pot. "I'll raise."

"Man, this is my last five," Melvin said as he called it.

"Well, I'm afraid I'm out of cash," the stranger said, "and I doubt you gentlemen take checks. Perhaps you'll accept this instead." He pulled a set of car keys from his overcoat pocket and set them atop the money in the center of the table.

Darius and Melvin exchanged awkward glances.

"You're putting up your car?" Darius asked. "I don't know who you think we are, but we don't play for high stakes like that."

The stranger gestured to the bar's main window. "Take a look outside and see if you change your mind."

Darius turned toward the window and his heart skipped a beat. Parked out on the curb was a shiny, red Corvette.

"Holy shit!" Melvin said. "*That's* your car?"

"It's mine for now. Whoever wins this hand becomes its new owner."

"Man, you know we can't match that raise."

"I don't expect you to. Not monetarily, at least. Instead, I'll accept one thing from each of your homes. I get to choose what those things are and don't have to name them until I win."

Melvin laughed. "I don't know what you think we've got in our homes, but it's nothing compared to that Vette. I'm in!"

"What about you, big winner? Are you in?"

Darius pried his eyes away from the car. There had to be a catch. Something about this man seemed off. Then again, Darius was a bit drunk. Maybe the stranger's oddness was all in his mind. "I don't know, man. How do I know that car's not stolen and you just want it off your hands?"

"I have the title and will give it to you if you win. Now call."

Darius glanced at his cards and felt a twinge of guilt. "Look, if you want to back out, take your car and your three dollars and forget the whole thing, you can."

"Man, the fuck are you saying?" Melvin asked. "Dude just put up a Corvette!"

"We don't play to screw anyone over. This is just a friendly game."

"I appreciate the concern," the stranger said. "Now call."

Darius shrugged. "Okay, I call."

"Now, let's see 'em," Melvin said as he spread his cards out on the table. A full house. Not bad, but not good enough for this hand.

Darius laid down his straight flush. "Sorry, Mel."

"Dammit, man! How do you always win?"

"Not so fast." The stranger placed his cards on the table one at a time. Four aces and a joker. "That's five of a kind, gentlemen."

Darius and Melvin both leaned in to get a better look.

"Okay then," Darius said, stunned. He hadn't known there were jokers in the deck. "Looks like you get to keep your car."

"And one thing from each of your homes."

"What do you want then?" Melvin asked.

"From you, Melvin James Smith, I want your grandfather's footlocker from his service in the Korean War."

"How'd you know about that? And how do you know my name?"

"Never mind that. I'll collect the footlocker in the morning."

"The hell you will! My granddad's photos, letters, and service uniform are in there. I thought you'd ask for a TV or a stereo or some shit. Why you gotta ask for something sentimental? It don't mean nothing to you."

"But it has value to you. I said you didn't have to match my bet *monetarily*. Emotionally is another matter."

Darius stared at the stranger with dread. It wasn't all in his mind after all.

"And you, Darius Tyrell Miller…"

His stomach tightened.

"…You've been winning big all night. I think it's time you lost big, don't you?"

"Who are you?"

"You should be asking what it is I want."

Darius thought of getting up and walking away, maybe even running, but he couldn't move. His arms and legs hung limp and unresponsive like they weren't attached. He shifted his eyes to Melvin, and he too appeared paralyzed.

"I'll give you all my winnings," Darius said to the stranger, "and I mean *all* of them, if you let us go right now."

"You're not getting off that easily. I said you'd lose big and I meant it. Right now, in your home, your wife is sleeping on the couch. In her womb is a child. He's not due for another two weeks, but that's close enough. I'll collect him in the morning along with the footlocker."

Darius's mind swam. How did the stranger know about Angelique and the baby? Was this a nightmare? Had he fallen asleep at the table?

"Man, you are some kind of insane," Melvin said to the stranger. His eyes were wide with fear, but the paralysis that held him and Darius was waning. "Let's get out of here, D."

They both jumped up from the table, leaving the money in the pot behind.

The stranger remained in his seat, silent and still, as they rushed out of the bar.

***

Angelique awoke a little after 5am to the baby kicking. She'd grown used to this. Around the same time each day, he'd wake her with those little kicks. The kid could've been an alarm clock.

"Alright, little guy," she said as she rolled out of bed. "I wish you'd do this three hours later. It'd be nice to get a full night's sleep."

Her night had hardly been restful. She had tried to wait up for Darius but dozed off on the couch while watching TV. It wasn't until he got home around 1am that she finally went to bed. He'd acted strange—scared even. He kept asking if she and the baby were okay and checked the whole house to see if anyone had broken in. Wouldn't say why.

She waddled into the bathroom where the first rays of morning light made the frosted glass of the window glow orange, like the stained glass of a church. She hung her nightgown on the doorknob and stepped into the shower. The warm water soothed her stretched and sore skin. She closed her eyes and started to drift off to sleep.

A strong kick jolted her awake. Another followed. And another until the baby was kicking furiously.

"Hey, settle down in there," she said.

Everything went still… *Too* still.

A sudden panic washed over her. She placed both hands on her belly, desperately trying to detect any movement inside. As though recoiling from her touch, her baby bump shrank beneath her hands, growing smaller and smaller until her belly was flat.

If it weren't for the water pelting her face, she would've thought it was a nightmare. But this was *very* real.

She ran from the shower, not bothering to turn off the water or grab a towel. She just ran, naked and dripping, into the bedroom and screamed, "DARIUS!"

Darius jerked awake and turned to her with eyes half-closed in a groggy gaze.

Angelique gestured to her abdomen but couldn't speak. Her breaths were more like gasps and soon turned to sobs. Tears clouded her vision, but she felt his arms wrap around her shoulders, felt him shaking with fear, and heard him mutter through his own sobs, "Oh God! What did I do?"

***

Darius and Angelique took a bus and a street car to Touro Infirmary's emergency room. A doctor there did an ultrasound and found nothing—no baby, no amniotic fluids—nothing. He didn't believe Angelique was ever pregnant. Since her regular doctor's office was closed for the weekend, it would be days before they could get hold of her medical records to prove him wrong.

Darius had told Angelique about the mysterious man from the night before, but whether she'd been listening, he couldn't tell. She was in shock, and truthfully, so was he. Now, as they left Touro and stepped out onto the street, the reality of their situation sank in and he felt lost. He looked at Angelique, and her expression told him she felt the same way.

"What do we do?" she asked in a small voice. "Do we go to the cops?"

"And tell them what? Someone kidnapped our unborn son using magic? They don't even take normal crimes seriously. There's a reason people say NOPD stands for 'Not Our Problem, Dude.'"

"Then *what do we do*? Track down the kidnapper ourselves? Do you even know where to look?"

"No, he didn't say anything about himself, not even his name. And his face was always in shadow." Now that he thought about it, he couldn't remember anything about the stranger's appearance—not his skin color, height, or build. It was like, beneath that wide-brimmed hat and long overcoat, he had no physical form at all. "Melvin was with me. Maybe he got a better look at the guy." Darius pulled out his phone and tapped his friend's name on the contacts list.

It only rang once before Melvin answered.

"Yo, Darius, you're not gonna believe this! My granddad's footlocker is gone! I've looked everywhere for it, and it was right here in my closet last night. That creepy motherfucker from the bar broke in and took it, man!"

"Melvin, I've gotta ask you something. What did that guy look like?"

"What'd he look like? He looked creepy as fuck is what he looked like! That big-ass hat and that coat like he was in an old detective movie or some shit."

"Other than his clothes, what'd he look like?"

"I don't know. Man, what am I supposed to tell my mom? Do you know how much my granddad's stuff means to her?"

"Melvin! *What did the guy look like?* Tall, short, Black, white—anything?"

"I don't know, man. I guess I never got a good look at him."

Darius's stomach dropped. "Okay, Mel. I've gotta take care of something. Bye." He hung up the phone and turned back to Angelique. "He doesn't remember what the guy looked like either, and his grandpa's footlocker is missing just as the stranger said it would be."

"I don't care about a damn footlocker! How are we supposed to find our son?"

"Look, the guy who did this, he's gotta be pure evil, like a demon or something. Maybe what we need is spiritual help."

"I can't believe you even spoke to him, let alone played cards with him. You gambled with our child like he was a fucking poker chip!"

"He didn't tell me what the stakes were."

"Well, I'm telling you I want my son back. I *need* him back."

"And we'll get him back."

She pursed her lips and stared down at the sidewalk, like she couldn't even look at him anymore. She might as well have stabbed him in the heart.

He placed a hand on her shoulder. "Hey, I mean it. We *will* get him back. And I think I know where to get help."

***

"Are you sure about this?" Angelique asked as she and Darius stood outside a shop on Magazine Street.

The faded, wooden sign hanging over them read, "Boudreaux's Voodoo: Healing Spells & Gris-Gris." Severed alligator heads and chicken feet lined the windowsill, and dolls of straw and cloth stood around them, propped up to face the passersby on the street. It all looked rather hokey to Angelique.

"We need someone who understands evil spirits," Darius said. "He had good reviews online."

"You sure those reviews are real?"

"Can you just give him a chance?"

She breathed a long sigh and then mumbled, "Alright."

They stepped into the shop, jostling a wind chime that hung above the door. A man soon entered from another room dressed in a 1930s-era vest, a pair of slacks, and a hat with a band lined in alligator teeth. He looked just as hokey as the rest of the place.

"Welcome!" he said with a sweeping gesture of his arms. "I am Boudreaux. How can I help y'all today? Looking for some healing spells? Want to get back at your jerk of a boss with a Voodoo doll? I'm guessing y'all aren't here for love potions since you two seem to be together."

Angelique rolled her eyes.

"Man, we need help with a crisis, so listen up," Darius said.

He related the entire story to Boudreaux, and Angelique wrestled with her anger as she heard the details again. She was trying—really trying—not to blame him for what happened.

Boudreaux's eyes grew wide. "Holy fucking shit, man! The hell d'you want me to do about that? I don't know anything about fighting demonic entities."

"Then what's all this?" Darius gestured to their surroundings.

"*This* is a shitty little tourist trap for out-of-town white people. None of this is real. I don't know a goddamn thing about *real* Voodoo. Hell, my name ain't even Boudreaux. It's Jamal."

Angelique was losing her wrestling match. "I knew this was a waste of time. Every second we spend in here is another second that our baby is in the hands of that monster, if he's not already dead!" Her voice cracked with those last few words, and tears welled in her eyes.

"Do you know any real Voodoo witch doctors that can help us?" Darius asked Boudreaux/Jamal.

"Hell no! If I did, they'd probably kick my ass for making a mockery of their religion. But I do know someone who may be able to help y'all. A friend of my aunt is like a conjuror or something. I think they call her an 'isht ahullo.' She's Choctaw, not Voodoo. A lot of people in the Native American community go to her, and believe me, she works miracles. She's the real deal."

"Where can we find her?"

"Hold on. I've got her business card." He removed an overstuffed wallet from his pants pocket and flipped through the assorted papers inside before landing on one.

Jamal handed the card to Angelique as she dried her eyes. It read, "Mona Peterson: Rosette Bakery and Flower Shop." The address was on a road Angelique didn't recognize.

"Your conjuror's a goddamn florist?" she said.

"Listen, if you've got a problem with some kind of evil spirit, she's the one to go to."

"I swear to God, if this turns out to be another waste of time…"

"Looks like she's out in the bayou," Darius said. He had the address pinpointed on a map on his phone. "If she's legit, she could be our best hope."

"*If.*" Angelique glared at Jamal, who held up his hands defensively and took a step back.

"Let's go find a cab," she said.

***

The ride out to Mona's was a long and expensive one. Darius told the driver not to wait for them. For all he knew, this process could take hours.

The bakery and flower shop was a little white shack with a mural of cutesy flowers springing up from the bottom of the walls. Wadded bits of cloth tied to strings hung down from the roof of the porch. Something appeared to be wrapped inside them, but what it was, Darius couldn't tell.

Angelique ran up to the screen door and knocked.

"It's open!" a woman's sing-song voice answered.

They stepped inside to find a small room with a rack of cookies and donuts on one side and a shelf of potted flowers on the other. A counter with a cash register sat between them, and behind it an open door that presumably led to the kitchen.

A short, stocky, bespectacled woman with streaks of grey in her long, black hair emerged from the door and smiled at them. She held a knife in her hand, which she quickly stuffed into a pocket on her "I Heart Avery Island" apron. "Y'all here for flowers or pastries, hon?"

"We heard that a conjuror named Mona works here," Darius said. "We're hoping she can help us."

"Well, I'm Mona. Usually only other Choctaws come to me for any kind of 'conjuring,' as you call it. Are y'all Choctaw?"

"No, but—"

"Our baby was taken by a demon!" Angelique said.

"A demon?" Mona raised an eyebrow. "Is this a joke? Y'all think it's funny to mock an isht ahullo?"

"No, ma'am," Darius replied. "We came from NOLA just to see you. We don't know who else to go to with something like this."

"Please," Angelique said. "I need my baby back. He wasn't due for another two weeks, and that thing took him right out of me!"

Mona drew a long, skeptical breath. "Okay, I'll bite. Tell me what happened."

Darius had lost count of how many times he'd told the story. He only hoped this time it would result in something more than a brush-off.

Mona at least seemed to listen. Once Darius finished his account, she nodded and said, "Y'all come with me."

She led them out to a yard behind her shack where four wooden poles, each painted a different color, stood in a circle around a fire pit with wood already there waiting to burn. A bucket containing a bound bundle of leaves lay at the foot of one of the poles alongside a lighter.

Tied to the bucket's handle was an eagle feather.

"I've never heard of an evil creature taking a child from the womb," Mona said as she picked up the bucket and the lighter. "Whatever did this must be powerful."

Darius and Angelique exchanged fearful glances. Was the stranger *too* powerful to defeat?

Mona lit the bundle of leaves and a fragrant smoke arose from the bucket. She scooped it toward her face and body, bathing herself in it like it was water. Then she entered the ring of poles and walked its perimeter, waving the smoke toward the outer edges with the feather as she did so. Once she completed the circle, she held the bucket out to Darius and Angelique. "Smudge yourselves before entering. Let the smoke wash over you and cleanse you."

Angelique and Darius imitated her movements with the smoke and then entered the circle.

Mona lit the firewood and removed from one of her apron pockets a small wad of cloth like the ones that hung from the porch. She unfurled it in her palm, revealing shreds of flaky, brown leaves. "The tobacco represents prayers. Take some and throw it into the fire. As it burns, the smoke will carry your prayer up to Nanapesa."

They each took a pinch of tobacco and tossed it into the flames. Darius silently pleaded for the safe return of their son but doubted prayers would be enough to make it happen.

Mona began to sing, though Darius couldn't tell if her words meant anything or were just melodic sounds. She danced around the fire in a stilted step-like pattern for a minute or two before coming to a halt.

"What is the name of the one who took your child?" she asked Darius.

"He never said."

"Who took the child?"

"I just told you, I don't—" Darius stopped as he realized Mona wasn't asking him.

She stared straight into the fire, or maybe *past* the fire, like she was looking into another world. "Kʋta hosh ʋlla ya̱ ho̱kopa tuk?"

"Looking for me?" replied a familiar voice.

Goosebumps spread across Darius's skin, but he couldn't see anyone around.

Thick, black clouds rolled in, darkening the sky overhead. As the sunlight faded, the shadowy form of a man in a wide-brimmed hat and a long overcoat appeared just outside the circle.

"That's him!" Darius could barely get the words out. His voice seemed to have left him.

"Where's our son?" Angelique shouted. Her hand clenched into a fist, and she took a step toward the stranger.

Mona grabbed her shoulder to stop her. "He can't enter the circle, and you shouldn't leave it."

"He has my baby!"

"You want your child back, give me something in exchange," the stranger said.

"Like what?"

"One of you can come with me in his place. A life for a life is a fair trade."

Darius felt nauseous. Was that the only thing the man—no, the *creature*—would accept?

"There will be no trade," Mona said.

The winds grew fierce and blew the trees, the shack, and everything around to the point they seemed they would break apart. But in the circle, all was calm. Even the fire remained steady, as though there was no wind at all.

"Return the child you stole!" Mona shouted.

"Stole? I won him fairly."

"Bullshit, man!" Darius said. "You cheated!"

"Have any proof of that? The child stays with me unless you have something to offer."

"Can you make him bring our son back?" Angelique asked Mona.

"Not unless we give him an ultimatum—something that will scare him."

"Scare *him*?" Darius said. "How?"

"He gets his power by taking things people care about and feeding off the grief he caused. We can deprive him of that."

"But I can't *not* grieve the loss of my son," Angelique said.

"No, I guess not."

Mona reached into her apron pocket and removed her kitchen knife. In one quick motion, she grabbed Angelique from behind and pressed the blade against her throat.

"The fuck?" A look of terror washed over Angelique's face.

Darius didn't have time to think, only react. He grabbed Mona's shoulder to pry her off, but she shouted, "Stop or I'll slit her throat!"

He let go of her and backed away. "Why're you doing this?"

Mona turned toward the stranger. "I'm guessing that child is the most important thing you ever took. Your greatest power comes from having the object of her grief. If I destroy her, that power disappears. One movement of this knife—"

"You wouldn't dare cut that woman," he said.

"Wanna bet?"

The stranger chuckled. "Sure. I'm a wagering man, as Darius can attest. And I know a bluff when I see one. I'll call it. If you cut her throat, I'll not only return the baby but everything I've ever taken. Now those are pretty high stakes for me. But I know you, Mona Marie Peterson. You wouldn't kill a mosquito much less an innocent person."

"You'll give back *everything* if I cut her throat?"

"Every damn thing. But if you don't, I keep it all, including the child, and no one—not an isht ahullo or anyone else—will have the power to bother me ever again."

"Let Nanapesa hold us to our words."

"Fine with me."

Darius's anger and fear boiled over. He lunged at Mona and took hold of her arm.

As she twisted away from him, the knife sliced across Angelique's neck.

Darius watched his wife fall to the ground and dove after her. He wrapped her in his arms and, for a moment, all he could hear was the pounding of his heart over his own mumbled prayers. Then laughter filled his ears—Angelique's laughter. He drew back to look at her, and a broad smile stretched across her face.

"She cut me!" Angelique said as she rubbed her neck.

The firelight illuminated a long, shallow scrape across her throat that barely bled.

Darius looked up at Mona, who smirked as she held up the knife.

"This is only sharp enough to slice through cake, honey. But I figure that cut on her neck is enough to fulfill our deal."

Darius's mind reeled. "Did you two plan this?"

"She whispered in my ear to play along when she grabbed me," Angelique replied.

"You cheated!" the stranger shouted.

"And you didn't?" Darius said. "Sneaking jokers into a deck so you could get five of a kind."

Mona pointed the knife at the stranger. "You said you'd give back everything if I cut her throat. A deal's a deal. Nanapesa will hold you to it."

The clouds parted slightly, and light cascaded onto the stranger— and *only* on the stranger.

"A deal's a deal," he said as his form dissipated beneath the glare of the sun.

The clouds vanished with him, and the beam of light expanded. Everywhere the rays fell, objects of all kinds materialized: A child's bike, sports trophies, college degrees, heart-shaped lockets, wedding rings on necklace chains, worn-out teddy bears, a familiar red Corvette, and an old, metal footlocker.

"Where's our baby?" Angelique asked, as her eyes darted from one object to another.

A muffled cry came from somewhere in the hoard, and Darius's eyes turned to the footlocker. He and Angelique ran to it and flipped open the latch. A baby boy, naked and squinting in the light, lay atop the old war letters and photos.

Relief swept through Darius like a wave, and the suddenness of it made him dizzy. He wasn't sure whether to believe his eyes or not.

Angelique cradled the baby in her arms and looked over at Mona with tears running down her face. "Thank you! Thank you *so much!*"

"It was a pleasure. That was the toughest evil creature I've fought in a while. Made me feel young again."

"We need to get a doctor to check him out," Darius said, "just to make sure he's okay."

"The nearest hospital is fifteen miles east of here," Mona said. "I could give y'all a ride, unless you wanna take that pretty, red car."

Darius glanced at the Corvette. Last night, he'd thought it was beautiful. Now he wished he'd never laid eyes on it. "No thanks. We can call a taxi."

Angelique blinked away her tears and held the baby out in front of her, like she was examining him. "Um, Darius, does he look *strange* to you?"

"Strange how?"

"Well, for one, his eyes…"

Both he and Mona moved in closer to get a better look.

The boy's fingernails were black and sharp like claws, and his irises were tinged with red.

Darius's relief turned to dread. He bent down and rifled through the contents of the footlocker. Every photo was warped and distorted, the uniform was torn to shreds, and the letters were illegibly smeared.

He now realized their mistake. The stranger said he would return what he took but not the way it was when he took it.

THE HEALER

A Tale from Mexico

By Caroline Johnson

CELESTIAL LIGHT FROM THE universe shines
through her skeletal eyes, full
of Day of the Dead fruit, sugar
candy, offerings, and sacrifices
to lithe spirits who follow her,
who linger like guardian angels.

And I am hurting. I need a curandera
fresh from the dry desert to kill my scorpions
to feed me tortilla soup, avocado, and tamales
made of corn that the *abuelas* spent two days
mashing and wrapping with husks.

I tell her of my surgery, my chemo,
radiation, new drugs, and constant fear.

She carefully lifts my veil of stars,
looks straight into my eyes, clasps
her hands like the Virgin Mary.
Despite her Catholic gaze I cannot
think of prayer. I go to a different
mass, my holy communion a wish bone
caught in my throat, while all the
madres, padres, hermanos y hermanas,
circle round her like gentle cherubs.

But she knows my secrets, does
what all good healers do—peeks into
the horror to pluck out the plum of suffering,
holds it up to the light so it transforms
from a heavy piece of rotten fruit
into a fawn with fragile shoulders

I watch as it stumbles away and grows wings.
I am as light as air.

SEIDR

A Tale from the Norse

By Marshall J. Moore

THE GODS GRANT FAVORS to no one. That is what you must remember.

Boons, yes, whether those take the form of knowledge or tools—or weapons, which are only a different kind of tool. Curses they dole out readily enough, whether justified or capricious, regardless of whether the punishment matches the offense.

But favors are gifts freely given, and the gods do not deal in these, for everything must have its price. That is a law by which even the divine must abide, as immutable as gravity and implacable as the rising of the sun. Any gain must be compensated by equal loss, each great triumph hollowed and hallowed by greater tragedy.

If you seek to bargain with the gods, you must steel your heart for loss.

***

Dawn has not yet broken when I awaken in the longhouse, its hearth fires having waned to little more than embers over the course of the night. A few of the village women tend to them, stoking the coals and feeding them fresh wood, so that by the time more sleepers awaken, the longhall will be warmed, the cauldrons bubbling with hearty soup and thick broth.

My stomach growls at the thought, but breakfast for me will be humbler fare.

I try to rise, but the arm flung across my chest arrests the motion. Dagny lies pressed to my side, still asleep. Her skin is soft against my own, for we are naked beneath our furs. My wife's hair lays fanned across the pillow, unbound from its customary braid and shining golden even in the dimness.

I raise my hand, meaning to disentangle myself from her, but instead find myself running my fingers along her arm, down her side, resting at last upon the gentle curve of her swelling belly. I linger there, wondering if the little life inside can feel its father's touch.

Were I free to do as I pleased, I would lie here all the morning long, content in the warmth of my wife's breath tickling my ear. But we are none of us free of obligation, and I have matters to attend to.

Dagny shifts as I disentangle myself from her embrace, mumbling something in the half-speech of those whose dreams have been disturbed. I slide out from beneath the furs, careful not to let any of them slip from her. With the renewal of the hearths, the longhall will soon be warm again, but the gooseflesh that prickles down my back is not a sensation I wish my beloved to suffer.

I would save her from all suffering, if I could.

In the dim half-light I dress, pulling on trousers and tunic before wrapping my legs in insulating strips of cloth, for it is the extremities that are first to catch frostbite. Even before I wrap them, my feet feel numb, and only partly from the cold.

Into my belt I slip my seax, and a bearskin cloak goes over all. Last of all, I sling my quiver across my shoulders, from which my unstrung bow and its complement of goose-feathered arrows peer out at the world.

Thus arrayed, I stalk on silent feet from the longhall, stealing into the world before the sun.

***

The seidmadr's lodge lies north of Weligbyr, in the foothills of the mountains. Yet when I depart the village, I head not north but west, deeper into the forests that surround our settlement in every direction save the east, where we are bounded instead by the sea.

MARSHALL J. MOORE

Autumn has not yet turned to winter, but this early in the day my breath mists before my eyes, and my footfalls are announced by the crunch of frost beneath my feet. When winter comes it will be a cold one, and likely a long one.

A poor season to bring a child into the world, and yet that is the fate which awaits mine. I will provide for him as best I can; a provision that begins well before the day he comes squalling into the cold world.

I stalk slowly through the forest in search of prey, bow in hand, arrow fitted to the string. This late in the autumn there is little to be found, but I remain hopeful. And more importantly, patient.

I stop only once, shrugging my trousers low about my hips to make water. Though my bladder feels full, it takes a long time for any to come, and even then it is little more than a thin trickle, scarcely steaming in the chill air. It has often been that way of late. At last, when I am sure no more will come, I shake myself clean and resume my hunt, for time grows fleeting.

Now more than ever.

***

The sun has cleared the treetops by the time I reach the seidmadr's lodge. It is a narrow, high-roofed cottage, sitting like a peaked hat atop its hill. Mountains loom behind it, their peaks already snowcapped against the cloudy sky. Bluish smoke rises from the lodge's chimney, sending an uneasy thrill through me. The seidmadr is home, then.

A part of me wants to turn around, to retreat to the village with what I have gleaned from the forest already. To leave matters beyond my ken untouched, for I am not a learned man; my wisdom and cunning do not extend beyond what little skill I have in the huntsman's trade. And even I know that when one goes seeking the gods, the gods take notice in their turn.

Yet I think instead of Dagny, sleeping and at peace, and of the babe that grows each day within her. The midwives say she is a month from delivery, perhaps two. By then it will be deep winter, and I must see that they are provided for.

I continue my climb uphill, towards the lodge. Before I have made it two steps, the door opens, and the seidmadr emerges.

From his reputation alone, I had expected him to be a slight, womanly man, for sorcery is not a masculine pursuit. The reality is almost the exact opposite.

The seidmadr stands over a head taller than me, a graying beard spilling over a chest that must once have been broad. Indeed, he has the look of a man who was once powerfully built, the advance of years having carved away excess muscle and fat alike until only toughened sinews remain.

He watches me draw near, frowning a little, squinting from his one good eye. The other is the color of milk, all clouded over.

"Hail, Frodi Seidmadr," I call, my words carried to him on a plume of breath. The sun has melted away the frost, but it is still cold upon the heights. "I have come to—"

"I know why you've come." His voice matches his appearance: deep and coarse, like there are splinters in his throat. His eye remains fixed on me, bluer than the smoke curling from his house, then flickers towards the village, which is just visible through the last of the autumn leaves. "Folk only come to me from Weligbyr when they want what I can offer them. What's your name, boy?"

"Yngvarr Olvirson," I say, a touch disappointed. I had half-expected him to have already divined my name, just as I half-expected that he had foreseen my arrival.

"Hmm." He strokes his beard, that one blue eye peering unblinkingly at me. For a moment I am seized by that mad desire to turn back, to forgo asking questions to which I may not want the answer.

"If you've come to me," Frodi says, "then you know that nothing in this life comes free. Especially not seidr."

"I know." I twitch my cloak aside, revealing the fruits of my morning's labors: three fat grouses hanging from my belt, felled quickly and cleanly by well-placed arrows. "Will this do?"

The seidmadr takes a step closer, squinting his eye for a better look. I hold the grouse towards him for his inspection, willing myself to await his judgment with patience. I wish I had brought something of greater substance as an offering: one of the elk that roams the woods, perhaps. But the grouse were all the forest saw fit to offer me.

"They'll do," he says at last, and the terseness of those words is wholly out of proportion with the relief that courses through me at this grudging acceptance. "For a stew, anyway. Come inside."

He turns, not waiting for me, and disappears into the black mouth of his lodge's doorway. I follow him inside, stepping over the threshold I have not dared to breach since I was a boy.

***

There is already a fire in Frodi's hearth, its flames licking the sides of a cauldron already bubbling with a rich broth. I catch the scent of leeks, carrots, and something else I cannot name. Some foreign spice brought to the seidmadr by someone gone a-viking, perhaps; Weligbyr is near enough to the sea that a few longships have travelled upriver to trade with us.

Frodi seats himself at the room's round table, gestures for me to use the stool opposite him. I do, placing the grouse on the table between us. The seidmadr's broad hands move quickly as he begins to pluck the birds, sending a cloud of feathers rising between us. I lean forward and do the same, eager to be seen as helpful; a guest rather than a beggar. The feathers are stiff between my fingers, the flesh beneath them cold.

"These are good birds," he says, breaking the silence that has settled between us as we strip the grouse of their plumage. "Hard to find this late in the season."

"I found them easily enough." Modesty has little place in a culture where any great undertaking is preceded by boasting.

"You must be a skilled hunter then, Yngvarr Olvirson." That blue eye flickers towards me, something shrewd shining within it. "Was that the pretense upon which you left Weligbyr?"

"It was," I admit, trying to keep either shame or defensiveness from my voice.

"Wise of you," Frodi says, but it does not sound like a compliment. "Can't have the villagers whispering behind your back that you're an ergi."

I bristle at that, tearing free a handful of feathers with enough force that it splits the grouse's skin. To call a man an ergi is to call him unmanly; one who engages in subtleties and manipulations instead of masculine forthrightness.

"Any man who says as much is welcome to meet me in holmgang," I say, heat rising in my voice. To call another man ergi is legal grounds for such an honor duel.

"And yet here you are," the seidmadr says mildly, his eye fixed on the nearly-stripped grouse in his hand. "Calm yourself, Yngvarr the Hunter. I would have precious little business if I labelled every man who came to my door as ergi."

"Every man," I repeat. It is known throughout the village that there are those who visit the seidmadr's lodge at times, though their reasons for doing so are their own. Most commonly these are village women, seeking some small charm or potion to ease what ails them or their children—or their husbands, who may thus save face by not going to the seidmadr directly. But sometimes men do make the trek up here, and not always seeking cures or fortunes.

There must be a look of apprehension upon my face, for Frodi snorts and pushes the grouse away from him, now fully plucked. "Put your mind at ease, Yngvarr Olvirson. Ergi or not, I've no desire to take you to bed."

Heat colors my face. "That's…not why I came up here."

"Didn't think it was." Seeing that I have finished plucking my grouse, Frodi hands me his, along with a knife. I take them both and begin cutting the birds up, the familiar motions setting my mind at ease as I carve meat from breastbone.

Frodi stands, filling the small space with his size. He reaches into one corner of the room, retrieves a long wooden pole with a fluffy cloud at its tip. A distaff; a tool for spinning wool into thread. *A woman's tool,* I think, but do not say.

"Ordinarily when a man your age comes seeking me," Frodi says, plucking a spindle from where it nestles amongst the cloud of wool, "it's because he wants to know whether he'll find fame and fortune when he goes a-viking, or to seek the god's favor in some great battle."

A skein of wool stretches from the end of the distaff to the spindle in Frodi's other hand. His fingers turn, skillfully spinning the skein about the spindle, transmuting raw wool into whole thread before my eyes.

"But the hoarfrost lies heavy upon the ground this morning," he continues, "so it is too late in the season for either raiding or warring. Tell me then, Yngvarr Olvirson: why have you come to me with three fat birds as payment? What service do you seek from Frodi One-Eye?"

This is it, then. The moment where I admit what I have known these last few weeks; where I speak aloud the fear that has slowly grown inside me. Just as our baby has grown in Dagny's womb; just as something else grows within me.

Yet when I open my mouth, that is not what I confess.

"You guess right," I say instead. "I come to you, Frodi One-Eye, seeking a foretelling, but not for those reasons."

This catches his interest, as nothing else I have said has done. That one eye fixes upon me, glimmering blue in the dimness of the lodge. "I see."

Thread continues to wind about the spindle in his hand, hypnotic in its rhythmic motion, so quick that it looks as though there are two strings instead of one. I shake my head to clear it, set the knife aside.

Putting the grouse on a plate, I join Frodi by the fire and sweep the chopped-up chunks of meat into the cauldron, adding the savory smell of cooking meat to the aroma filling the room.

"Do you want me to tell you the time and manner in which you shall die, Yngvarr the Hunter?" he asks, not looking at me. "For if that is what you seek, I can tell you. But be forewarned, it is knowledge that shall do you only ill. For I have told others of their fates, and nothing they do has ever sufficed to avert—"

"No," I cut him off, agitation rising in me like crabs in my belly. "I already know how I will die."

Silence hangs heavy in the air between us once again. All is still in the lodge save for the spindle turning in Frodi's hand, slowly pulling skeins from the cloud of wool.

"You look well enough," he says after a time. Then, as if unable to keep himself from asking: "What is it that's killing you?"

"Man's flow," I say, and the admission stings. A disease of the manhood; what greater sign of ergi could there be?

Frodi nods, something almost like sympathy in his eye. "Which kind?"

I make a rude gesture towards my groin, which earns a barking laugh, swiftly silenced.

"How long?" he asks, a sort of detached concern in his voice. The tone of a man who has had much practice pitying the doomed.

"Long enough," I say, thinking of this morning's thin and unsatisfactory stream of piss, of how where it hit the ground the hoarfrost became speckled with blood.

"That's hard." Frodi does not bother to disguise his pity, yet somehow this does not rankle as it would coming from another man. Perhaps it is because I know that nothing said in this lodge shall be repeated beyond these walls, or perhaps it is because as seidmadr he is an ergi by his very nature. Either way, it is a comfort, though a strange one.

"A hard way to die," I agree, and my mouth feels suddenly dry. "Especially…"

I cannot finish the sentence, but that does not matter.

"Especially for a man who is used to being strong and hale," Frodi says, nodding. "Especially for a man with a child on the way."

I smile. "So you foresaw my coming after all, Frodi Seidmadr."

"Perhaps." He tucks the spindle into the distaff and sets it carefully aside, then rises, retreating into the darker recesses of the lodge. He returns with two horns, hands one to me. "Or perhaps a man who would risk his reputation in coming to me when he already knows what fate awaits him could only be doing so upon another's behalf. You did not come here to bargain or beg, Yngvarr, which is more than I can say for many who have sat where you now sit. Not for yourself. Not for more time. So you must have already drunk deep from life's cup indeed."

I say nothing, for he is right. Instead, I raise the horn to my lips. I toss it back and drink deep indeed, as if to prove the truth of what Frodi says. The mead tastes at once sweet and briny, layered like honey over the unmistakable sting of alcohol.

"Our child will be born soon," I say, wiping the back of my hand against my lips. "I will be there, I think, when he comes. I hope. But not for long after. *If* he comes."

"I see," the seidmadr says, staring hard at me with his one good eye. "Your first child, but not your wife's first pregnancy."

I nod. "We…she has miscarried before. Never this far along, but…"

"You want what all men want for their wives and sons," Frodi says, then frowns—not at me, but at some inner thought he does not see fit to share. "All good men, anyway. Their safety, their health."

"Their happiness," I say, raising the horn. Frodi raises his, and we drink to that.

"So," the seidmadr says, more to himself than to me. "You come to me asking for foreknowledge. Not for yourself, but for those you love. A worthy act, Yngvarr Olvirson."

"Will you do it, then?" Despite the mead, my throat feels dry as I ask. "Will you tell me if my Dagny will be alright? If our son will survive?"

Frodi does not answer, not at first. He turns to the fire, turning over the burning logs with an iron poker. He looks more than ever like a great shaggy bear, squatting on his haunches as he paws at the licking flames.

"Here is the thing about fate, Yngvarr," he says without turning to look at me. "It is fixed, now and forever. What shall be will be, and not even the gods can alter it. Odin dreams that the wolf-pup Fenris will someday grow so large he will devour the sun at Ragnarök. So old One-Eye tricks the monster into permitting himself to be bound, even though it costs poor Tyr his hand—and more than that, the wolf's trust. Now Fenris is grown large enough to swallow mountains, and when Ragnarök comes and he slips free of the chain Gleipnir, he will devour the Sun, aye—but also the Allfather who betrayed him trying to prevent that very fate from coming to pass."

"I know this story," I say, frowning. "But its ken is lost on me."

Frodi snorts, his disappointment evident. "It's said the hunter's hands are ever upon the bow rather than the lyre, so I suppose I cannot hold a lack of poetic understanding against you. Yet I'd hoped my meaning would be plain enough."

He turns back to me, and for a moment all I can see is his blue eye shining bright in the darkness. I think again of crafty old Odin, king of gods, who himself mastered the art of seidr. The Allfather who walks Midgard in man's shape, it is said.

"I put the question to you plainly," the seidmadr says. "If I tell you the fate of those you love, and you do not like what it is I tell, what will you do?"

I open my mouth, but he cuts me off with a raised hand, palm towards me.

"Think carefully," he advises. "I have had men rage at me in denial, try to bargain or beg for another outcome, or disbelieve me entirely. Yet I promise this, Yngvarr Olvirson: the fate I foretell shall come to pass, as sure as Thor will strike his hammer when my hand falls."

He lowers his hand. Sure enough, despite the clear sky outside, thunder booms against the mountains.

Only when its echo has faded into the distance do I give him my answer.

"I must beg your apologies, Frodi Seidmadr," I say. "For I have lied to you."

A bushy brow rises above a blue eye, but he does not interrupt.

"I lied to you," I repeat, heart beating against my chest like Eitri's hammer, quick and hard. "I seek foreknowledge of my family's future, but not for their sake. For my own."

His answer is a single word. "Why?"

I do not reply immediately. Instead, I look around at the dim walls of the lodge. Wonder for the first time what sort of man chooses the seidmadr's path, who shuts himself away from clan and kin to live upon the margins of the world. I wonder whether Frodi was always such a man, or if something drove him to become one instead.

"Have you ever loved someone?"

The words slip from my mouth without first consulting my mind. As soon as they do, the room grows chill, despite the cauldron on the hearth.

Chill too is Frodi's voice. "You are bold to ask this, Yngvarr the Hunter."

"Boldness is easy for a dying man," I say. "Yet you need not answer. But if you have ever known another's loving touch, Frodi, then you know what it is to worry for their safety and their happiness, regardless of your own. I..."

There is a lump in my throat. I swallow it down, force myself to continue speaking. "I would not go to my grave fearful of what awaits those I love."

"Yet you still have not answered my question." Frodi takes a long-handled ladle and stirs the cauldron. "What if I tell you that your wife will die in childbirth before the man's flow takes you? That your son will not survive her, and that you yourself will take your grief and hang yourself from a tree with it? What then will you do, Yngvarr Olvirson, if the fate ordained for you is as dire as that?"

There is a gnawing pit in my stomach; a black hole of fear akin to what set my limbs trembling before my first raid, only far, far greater in magnitude.

I breathe deeply, tasting the stew upon the fire, and close my eyes. Behind their lids I see Dagny, her hair as golden as Freyja's as it fans across our pillow.

"If fate is as cruel as you decree it," I say, my eyes still closed, "for her and for me and for our son. Then all that remains for me is to hold her close–to hold them both close—for what little time is permitted us."

Silence stretches between us, yet I do not open my eyes, for I do not want to see what lies upon Frodi's face.

"A wise answer, Yngvarr Olvirson," he says at last, and his voice is somehow changed. Cracked and cunning, the way I expect an old fox might sound if it could speak. "Very well. I will grant you what you seek."

I open my eyes, blinking against the firelight, which seems to have grown somehow brighter. In a moment I understand why: Frodi has moved the cauldron from it, and even now is stirring the embers, stoking the flames into new life. The fire casts one half of his face in harsh relief, illuminating every deep line and groove of his wrinkled features. The other half–his blind eye included—lies wholly in shadow.

"Watch closely," he says in that strangely cunning voice, as he retrieves his staff and spindle. In the half-light they do not look like tools unbecoming of a powerful man. A distaff is still a staff, after all.

I nod, staring as the winding thread grows ever more hypnotic. With each turn of the spindle the thread shudders and dances like a harpstring. And in the space between those dancing cords, a vision appears.

Dagny, her golden hair tied into a high braid. A baby in her arms, red-cheeked and chubby.

A cry escapes my lips, and my vision blurs. Yet I refuse to blink, for fear that in that moment of blindness the vision will fade.

It does not.

"Fate is hard," the seidmadr says, in that old fox's voice, "and fate is cruel. But the universe is not wholly without justice, Yngvarr Olvirson. The illness growing even now inside of you has robbed you of many years you might have spent whole and hale. That stolen time cannot be recovered, but what is lost to you shall be given to your wife, and to your son. This I prophesy you with the eyes of fate, and may neither gods nor men gainsay it."

Relief floods through me like spiced mead drunk upon a midwinter night. For so long I have felt like a man trapped beneath a crushing weight, unable to move that which presses down against him. Powerless. Weak. Yet with the seidmadr's words, with the spindle's vision, that weight has been lifted. Lifted from me by the distaff when I was helpless to lift it myself.

If this is ergi, than I will accept the label of unmanliness gladly.

Frodi watches me, unspeaking, blue eye glinting. I should thank him, I know. Should more than thank him; should fall upon my knees and swear to do him whatever service still lies within my failing power. But when I find my voice, what comes out is: "How long can I look?"

The seidmadr smiles, his hand turning the spindle in its steady, unwavering rhythm. "Until your thread runs out, Yngvarr Olvirson. But until then, as long as you like."

Thus reassured, I blink away the tears I have not permitted myself to shed. The vision between the spindle's threads remains. I feast my eyes upon it, drinking in the sight of my wife, as beautiful as she has ever looked in life. Of our son, healthy and happy in her arms.

Of a future I will not be present for, but of which I have been granted this one, precious glimpse. It is not enough, but it is what I have been given, and for that at least I am grateful.

The spindle turns.

THE GHOST OF SUMMER SUNS

A Tale from Italy

By N.R. Lambert

SQUINTING OVER THE BOXY old camera Nonna gave me—no film, but I like to wind and click the buttons—I watch through the grimy, cracked lens as she finishes with the shovel. Behind her, the late June sun lingers on the Tuscan horizon like a dropped scoop of her arancia sorbetto melting on the terrace flagstones. She kneels and pulls a clay jar from her basket, carefully placing it in the hole.

"What are you planting?"

She pushes a mound of dug up soil over the jar before she answers.

"It's a *who*, not a what."

"A who?" This stops my bare feet from kicking against the low stone wall.

"Sì, luce mio, a who."

"But who is the who?"

"So many questions, you sound like an owl." She pulls the last mounds of sandy dirt over the hole with both hands, before pushing herself up to stand with a grunt. "It's another day's story, Oriana."

Smacking her hands against her skirts, she casts a shower of dust sparkling into the last rays of sunlight. The moon, all skinny and small, is already tipping over us, and the rising trill of crickets washes in with dusk's shadows. Nonna taps the mound with her shovel, then pulls a fistful of something from one of her apron pockets and sprinkles it over the mound like rain. Seeds of some sort.

The sun is just sticky juice on the hills now, but it's still enough light to see that she's been crying when she joins me at the wall.

"Nonna?"

She tilts her head back and points up over our heads.

"See that star there, the bright one just out of Virgo's reach?"

I follow her finger and find the star. "Sì, what about it?"

Nonna doesn't answer right away; she pulls me close for a hug.

"I want you to remember that star… eventually. But right now, I need you to forget, luce mio." She leans over and touches her lips to the top of my head, whispering words in a language I've never heard before.

***

"Did I ever tell you the real story of Ceres?" Nonna spits a cherry pit into the darkness lapping up against the terrace's lamplight. She eats at least half of what she pits, I'd bet, and so it takes twice as long to get enough for the cordial. But I promised to help, and it's not like I've got anyone calling on me to go out. My friends are all suddenly very busy with dances and dates and I'm stuck with Nonna pitting cherries.

I look up. Lit by Arcturus, Virgo reclines over us, as if she's also waiting for Nonna to continue.

"I know the story, Nonna. Everyone knows it. Ceres is just another name for Demeter or Virgo, right? Fertility and farms and stuff. They still teach mythology."

She scoffs. "You only know it the way the books tell it then."

"What difference does that make?"

A soggy overripe cherry smacks me in the shoulder before sliding to the flagstone with a *plop*. For a woman who claims she has trouble seeing, her aim is good.

"Ceres is more than fertility or crops." Nonna spits another pit into the night. "Before men decided to lump every goddess together and call her 'Virgo,' Ceres was a shepherd of souls. She helped the departing cross over."

"That doesn't sound like—"

"Sta' zitto! Let me finish. Every year, about a week before il Giorno

99

dei Morti, the feast of souls, Ceres opened the gates between the living and the dead and escorted the spirits of the departed through. But one year, as she opened the gates, she spied someone she loved very much waiting to cross. She couldn't bear to lose this light from her life, so she prayed and begged the gods for more time.

"Of course, even they could not undo mortality. But seeing Ceres so heartbroken, the gods had pity and gave her a different gift. They allowed Ceres to take the little time the child had left in that plane and stretch it thin, thin, thin—like silk—to make it last as long as she could. So that's what Ceres did. She took that little girl's final moments on Earth and made them a lifetime.

"Then, when the last grains dropped through the hourglass, Ceres performed her duty, even though it broke her heart. She held the little girl's hand while she passed from this plane into the next. But just before she closed the gates between their worlds, Ceres took a piece of her broken heart and hung it in the sky before her. And ever since then, for a few days at the end of October, Ceres' heart marks the spot where the sun set on that little girl's long last day, so the world would see and remember the light that lived there not so long ago."

"Nonna!" I almost knock over my basket of cherries. "That's such a sad story! No wonder they don't tell that to children."

"Bah! They don't tell it because they don't remember," she pops another cherry into her mouth and smiles. "Have more, luce mio, the season is much too short."

✳✳✳

The taxi throws up a cloud of dust as the driver makes a sloppy U-turn and heads back toward the village. Everything looks the same, like I never left. Like I haven't been gone for years, too busy studying, working, falling in love, falling out of love, studying more. Even Nonna seems unchanged, rocking on the terrace, broad straw hat shading her face and whatever book she's reading today (mysteries, always, I send new ones whenever I find them in the university's used book sales).

"Ciao, luce mio!" She calls to me as though my visit isn't a surprise. As though she was expecting me. As though she knew just a few hours ago I'd walked out of my law exams in a cold panic, shoved an irrational assortment of skirts and books and shoes into a bag, and taken several too-expensive trains to see her. I drop my bag at the edge of the road and walk—then run—up the flower-lined drive to greet her.

She wraps her arms around me, and I feel in my bones that everything will be okay, at least for now. Even if I did just throw away years of school and my chance at a perfectly good legal career for the most fragile wisp of a dream. She guides me to the shady bench under the eaves, away from the judgy glare of the late afternoon sun, and pours me a glass of limonata from a sweating ceramic pitcher

She doesn't ask, but I answer anyway.

"It was wrong. I knew all along, deep down, you know? But I was too afraid to face it, to say it—that I'd been wasting my time and everyone else's. All of a sudden, I just felt like I couldn't waste even one more minute on it." My whole body is vibrating. Nonna tips up my hand with the limonata and I pause to take a sip, and then a breath.

"I met this editor a few weeks ago, she bought some of my pictures for a special issue. She said I had a gift and if I was interested, I could work for the magazine. I'd be traveling, taking photos… I'll probably be broke, and it's probably a mistake, but still…" Another gulp of limonata to wash down the panic; it doesn't really work.

Nonna smiles and clasps my free hand in hers, her sun burnished skin like olive wood, "Following your heart is never a mistake, luce mio… but probably, you could have finished the test first."

I laugh, still shaky, but already feeling a bit steadier. "I know. I just… I felt like I was running out of time."

Nonna nods and sips her limonata. "We all do."

SEERS AND SIBYLS – *Italy*

"Ecco, Oriana." Nonna hands me a bouquet of golden daisies, gathered from the same field behind the chapel where I used to collect armfuls of the "sunnies" for her when I was small. The flowers seem to light the entire terrace and all the guests, though I know it's just the Italian sun doing its thing.

"Grazie, Nonna." I have to bend to kiss her forehead now. As a child, she already seemed as old as Etna, but I know her being here today is a gift from the universe or some god, and I am so deeply grateful in that moment that I begin to cry.

"No, no, luce mio." She reaches up and taps away my tears, smiling; then one of the other village women, chattering gleefully, pulls her over to a new group of guests. This whole day feels locked in time, carefully pressed between sheets of wax paper, even as the first milkweed seeds drift past Nonna's garden, leading autumn in.

Though the size of the terrace means we're never more than a few yards apart, I find myself looking for Donato again and again. He must be doing it too because we keep catching each other's eyes and just laughing, the absurdity of so much joy.

When Nonna first suggested that we have the wedding at her house, I realized I never imagined it being anywhere else. I've never felt more at home than here, until I met Donato, or rather, until true-me finally met true-him.

There was always a curtain drawn between us, even though we'd played together as children, flirted on the same beaches as teens, toasted at the same dinners as adults. We maybe even shared a quick kiss during a party game long ago. But once that curtain parted, once we really saw each other, we couldn't look away again.

Nonna takes Donato's hand and puts it in mine. "Pronto?"

She squeezes our hands together before turning to the guests and herding them to their places. When she smiles, she glows.

It's sunset when we begin; our photographer—a colleague and a dear friend—is probably both loving and hating me for the tricky lighting. But I can tell Nonna is pleased with the timing, even though her eyes keep drifting to the dimming horizon at our backs.

***

I'm behind the chapel, swaths of daisies gone to seed dotted with worn headstones so smooth you might forget human hands ever touched them or lay beneath them. I reach for my camera bag, but it's not on my shoulder. Confusion creeps over me. I don't know how I got here. Or when... Feeling unsteady, I sit on the edge of the stone wall and look up to see Nonna walking toward me.

Impossible. It's been too long. Hasn't it? She can't still be here, and yet... she looks exactly the same.

"Luce mio," her smile is a sad one today. Dusk blooms behind her and the breeze swirls a ghostly stream of milkweed and dandelion wishes around us.

"I don't understand."

She bends to kiss my forehead with an ancient word on her lips, and I remember.

All of it. Where my real life ended and where the dream life she gave me began—a gift to draw out our time together as delicate and thin as a cobweb so I could gather all the days she could give me, all the moments I lost before I ever lived them.

I look down. I am small again. Back to the beginning... and the end. I swing my legs against the low cemetery wall.

Nonna reaches out. "Andiamo, luce mio, help me with the seeds before you go."

She takes my hand, leading me through the field, to the gate beyond, as Virgo prays at the purpling horizon. The chill in the air feels good, though it slows the field crickets' song. Nonna kneels before me, squeezes my hand, and holds it to her heart. She presses something into my palm.

I uncurl my fingers, expecting the seeds. But instead, find an impossibly bright shard of light, shining more vividly than anything in the darkening sky, and already, I am gone.

PYTHIA

A Tale from Ancient Greece

By Susan Jordan

DELPHI MEANS WOMB, MOST ancient oracle
Of Gaia, Earth Mother
Of Delphyne, womb of creation.
Her Stone marks the center,
The omphalos, world's navel,
The snake Python "Deep Origin"
Is her son who dwells in the uterine cave,
Where inspiration rises to the priestess,
The Pythia, Pythonissa.
Then the patriarchs said their god Apollo
Killed the Python, murdered Delphyne.
He's taking over now, it's time
For a new order.
Accept or die.

ACOLYTE

A Tale from Ancient Egypt

By Jeremy Megargee

WHEN THE VISION COMES, it burns. Nassor thrashes on the bedroll, teeth clenched, eyes rolled up into unseeing whites. He sees his village, but not as he knows it. The tranquility is washed clean, and nothing is familiar. Everything is smeared in a dripping red lens, and the ground screams. The people that he knows are transmogrified.

They've been flipped inside out, walking ruptures, and the sensitive glistening meat of a person that should never be allowed to see sunlight is exposed. And yet, no death comes. These pitiful lumps of limping flesh still breathe, and with each forced shamble, entreaties for a merciful end are flung up into the stratosphere. It rains eyes, soft jellied balls that plop against the soil, layers accumulating and rolling together in a soft wave.

This is inversion. A betrayal of the code of existence.

Nassor seizes in place, scratching at his eye sockets, and when he awakens, he will find a few superficial lacerations across the lids and brow.

He craves order, as all people do, and he is shown that this is what occurs when order is shattered. The chaos leaks in. It boils thoughtlessly across land and sea, and all things sacred sink down into the profane.

It is a heralded event, and a god has the power to call it down. Nassor is allowed only glimpses of the god. Iridescent scales that glitter with uncomfortable colors. Endless coils that compose a body, enough length to wrap up the entire world many times over. Sapphire slits for eyes, and a soulless gaze that cuts across dimensional barriers.

JEREMY MEGARGEE

It is the forked tongue that is the worst, and it flickers out in Nassor's direction, the sheer size of it causing a foul bitter wind to lick across Nassor's astral form. This is the god that keeps locked the door that opens into pandemonium. If his whim is to open it even a crack, Nassor's vision will become reality. This knowledge assaults the dreamer, and his limbs contort against the possibilities of such a rancid release, fingers curling inward like claws.

This god keeps the door that holds back chaos closed for now, but he is a fickle god. Voracious in nature, and playful even in his void of voids. Nassor is made to see, and Nassor is made to understand.

The god wants something from him.

***

He awakens with dawn still a glowing slit on the horizon. All others still slumber, and for this, he is grateful. It would be best for his children and his wife to never know that such malformations exist beyond the veil. Nassor is drawn to the Nile for a purpose unknown. His legs carry him to the banks of the river only because this function was somehow implanted in him after the vision departed.

The water is bluish gray, softly rushing in this quiet birth of daylight, and Nassor just stands and looks at it, finding a small amount of solace in the cool mud caked beneath the soles of his bare feet.

Nassor doesn't notice the serpent at first. The enormous snake is half in shadow, its exposed length drinking in the first few sips of sunlight. It watches him with languid appraisal, giant diamond-shaped head lifting to acknowledge the man's arrival. The snake's body is coiled up underneath it in the shallows, and the sheer weight of what lurks there causes Nassor to take a cautious backward step. He has seen large constrictors before, but he's never known one like this to exist in Africa. He cannot compare it to stumbling across a python in the bush. There is an *otherness* at work here, and Nassor knows in his heart that he was meant to find this unnatural traveler.

The man doesn't know what the appropriate reaction is, but he notices similarities to the physiology of the god from his vision, and so he assumes some level of dark worship is called for. Nassor begins to crouch down with the intention to kneel, but to his surprise, a hissed whisper stops him.

Words accumulate from the darkened glottis, and Nassor leans forward to properly hear them.

"No, clever ape. Do not kneel before me and kiss the mud. Think of me as a priest. Soothsayer, conduit, and more, but I am not the god you see in your dreams. Merely the tongue that speaks *his* will."

Nassor gathers his senses back to him and nods, standing there awkwardly with his hands at his sides.

"What is his will? And who is this god?"

A shifting from those massive coils, and the serpent's head lifts higher, weaving left to right.

"He is the doorway, rusted and forgotten. He is the lock that holds back experiences that would eradiate the threads of the human condition. The only thing that is able to wrap up havoc and make it toothless is the god I speak for. Would you say his name?"

The serpent yawns, hooked fangs glistening in a raw gullet. Nassor nods his consent.

"Say it then, and cradle it close. He is Apophis, and beneath all the oldest deserts he waits."

Nassor speaks it, tasting the god's name on his tongue. It sits there like sand lapped up dry from the surface of a dune.

"Apophis…"

"He's taken notice of you. This is a rare event. He stirs seldom and has no interest in mortal affairs. But he's puckish this millennium, and he has chosen you for a trial. A succession of offerings."

"Offerings? I'm lowborn, and I have little to give."

"You misunderstand. Not treasures. Apophis seeks offerings that are alive and breathing. Such was the way with him before you or your ancestors were ever born. Gifts were bestowed. Sacrifices were plentiful. He misses those days, and he has grown nostalgic."

Nassor feels the hair standing up on the back of his neck. He wishes very much that anyone other than him would have been chosen for this trial.

"Offerings hold back chaos. They prevent the unlocking of the door and the inversion of the universe. A small price to pay, don't you think?"

There's a veiled threat in the snake's delivery, but it's coated in counterfeit charm. Nassor knows this isn't a request, but a firm demand.

He rubs his hands together and wets his dry lips.

"What sort of living things does he want?"

***

"Bring me a sunbird with a breast of red. A symbol of transcendence, and that is where we'll start. Think on that little life as you carry it forth to my open maw. We whet the appetite, and we test your devotion."

Nassor thinks on these words as he walks closer to the serpent, the bird agitated and warm in his cupped hands. It chirps for the freedom that it has always known, but that chapter has ended. He thrusts his hands forward, and the anaconda unhinges its jaw, taking in the sunbird as it flutters and sheds vibrant wings. It vanishes down into the deep of the snake, that corridor of dark, and even when the serpent's mouth closes, Nassor can hear the bird singing deep in the innards.

It's a haunting song, and it lasts for far longer than he'd like. The serpent sleeps after the feeding, and Nassor notices a small red feather stuck to his palm.

Sundown creeps in as he stares at it.

***

"Have you seen the core of innocence, Nassor? It exists in all things born, but only for transient moments. The perfect host for innocence is a creature freshly birthed. That level of purity and beauty isn't built to last. Apophis misses that flavor. He eats through me, and he wishes to reacquaint himself."

"Fetch a baby gazelle that moment it slides from mother's womb. Bundle it with placenta and afterbirth still shining on its coat. Legs shaky, and it'll never learn to walk. It formed in claustrophobic darkness, and to darkness it will return to disintegrate. Do this for your god and make haste."

The helpless animal feels fragile in Nassor's arms. It's sticky, and he had to run far across the plain to separate it from its mother. The tiny gazelle has big curious eyes and a wet snout, and it keeps rubbing its nose against his arm. Nassor cannot look down at it. A flood of guilt is barely contained in his chest, and if he looks closely at the newborn animal, the dam will form great fissures and get closer to breaking.

It is mercifully quick. The confused animal child slides down into the serpent's open gullet, and it forms a small bulge deeper in the length of the snake. Only after it has been consumed does it start to bleat for its mother, that lonely sound coming from beneath the weight of scales of meat.

Nassor scrubs hands across his cheeks, noticing that he has been neglectful about shaving. It is difficult to focus on anything but the retrieval of these offerings. Apophis dominates his mind, and the threat of the vision that could manifest if he doesn't serve his god well.

"Why can't you kill them first? You eat them alive. It's cruel for them to still be inside you, frightened in the dark…"

"Question not, acolyte. Apophis likes to draw out a feeding. The best banquets require a level of patience that few have. Once delivered into the depths of the wet burning dark, life is savored intimately."

Nassor sighs and bows his head, but he can't stop thinking about the bird and the baby gazelle together in the hell of the constrictor's stomach, cramped and corroding.

He starts dreaming of tight places where light is reduced to a myth.

***

"She trusts you, Nassor. That is why Apophis wants her."

Rana has been in his village ever since he was a boy. She's a street dog with no specific home or master to lay claim to, but beloved by all, and fed and sheltered by every class of people, elders and farmers included. She comes willingly when he calls, trotting along at Nassor's side and eager for adventure.

He feels a strong affection for this dog. But a sermon was delivered onto him from the glottis of the priest, and Apophis demands that affection to be snipped into remnants, scissored from his heart and cast behind his shoulder. He glances down at her, deep purple hollows under Nassor's eyes, and it wounds him to see her tongue lolling happily at the mere fact that she is in his presence.

They arrive at the banks of the Nile, and he contemplates snatching Rana up into his arms and running for the treeline. It isn't too late. But the fear of what may come holds him in place. He has seen the kaleidoscope of chaos, and if it bleeds through, all is lost. The offerings hold it back, and as difficult as they are, he must maintain his resolve.

The serpent lunges from a nest of shadow, gargantuan diamond-shaped head snapping into the dog's leg. The fangs sink in deep, and it starts to drag Rana backward along the muddy bank. She's barely able to get out a yelp, and then the serpent is detaching its jaw, inching that mouth up over her body in an effort to swallow Rana whole. Her hindquarters vanish into the darkened gullet, and then only her torso and head are visible.

She's staring at Nassor, willing him to step in. Her eyes are large, trusting, and infinitely sad. She's digging her forepaws into the earth and trying to fight to escape the snake's mouth, putting all of her strength into the act. Nassor takes a half-hearted step forward, his throat working, the emotion inside of him sending tidal waves up against the dam of guilt. He didn't expect this sight to hurt as much as it does.

The process continues, painfully slow, and soon her big sad eyes vanish behind the snake's blackened lips. When it is over, Nassor hangs his head, the weight of his betrayal feeling like a stone in his chest. There's an awkward writhing ball in the serpent's midsection, and he knows she's there.

From within, Rana whines.

***

"You cannot ask this of me, priest. I have been faithful, but this is a line that cannot be crossed."

Nassor crouches in the dust and gazes deep into the cookfire, the flames reflecting in his obsidian-colored irises. The conflict twists in his insides, and he keeps hearing the words that hissed from the priest's hungry mouth.

"Do you know what happens if Apophis were to dip his ladle into the soup of chaos, clever ape? Can you comprehend what occurs when even a few cupfuls spill over the rim? It would unmake the world as you've come to perceive it. Up becomes down. Fire becomes water. Life becomes blistered begging Death that cannot rest. Your actions protect the threshold. Your sacrifices save mankind."

"Why me? Let another take this on. I don't have the will."

"Nor did Abraham, but it is your burden all the same. Gods speak, acolytes listen."

There is no denying what has been asked. Nassor's faith quakes inside of him, and he wishes that this universe was godless. This task will scrape him clean. It will kill the man that he was, and he doesn't know if even a vestige of his spirit will survive.

Apophis slithers through his broken thoughts, and nothing

remains but this. Nassor has been assured that this sacrifice will be the last.

***

His wife walks ahead of him, olive skin, hair soft like the hour of midnight. He holds the little hands of his daughters, both of them toddling along with him side by side. They're going to the river to bathe as a family.

This is the lie he feeds himself. Off to the river to bathe. It is dark on the edge of the Nile. In Nassor's soul, it has never been darker. He mumbles prayers to himself, and they tangle together in his mouth. His mental state seems undone, and he forgets which gods that he worships.

His wife turns to him, a smile dawning on her lips. The weight of the serpent's head smashes into her lower back, locking onto skin with a sly ambush. There have been so many nights when he has caressed her skin, the softness of it moisturized with oils. She is yanked backward into the gluttonous shadow places of the river. She is pulled from his life, and thankfully the night is moonless, so he is spared from a full view. But he hears her bones cracking and crunching as she is folded like an accordion to fit into the snake's widening jaw.

His hands rest on the faces of his daughters, obscuring their eyes. Their small bodies tremble in the mist that drifts in off the water.

"Papa, where did mama go?"

"She's swimming. Do you want to swim with her?"

Nassor chokes down a sob. He has not blinked. He feels like he has lost the ability to blink.

"Do you want to *be with her*?"

His little ones nod their heads, and so he takes their hands and pulls them through the mud. They trip and crawl. He leaves them there amongst shells and driftwood. They're crying, mucus running from nostrils. The devil in the dark wastes no time. It finds them, and it swallows them.

Nassor has fallen to his knees, and he is taking up handfuls of mud, smearing the black gloop across his open eyes. He does not want to see. He is breathing in the mud, hyperventilating, his brain a breeding pit of serpents.

He hears dim noises that won't relent. The haunted song of a sunbird. The weak bleating of a gazelle. The barking of a mournful dog. The shrieks of a wounded wife, the weeping of swallowed children.

This is the music that Apophis makes for his acolyte. The tributaries of chaos that rush through him like the roiling Nile. The serpent slithers from its resting place, enormous distended belly dragging along behind it. It rides the old river, and soon it's gone. Nassor refuses to look up. His mind is inside out, and his faith is consumed.

God has abandoned him.

A BLESSING AND A CURSE

A Tale from Nigeria

By Nwajesu Ekpenisi

WOMAN SITS AT THE table in her dimly lit chamber, surrounded by flickering candles and the pungent aroma of burning incense from a calabash. The air around her hums with a power that is ancient and timeless. Her eyes are shut. She takes a deep breath, letting the energy of the room wash over her. Her earth-coloured pellegrina gown draped elegantly over her curves. A palla, emblazed from her head, flows down her back like a river of pure light. There's something unique about her. She has always been fascinated by the world of the dead and can make contact with the spirits of the departed. Her gift—as long as she lives—makes her privy to the darker aspects of human nature.

***

At nine, in her dreams, she'd see herself standing under the kaleidoscopic shades of blue and gloomy black skies, interacting with her deceased loved ones—her father, grandparents, late aunts and uncles. Other times, she spoke with random people from the village that she knew were dead.

At twelve, she didn't only dream of the dead; she could see them roaming the village, she could communicate with them. When she walked around, she heard voices of spirits clamouring to possess her. Once, she ambled to the entrance of the village morgue and lay there until her mother, with tears cracking the sides of her face, cried over her, thinking she was dead. She even received messages from the deceased for their loved ones too:

115

SEERS AND SIBYLS – *Nigeria*

—Tell my mother that I was poisoned by my younger brother; my best friend shouldn't be accused.

—Tell my family to bury my body inside my new building.

—Go to my wife and let her know that I miss her.

These messages were never delivered because she felt that they were mere phantasms. And although it scared her, it also thrilled her. But she kept everything she saw and heard to herself.

At sixteen, she began seeing beneath things: fetuses burgeoning; love stories sprouting and flourishing; marriages crashing; flashes of gory images and charred bodies; strange shadows lurking around people, making her want to warn them about the alarming proximity of their death. Many lives were lost due to her silence, and a feeling indistinguishable from being an accomplice weighed down on her. She had always dreaded the outcome of her visions. She feared being wrong. However, her fear extended beyond that, as she was also scared of being right. To her, being wrong would only make her a deceiver, but being accurate would make her even worse—an executioner.

Visions are significant if the impending dangers predicted are avoided. These visions Woman sees, this gift she has, started from her great, great grandmother who was herself a conduit between the living and the dead, so her mother told her.

At twenty, she crept through dense bushes, the thorns scratching at her skin as she fled the village at night with the help of her mother, who saved her from being lynched by the villagers. On the night of the attack, spurts of *Kill the witch! Kill the witch! Burn her!* came from an angry mob outside her house. They called for her blood, blaming her for the death of one of the clan chiefs. While passing through the man's house on her way back from the farm with her mother, she had had one of her erratic visions—the man falling from a tall palm tree, his neck twisted, legs splayed, bones squashed, and his eyes pierced by the sharp edge of a twig—and predicted his death two days before it happened. A gift, indeed, can be a blessing and a curse. She wished she was able to control the visions. She wished she had willed him to live his last days happy. She wished she hadn't foreseen his death and had allowed him go untethered into bliss.

The voices of the men outside grew more and more frenzied as they attempted to storm the house. She sat huddled in a corner, her heart beating frantically and her eyes burning with tears, until her mother took her into their bedroom and helped her escape through the window.

***

Currently, Woman is thirty and lives in a mystical chamber filled with the ancient wisdom of the ages. The walls are adorned with intricate carvings and hieroglyphs, depicting the stories and prophecies of the sibyls of old. A thick, musty scent fills the air, as if the very essence of the past has been trapped within these walls. In the centre of the room stands a large, ornate table, its surface covered in parchment scrolls and ancient books. As you step inside, you can feel a sense of reverence and awe, as if in the presence of something truly special and powerful.

In her chamber, a young Man sits opposite her, his heart heavy with grief, his face a mishmash of sadness and frustration. The rugged, stubble-bearded Man is clad in a brown Gucci polo and trouser, a shade darker than the colour of his skin. His sandals lie close to the entrance of the door. He's barefoot. He had heard of Woman's reputation for communicating with the dead from a friend, and he had decided to seek her help in finding the truth about his mother's demise. Man is desperate and has unanswered questions, but he waits patiently for Woman to speak. Woman speaks and Man introduces himself.

"What brings you here?" Woman opens her eyes and asks. She can see through him like a crystal clear object, how the grief he feels has sucked out his oomph and will to live. She knows why he has come but she asks anyway.

"I want to speak with my mother," Man replies.

"Communication with your mother requires no special gift," Woman tells him, placing her ring studded fingers on the table. "The purpose of your visit is to listen to any words she may have to share with you."

Man knows this. He bobs his head in agreement.

The ritual begins. She pushes aside the parchment scrolls and books on the table. She dips an aspergillum into the calabash which contains a putrid organic potion. She sprinkles it on Man and around the room. Man catches some of it in his slightly parted lips. His face creases into a frown at the bitter taste of the concoction.

She turns to Man and says, "Please, give me your hand."

Man reaches out, and as soon as their hands touch, he feels a surge of energy pass through him. The life of Man is open to Woman like a book. Chapter by chapter, page by page: A child deprived of fatherly love; a teen who survived verbal and physical abuse from his father; a broken youth who knew his mother's love and endured his father's hate; rejected, lonely, confused; a man who journeyed far from home, searching for healing, craving to be accepted; a soul poisoned by bitterness; a heart yearning for vengeance.

Man lost his mother few months ago, and he still can't shake off the feeling that something wasn't right about her death. His mother was all he had in the world, and now she's faded away like the stars of the morning.

Woman starts chanting in an ancient language, her voice growing louder and more powerful with each word: *Spirits of the dead, hear my call. Come forth from your slumber, rise tall. With words of power and magic, I summon you this time. Mother nature, hear my voice, through the veil of death, I invoke. Oh spirit of the dead, heed my call, and rise from the grave. Within these words, I conjure you once more.*

The candles flicker and dance, as if they are responding to her call. She reaches out with her mind, feeling for the spirit of the dead. She asks Man, "What's her name?"

"Alice Okeke," Man tells her.

NWAJESU EKPENISI

Woman repeats the name thrice. She guides Man and asks him to speak into the calabash. He obeys and suddenly, a cold gust of wind sweeps through the chamber, extinguishing the candles and sending the incense smoke swirling. Woman's body begins to shake, her eyelids fluttering, as the spirit of the dead makes its presence known. The dead whispers to Woman, its voice like the rustling of leaves on a windy day. Woman's eyes fly open, revealing only her sclera. She stretches out her hands, as if she were grasping for something unseen. The spirit of the dead is now fully manifest, its ethereal form swirling around Woman. But Man can't see the spirit. He only feels a familiar air gust round him. Woman's lenses are back.

"She's listening. Speak now," Woman says to Man.

"Tell her I miss her."

"She says she misses you, too. She says she never wanted to leave you all alone in this world." Woman tells Man that his mother says he looks so pale with his unkempt hair and unshaved beard.

"I'm still mourning you, mum."

Woman smiles and tells him that his mother understands and that she wants him to look after himself now that she's no more. Woman tells him that his mother wants to know if Ebuka, his lover, still visits him, if they're still together.

Man grimaces. "Yes. He even followed me home from Lagos for your funeral." He sneezes. "Mum, it wasn't even a week after you passed, father brought another lady into the house." The veins on his temple pulsate, giving away the thunderstorm brewing inside him. "Dad said you were involved in a hit-and-run accident. I want to know the truth. Was it really a hit-and-run accident?" he asks both of them.

"No, it wasn't a hit-and-run accident," Woman says, staring into Man's enraged face. "She was murdered." Woman can feel the hate he feels.

Man has always suspected, but he has never been able to prove it. "Who's behind it? Do you know the driver?" Tears burn his eyes. "I promise I'll make that person pay!"

SEERS AND SIBYLS – *Nigeria*

Instantly, Woman tumbles into a whirlpool of floating visions. The images come in flashes, each one more surreal than the last, like a mirage of fragmented memories and illusions—she sees Man storming out of her chamber; she sees Man with a dagger; she sees a corpse lying flat at Man's feet, Man's hands coated in blood; she sees Man apprehended and handcuffed by the police; she sees Man donning the orange jumpsuit of a prison garb.

She snaps back to reality. She's hesitant. Not all secrets of the dead are meant for the living. She fears that the truth will only exacerbate the situation. Truth, at times, can be dangerous. So instead, Woman tells Man that his mother wants him to move on.

Man is insistent. "Please mum, tell me. Please." He's weeping and pleading.

Sometimes, ignorance is truly bliss. Some secrets are better left untouched, unrevealed. It's not always best to reveal some truths. They will find a way to reveal themselves. Woman calms Man down. She knows the consequences that will follow if Man finds out the truth. The silence in the room lengthens.

Outside, the sky is overcast. A gust of wind sweeps through fallen leaves, lifting them off the ground in a violent swirl. Dark clouds cover the sky and thunder rumbles. Man hates being drenched, so he stands up and takes his leave. Woman may have tried to keep the secret of the dead buried, but she can't shake off the feeling of unease. She hears her name after she closes the door behind Man. She recognizes the voice—it's Alice Okeke.

"How could you?" Alice asks.

"How could I what?" Woman is familiar with the ways of the dead. The dead see things only from the perspective of being dead. Spirits can be clumsy at times.

"Why did you lie in my name?" Alice's voice reverberates. "That was the only way he could have found out the truth."

"You should be appreciating me that I saved your son," Woman says, "Didn't you feel his rage? Don't you know what your son is capable of doing if he finds out the truth? Do you want him locked up in prison for the rest of his life?"

"That doesn't justify your lie!"

"I lied to save him." Woman hears a piercing squall and covers her ears with her hands. She sees Alice appear out of the calabash on the table; her appearance resembles a grotesque, smoky, shadowy figure.

She rebukes Woman for not telling her son everything: that her soul isn't at rest, that his father is responsible for her death, that he ran her over with his car the day she confronted him about his affair.

"You amaze me, Udodi," Alice calls Woman by her name.

"If your son finds out the truth, he will murder his father! Is that what you really want, Alice?"

"I don't care!" Alice snarls, her voice like the sound of raging waters. "I want revenge!"

"Alice, the path of revenge is a dark and treacherous one. How could you call yourself a mother if you let your son tread on that path?" Woman probes.

"You're an ordinary messenger, not a saviour!" Alice howls. "Do you know what it feels like to be betrayed by the one you love? Oh, you don't. Do you even know what love means? You miserable woman stuck in this wretched chamber."

"There's no point arguing with you. Your son is gone with what he thinks is the truth," Woman says, turning to light the candles and to sever the connection.

"He will return. I know my son." Alice stops Woman. "He won't be at peace until he finds out the truth. And if he returns here, you must tell him the truth!"

"I won't!"

"You will!"

"I—"

A knock at the door interrupts them. Woman hurtles towards the door, her footsteps moving against her will, pulling her away from the means to sever the connection. She swings it open and sees Man, drenched.

"Please, it's raining heavily. Can I stay here till it stops?" Man wipes his damp face.

Woman stares blankly at him. She agrees. As she shuts the door, Alice's voice fills her head. *Tell him the truth!*

Since Woman doesn't want to reveal it, she demands Woman let her in, declaring war against her in a spiritual duel that Woman is now losing. The knocks on the door of her soul are draining her of the meager strength she has left. The flashes of man coated in blood keep coming and going.

"But why did my mother choose not to reveal the culprit?" Man asks, sitting down, expecting a response.

Woman glances at him but says nothing. The voice, this time, has eaten deep into her, so much that she begins to lose control of her own body, involuntarily letting Alice in. She's struggling to gain her ground and losing at the same time. Her head throbs. She's too weak to navigate the force surging through her, spiraling into a maelstrom of confusion, blurring the lines between her world and the ethereal realms. She shrieks and crumbles to her knees, her head downcast. Man fidgets.

"Chibuikem," Woman calls. She calls him by the native name given to him by his mother. A name he didn't disclose to Woman. "Nwam, my son."

Man's gaze flits to Woman whose voice is now different. Familiar.

And the word—"Mum?"—slips out of his lips. Now, the truth must be revealed and what must be must be.

CASSANDRA'S ACCOUNTING

A Tale from Ancient Greece

By Jennifer Bushroe

AFTER APOLLO CURSES HER
Cassandra is silent for three days
untangling the twisted threads
of vision and thought and speech
knowing the future yet revealing none of it

The first thing she says is
less a prophecy and more a promise
You won't occasionally think in lies
which is the closest she can come to
I will always speak the truth

With each word she tests people's belief
finds subjects and objects heavy like warp weights
on which to loom actions and descriptions
I won't craft a vase
I won't eternally resent Apollo

Later
she shatters a vase against a wall
she neglects the god's temple
and Cassandra is still a liar but
at least people now know which thread to follow

It is up to them to trace the weft
to the taut and unbroken truth
Eventually the inverse won't be enough

SEERS AND SIBYLS – *Ancient Greece*

She will warn of Paris *rescuing* Helen *delivering* Helen
but that is how her brother will already see it

Perhaps Cassandra should leave
before her father locks her up
before the war
before her own abduction
Yes she should leave

head to Delphi
sit outside the oracle's shrine
cast off her titles of princess and priestess
declare herself Falsity
the goddess of untruths

She will speak directly to her supplicants
because seekers actually listen
They will ask
Will my crop come in
Should I make the trade

When will I recover from this sickness
She will say
The rains will be delayed
He will try to cheat you
You might die tomorrow

And it won't matter which part isn't true
or that she never answered their question
because they will walk away smiling
the lie as sweet as ambrosia
their hope sweeter still

UNTIL PROPHECY'S END

A Tale from the Celts

By Laura Marden

A COLD WIND SHOOK *the bare branches of the forest, and the remaining leaves clacked like dry bones. But even the dismal clamor couldn't drown out the heaving of Veldicca's lungs as she paused at the crest of a hill to catch her breath. Below, the grade dropped sharply into a hazardous bank of slippery rocks and loam. Veldicca shifted her daughter's weight higher on her hip, wrapping her aching arms around the small child and pressing a kiss against her rosy, windburnt forehead.*

Mairenn's youthful brow pinched in worry, even in her sleep. The girl had been crying for days, ranging from angry screams to sad whimpers. She wanted her father, her brothers, her home; it was all Veldicca could do to keep from surrendering to her daughter's demands and retracing her steps back to the village.

But Mairenn couldn't go back. Tears welled in Veldicca's eyes, recalling the druidess' words.

The child's destiny will be met with much blood and terrible struggle. She is linked to her village—each will share the same fate.

She tucked the shawl tighter around Mairenn's sleeping form and started down the hillside. The cold wind reminded her of the approaching winter, and Veldicca tried not to think about the foolishness of her escape as she sought out footholds beneath the leaves. Her back clenched with the effort it took to not jostle her daughter awake with every misstep.

Despite her best efforts, she lost her footing. The ground rose up to meet Veldicca far faster than she could manage, and she wound her body around her daughter's, cradling the child's head with hands that bruised against the tree trunks she tumbled into. When she landed at the bottom, a small hand reached out from the disheveled shawl and touched Veldicca's cheek.

"Mama?"

SEERS AND SIBYLS – *Celts*

Mairenn's blue eyes, large with fright, peered into her mother's, and Veldicca checked her for any signs of injury. Finding none, she lay in the pile of leaves churned up by her fall and wept into her daughter's hair.

***

Ailidh stopped to take in the forest around her. For two days, she had wandered these woods, but there was no sign of the dwelling she was sent to find. She slumped onto a fallen tree, resting against the cushiony moss covering the trunk. With a sigh that came out more like an angry hiss, she pulled her shoes off and massaged her feet.

Ailidh felt certain she was on the right trail, but she should have already arrived. The druidess had read the path in the pattern of bones she tossed on the floor in front of Ailidh's hearth: *turn north when you reach the waterfall and walk until you reach a fast-moving brook. Follow that upstream for a day, and you will find a forest hut wherein dwells the one who will save us all.* She glanced up at the sun hanging low in the sky and wrapped her sore toes back into her stiff leather shoes. She couldn't afford to waste more daylight.

As she bent to tie the leather thongs at her ankles, Ailidh heard the flapping of wings and felt a light breeze ruffle her hair. Looking up in alarm, her eyes landed on a falcon settling in the branches above. It stared at her with glinting golden eyes, twisting its head from side to side.

"Thinking about taking my head off, were you?"

The falcon shook out its feathers and fluttered to another limb. "Ah. I see you're going the same way as me." She meant it as a joke, but the bird kept pace with her as she walked, flying from branch to branch, always a little bit ahead. Ailidh watched it with such curiosity that she didn't see the hut until she tripped over the low boundary fence surrounding it. The falcon gave out a piercing call and dove towards the ground. Right onto the outstretched arm of a woman.

Dipping its head, the falcon ate something from the woman's

hand, and she stroked the speckled brown feathers of its wings, cooing gentle words that Ailidh couldn't hear. She looked the same age as Ailidh's mother, a few streaks of gray in her black hair, and wrinkles pressed into the skin around her inquisitive eyes. "Who are you?"

Ailidh took a hesitant step forward. "Ailidh. I've come to request your aid."

The woman scoffed. "Who told you that I would be able to aid you?"

"The druidess of my village." Ailidh swallowed as the other's face darkened. "She said the one who could help us dwelt deep in the forest and told me where to find this hut."

As Ailidh's voice trailed away, the woman threw her arm up, launching the falcon above her head. Both watched the bird catch itself midair and fly off into the cloudless sky. When the sound of wings died down, the woman spoke again. "The druidess was wrong."

Ailidh dared to take a few steps closer. "What do you mean?"

The woman whipped her head toward Ailidh, annoyance burning in her eyes. "I mean *leave*. And don't return to this place. Ever."

Anger sparked in Ailidh's chest. First the druidess and now this stranger; no one would give a proper answer. Ailidh would not waste days of travel only to be turned away.

"You don't understand." The words spilled from Ailidh's mouth. "Every village along the southern river is in danger. Marauders are taking everything from us; our food, livestock, our families. We have people—good warriors—willing to destroy these bandits, but we don't know where to look. No one who's gone out to search for their encampment has come back. My brother—"

Ailidh's next words caught in her throat. But instead, one look from the older woman showed she understood. She lost her severity and coldness, and even at this distance, Ailidh could see tears pooling in her eyes.

The woman cast her gaze at the ground. "If I could help you, I would. But the one you're looking for isn't here anymore."

SEERS AND SIBYLS – *Celts*

Fear, grief, brokenness; all were expressions Ailidh had grown to know too well in recent months, and they were all reflected in the other woman's face. Her fingers curled, and she imagined taking the woman by the shoulders and shaking her until the riddles stopped. But Ailidh realized the futility of it all, recognizing defeat in the way the older woman hunched her shoulders to her ears. Without another word, Ailidh left.

She walked until she found a boulder where she could sit and try to keep from crying. She didn't know what else to do except return to her village. Back to face the elders, her friends and family, and tell them she had failed, that they put their trust in the wrong person. When the chieftain chose her for the journey, Ailidh was humbled by the weight of her responsibility. People who knew her since birth depended on her in desperation and with hope to stop the scourge threatening to destroy all they had worked for. In the end, Ailidh was foiled by nothing more than a sad, stubborn old woman.

She heard the rustle of wings nearby, and Ailidh looked up as the falcon landed on the stone by her side. It cocked its head, twisting its neck at strange angles to look her over.

"What have you come to gawk at?" Ailidh used a corner of her sleeve to wipe away her tears. The bird merely dipped its head and kept staring. "I know feeling sorry for myself does no good, but I can't do anything else," Ailidh said. "Your friend back there won't talk to me. I don't even know why the druidess sent me to her. How could an angry woman living in the middle of the woods help anyway?"

The falcon looked away from her and preened itself, nibbling and grooming each feather with its curved beak.

"Are you even listening to me?" Ailidh's voice was sharp. "I made an oath to the gods that I wouldn't fail my village—my family. But I don't know why they chose me. I don't know what I'm doing."

Downy fluff fell from the bird's chest and drifted to the mossy surface of the rock. She picked up one of the feathers, running its soft fibers between her fingers and regarding the beauty of each strand.

"I suppose you understand that feeling. The way your mother taught you to fly when she pushed you out of the nest before you were ready."

The falcon stopped grooming and looked at Ailidh with an expression akin to accusation. She wasn't sure at first why the bird's gaze made her feel like she had said something wrong. Ailidh kept twisting the soft down. With a sigh, she admitted the truth. "But you were ready, weren't you? You just didn't know it yet."

The bird tapped its talons against the rock with an impatient clicking. Ailidh held the feather out and released it, watching it spin in a drifting descent and finally come to rest a few paces away, beckoning her to pick it up again.

Reaching for her satchel, Ailidh opened it and took stock of the contents. There wasn't much, but she had dried meat and bread, enough to last a few more days if she was careful with her portions.

"If your friend won't help me, then I'll find the thieves' den myself." Once she said the words out loud, it felt imperative to follow through. "Only." She wavered. The falcon dipped its head, curious and expectant. "I don't know where to begin looking."

Burying her face in her hands, Ailidh tried to sort out her thoughts. The falcon dropped to the ground in front of her and picked at the hem of her dress, tugging with its beak. Instinctively, Ailidh shooed it away. The falcon flew to a high perch in a nearby tree and looked down at her, letting out a short chirp.

Nevermind the bitter woman, she wasn't the reason for the druidess' instructions. It was her falcon. She wondered if that was all too strange to be true, but Ailidh was in service to the gods. It was best not to ask too many questions; she wasn't likely to receive answers anyway.

"You would be my eyes? Lead me to the place where the murderers hide?"

In response, the falcon flapped its wings and sprang into the air. It wove deftly between the trunks of the trees, and Ailidh had to run to keep up.

***

Veldicca remained in the place she had fallen, rocking and humming to calm her daughter. She knew this was her fault. When her womb had seemingly closed, Veldicca was still young and full of longing for more children. But her prayers to the gods went unanswered, and she could well remember the day she had taken a spiteful stab at Brigit. Offering her final sacrifice to the goddess, Veldicca couldn't help but utter bitter words under her breath. If you had given me a child, I would have seen that she served you well. *How then, was she surprised over the next few months as the swell of her stomach grew and she felt the quickening of the baby inside.*

Footsteps crunched close by. Veldicca's head whipped up, and she dashed the tears from her eyes. There, a stone's throw away, stood another woman. Snarled and gray, the crone's loose hair hung down her bent back. She wore simple black clothes and carried a polished staff. Pouches and trinkets hung from her belt, and Veldicca could see the silver earrings and fine brooches pinning the old woman's dress; gifts from townspeople grateful for a magic spell or reading of their fates. The strange visitor before her was another wisewoman.

"You've wandered far from home," the crone called out.

Veldicca struggled to her feet, turning her body to shield Mairenn from the intruder's eyes. "Leave me," Veldicca shouted. She glanced around, but there was nowhere to run; the late autumn forest was bare of any cover to hide her and her child.

"Where will you go?" The druidess asked. "Do you really think you and the girl will survive the winter on your own?"

"At least we will make our own way in the world. I'll not leave my daughter to suffer a fate she didn't ask for."

The lines of the crone's forehead deepened. "So you will force her to suffer death at your hands?"

The tears returned to Veldicca's eyes. She was strong, clever, and capable of foraging and laying snares, but even the best hunters starved in winter. Before leaving the village, Veldicca had convinced herself they would survive because she would pass on the greater portions to Mairenn and bear the worst of the hunger herself. Now, the crone's admonition exposed her for the fool she was, and her cheeks flushed hot, even in the cold air.

***

The next morning, Ailidh sat up stiffly from her bed of damp leaves. They had rested at dusk, when Ailidh could no longer see the falcon ahead of her in the low light. She felt certain that she'd traveled farther in that afternoon than in the previous two days.

Talons scratched against bark, and Ailidh peered up at the falcon. She yawned and ran her fingers through her hair, now snarled and speckled with debris from the forest floor.

"I know where I am," she said out loud, even though the falcon couldn't understand. "I recognized the meadow we passed through at sunset last night; it is well known to my village. My family would take special trips to forage for berries there in the summer." She sighed. "Though, it hasn't been safe in years."

The falcon spun its head away from her, suddenly alert and tense. It let out an ear-splitting shriek that made the hair on Ailidh's arms stand on end. She fell silent at once, and then heard it too. Voices and the heavy tread of feet.

Ailidh ducked down behind a holly bush. Its waxy leaves poked into her flesh, but it was the only foliage nearby thick enough to hide her. Mere paces away from the place she had slept, two men swaggered past. They each carried spears, and one also had a long-knife hanging from a baldric over his shoulder. Ailidh quivered in her hiding place, wondering again why she'd been sent when there were brave warriors in her village who wouldn't cower in the face of danger.

The bandits disappeared from sight. Tiptoeing through the dried leaves, she approached the place the men had come from and found a hunting path, oft-trod and easy to follow. The falcon dropped with a trill onto the ground by her feet.

"I think I know where their camp is," said Ailidh. "Come, there's another way."

Ailidh crept away from the path. The gully she was looking for ran beneath a cliff of exposed stone. Her brother had been able to climb all the way to the top, as had she, after many tries and not a few scrapes and bruises. Ailidh recalled that the small ravine cleaved the forest terrain for close to a mile until it spilled out into a glen with fresh water and high, protective hills; a perfect place if you didn't want to be found.

The stone wall appeared where she remembered, and she adjusted her course to travel alongside it. The debris at the bottom of the gully had been washed aside by rain, exposing patches of bare dirt so she could travel silently. She increased her speed to a cautious run.

As she hurried, she felt safe with the falcon's sharp eyes watching her from above the treetops, and for a brief time, Ailidh's fears melted away. The elders' trust in her would be founded after all, and she could return to her family knowing that she had helped dispel the dark cloud from their lives.

Abruptly, the falcon swooped down and cut her steps short. They were close to the glen. Dropping into a crouch, Ailidh fought to listen over the sound of her own breathing. It took several moments, but eventually, she heard it; men and women's voices, the sharp cracking of an ax, dull taps from a hammer.

She turned her smile on the falcon. "We found them."

With a chirp, the falcon winged upwards and away, and Ailidh was left alone. She was puzzled over the bird's sudden departure, but wanting to get a better look for herself, she searched about for a good vantage point. Her eyes landed on a high ledge at the top of a nearby hillock, and she scaled the leafy incline, careful to remain behind the rise of the hill so the occupants of the camp below wouldn't see her moving through the trees. Ailidh was not disappointed. She lay on her stomach at the crest of the ledge, the entire glen spread out below her, and she could now see how the bandits seemed to disappear into the forest, returning to this hollow like rabbits to a warren.

Several dugout cabins faced a fast-flowing stream carving its way through the dark soil. The space was narrow, with barely enough room to walk between the doors of the dugouts and the steep embankment of the stream. Between the lodges, people carved tools, cooked food, and patched clothes, much like any other community. She estimated that there were around thirty to forty men and a handful of women and children. Ailidh felt a pang, realizing that the latter were likely taken away from their homes by force, but would be caught up in the attack nonetheless.

Leaves rustled behind her as the falcon landed and she shook away the darkness that had entered her mind. When she turned however, the falcon was nowhere in sight. Instead, her heart plunged, seeing one of the bandits coming towards her, spear lowered and ready to attack.

Throwing herself sideways, Ailidh slid down the grade she had just climbed and picked herself up at the bottom of the ravine. She sprinted away, the snapping of twigs and heavy footfalls of the man chasing her loud in her ears.

Her toe caught under a thick root of an oak tree, and she fell hard, knocking the breath out of her lungs. At the same moment, the man's spear hit the tree next to her with a *thwump*. He pounced on her, pinning her under his weight. Dirt wedged under her fingernails as she clawed at the ground, trying to pull free. And failing.

***

Veldicca flinched when the crone lifted knobby fingers towards her.

"It matters not. Brigit has made known her intentions towards the girl, and the goddess will not let her die." The druidess' voice slowed, and she dwelled on every word. "But, you tried to break your promise. You will live apart from your village and your kin until the girl has fulfilled her purpose. You will not see your other children until the prophecy comes to pass. Brigit will not let you forget who the girl belongs to."

The crone dropped her head and leaned on her staff as though the words had drained her of all energy. Veldicca was left speechless, chilled to her very bones.

"Mama."

Mairenn's voice trembled and she clutched at her mother's collar. She cried out, high-pitched and full of fear. As Veldicca bent to comfort her child, she suddenly felt a sting of pain on her neck. She brought her hand up and her fingers came away bloody. Mairenn must have scratched her.

But when Veldicca tried to take Mairenn's hands to calm the child, she recoiled. The small fingers were gone, and in their place were sharp talons. Veldicca collapsed to the ground, laying Mairenn down to see what was happening. Sickness gripped her stomach; panic clouded her mind.

She watched helplessly as Mairenn shrank. Feathers sprouted from her head and body. The girl's cries of "Mama! Mama!" turned into the shrieks of a frightened animal. A moment later, Veldicca's daughter disappeared, and she held a young falcon in her hands.

The bird squawked, flapping its undeveloped wings and clumsily trying to walk about on the small heap of clothes it had once worn.

A cry tore from Veldicca's chest; a terrible choking sound that reverberated through the trees. She held her daughter against her breast, rocking back and forth. Sobs wracked her body, but no tears came. Veldicca looked around with wild, desperate eyes, but the crone was gone. She could only hear the wind shaking the branches like a death rattle and the pitiful chirping of the bird in her hands.

***

As Ailidh struggled, a scream that was not her own rent the air. There was a hollow *thud* and the man flew off of her from the force of the blow. She looked up in time to see the falcon banking for another strike. Twisting around, she crawled backwards, away from the stunned man who was trying to sit up. Blood ran from deep gouges into his face.

The falcon arrived in a flurry of wings, razor-sharp talons outstretched towards the man's eyes. Ailidh didn't see the dagger until it was too late. Even though the man slashed blindly, the blade found its mark, biting deep into the falcon's breast. The limp bird hit the forest floor with a crunch of dead leaves, and the dagger went flying into the brush.

Ailidh managed a cry of dismay before she turned back to the bandit. He fumbled for the weapon, swiping away blood so he could see, cursing at the pain now that his initial shock was wearing off.

Ailidh saw the glint of the blade within her reach; she stood frozen to the spot. She wanted nothing to do with this part.

"The Morrígan give me strength," she whispered. Ailidh grasped the dagger.

The bandit rummaged around in the loam with his back exposed. Standing over him, she lost her resolve for a moment, but a spark of anger flared in her heart when she remembered the man belonged to the ones who had killed her brother. She tightened her grip on the hilt and plunged the dagger into the side of her assailant's neck.

The man arched backwards, nearly knocking her over. Jerking the blade free, Ailidh retreated, and the man toppled, sputtering on the blood filling his throat. Even though it was over in the space of a few breaths, the seconds dragged on. Ailidh's initial dread faded to a cold numbness while she watched the man writhe, and then go still.

At once, she began heaping leaves and fallen branches over the corpse, trying to disguise all traces of the fight. If she had any favor with the gods, a wolf would drag away the carcass before the other bandits found it.

When the job was done, she stood back, satisfied that she had concealed the body to the best of her abilities. She thought of the falcon lying somewhere behind her. It wouldn't do to leave such a brave animal, a creature that had saved her life. She would take the bird with her until she found a quiet place beside a stream to build a cairn and give it a fitting place for its final rest.

She turned, expecting to see the crumpled mound of feathers, but was dumbfounded. The falcon was gone and in its place was the body through a fog of exhaustion. The whole time, Mairenn kept her trembling hand clasped around Ailidh's, refusing to let go.

od smeared across her torso, and lying

gled up in Ailidh's mouth.

ishment and crouched over the body, allow rising and falling of the woman's e of a heartbeat, the injured woman ises peered up at Ailidh before closing

dh at the same time. She tugged the pins oped the garment around the stranger ith strips of fabric Ailidh cut from her t whispering, "Please, stay alive. Please,

***

e edges of the night sky when Ailidh, cher fashioned from fallen fir branches, te her village stood. She saw the outlines ess, heard the barking of dogs, and saw watchman searching for the source of ed in the middle of the path, using the alongside the stretcher and take the

She would have cried with relief, but she t. The watchman called out to someone idh recognized the voice of her cousin she and her companion would be er father's house to recover. awake at Ailidh's side. She coughed and in her chest. Ailidh put her other hand eady her. n's voice was strained, afraid.

WISE SERPENT

A Tale from the Ancient Hebrew

By Joseph Mathias

…И жало мудрыя змеи
В уста замершие мои
Вложил десницею кровавой.

*And with his bloody right hand
he placed a crafty serpent
between my frozen lips.*
— Alexander Pushkin, "The Prophet"

I HURTLED HEADLONG FROM my birth,
and writhed upon the dust of earth;
and scarce a hundred heartbeats passed
between my first breath and my last.
Outstretched and prone and numb I lay,
and cringed upon myself straightway,
nor knew if mine might be the form
of seraph fallen or groveling worm—
until a rod before me fell,
and bent, and quivered, and became
a serpent long and terrible,
whose shape as mine must be the same.

And as he drew his great coils out,
and fixed his glassy eye on me,
both gods and men stood roundabout,
the outcome of our strife to see.
I reared my head, I worked my jaw

SEERS AND SIBYLS – *Ancient Hebrew*

till loose it hung and out of joint.
The venom galled my velvet maw,
and filled my fangs from root to point.

But even as I made to strike,
my foe flicked forth the living flame
of his forked tongue, and it became
two serpents more, and dread alike.
And human wiles were in their eyes,
and human speech was in their mouths.
And this one spun persuasive lies,
and that one framed misshapen truths.
And as their sleek coils circled round,
entrancing shapes danced in their skin.
And shrinking back, no chance I found
to strike them as they hemmed me in.

But overhead a voice arose:
"Make wide your mouth against your foes,
and I will fill it." This I did;
and from my parted lips there slid
a speech more subtle and fluent yet.
For I too had a parted tongue,
which on its right fork could beget
invention, fancy, and wild song;
but into these, its left side poured
the immutable eternal word.
And when my hissing mockers struck
their heads on this, its substance smote
their skulls to bits; their thin fangs broke;
and limp they both slid past my throat.

But at the voice's next command

JOSEPH MATHIAS

I stretched out rigid as a rod,
and passed into the prophet's hand,
to work again the words of God.

BERGDIS AND MIMIR

A Tale from the Norse

By Stephanie Ellis

"THEY'RE BACK! THEY'RE BACK!"

The boy's cries were met with a cheer by a few and silence by others. Heads turned to see Thorkel's raven banner closing in on the settlement, the tramp of feet a drumbeat across the pastures.

Anxious women looked to Gudrid for reassurance. Their *spakonur* ignored the murmurs around her and their accusing stares, kept her eyes fixed on the approaching warrior band.

As Bergdis counted the arrivals, she realised Gudrid—always so reliable in her prophecies—had been completely wrong on this occasion. *How?* The men spilled into the village and it was clear that none had been lost as Gudrid had foretold.

Thorkel took in the gathering and smiled—until he caught sight of his wife. The curve of Noora's belly was obvious. Her stomach had been flat when Thorkel had taken their men on yet another raid several months ago. Everybody knew they had been gone too long for Thorkel to be the sire. It only remained to see what he would do. Bergdis scanned the small group for Erik, Thorkel's brother and the father of Noora's baby—he was nowhere to be seen.

"It appears my brother has looked after our people extremely well," he said. "Wife, it seems you have kept your promise to obey Erik in all things." His tone was even, without a hint of outrage, almost as if he'd expected it.

Noora shrank back at his words. Bergdis reached out to her sister and squeezed her hand, offering what little reassurance she could give with her touch.

"And as you can see, we have kept our promise to bring back the wealth which will see Jelling prosper."

Unknown men and women, shackled behind the warriors, shuffled forward to set chests at Thorkel's feet, which he immediately ordered open to display the plate and jewels within. Alongside the chests were dropped pelts of wolf and bear, and bolts of cloth. Bergdis wondered at the place they had raided, what manner of folk were as wealthy as this except kings?

"Odin keep us safe," she whispered, touching the amulet at her neck. Grey clouds had gathered on the horizon and a strong wind swept up the valley from the direction of the sea.

At this, Gudrid finally acknowledged her presence. "I doubt he will. He knows what I have done." Her voice, too, was calm.

The crowd had broken up as families reunited and others stepped forward to examine both Thorkel's plunder and his captives. It left Bergdis alone with Gudrid. She tugged the woman's sleeve, pulling her back a little so they could talk without being overheard. Noora was standing obediently beside Thorkel.

"What did you do?" Bergdis's stomach was in knots. There had been no hint of secrets this past summer, an idyllic time in which they had watched sheep and tended their crops and lived with Gudrid's promise, that Thorkel would not return and Erik would become their chief.

"What he made me do. I said what he told me to say when he was away."

Bergdis was incredulous. "You lied to us? You betrayed your gift?"

"How could I not when Thorkel promised to kill you and your sister if I did not do as he said. Now, he will kill only one of you."

The fear in Bergdis's stomach solidified into ice as Gudrid continued, revealing she told Thorkel his brother would strive to take his wife and his place as chieftain.

"He knew and yet let it happen? Why?"

"So that he would be shown to have right on his side when he kills his brother. Remember he has only been allowed to continue as chief under caution from Jarl Harald."

There had been a third brother, Olaf, whose death had been mysterious and caused much discontent at the last Thing. Yet Harald needed Thorkel and his men and so had dismissed the accusation as mere hearsay.

"He'll be after Harald's position next," said Bergdis. "Ouch!"

In the few moments Bergdis had taken her eyes off the milling villagers, Noora had rejoined them and grabbed her hand, squeezing hard enough to hurt. Bergdis shot her a look and spotted Thorkel bearing down on them. She swallowed, sent another prayer to Odin that he had not heard her words. The women around her scattered at their chief's approach.

"Take Noora to my house," he commanded the two men who accompanied him.

My, not *our* as of old. Her sister's fate was already written. She could do nothing but watch them drag Noora away, Thorkel striding ahead. Only Gudrid remained at her side.

"Erik should challenge him! Why does he not defend her?"

Gudrid scoffed. "Because he is a coward. Why do you think Thorkel left him here? He's a liability on a raid—and to the village."

The woman had a point. Erik harboured the spirit of Loki; a sly trickster, his mischief was rarely traced back to him. It was for others to pay for his schemes, often with loss of limb—or life. Bergdis had never really liked him but that summer he had been charming and pleasant, and she had given him the benefit of the doubt, whilst her sister had given him more.

"So you were set to trap him—and Noora was the bait."

"Your sister was a fool for yielding to him so swiftly."

"But Erik appears to have fled, his horse has gone. It is Noora who will face punishment."

Bergdis pulled her cloak tighter about her shoulders and watched her father enter their family's hut. She would not sleep under that roof tonight. She did not want to hear her mother's cries and terrified mumblings about her daughter's fate. Instead, she turned her back on the village.

"Where are you going?" called Gudrid.

"Why don't you tell me?" she answered, keeping her face set on the track ahead. The path was fading with the light, but her feet seemed to know the way and she allowed herself to be directed wherever they took her. She passed the mounds at the edge of the village, the rune-carved stones denoting their border, then further still to the edge of the wood. As her eyes adjusted to the gloom, she heard the first of the wolves. If her absence was noticed, nobody would come looking for her. They never did when the wolves sang.

Yet Bergdis was unafraid. A memory had settled over her of walking this path before, many years ago as a young child, and a voice had told her she would return. It had not been Gudrid's voice.

On she went, further from Jelling and safety, and deeper into the embrace of the mountain. The trees remained sparse on the path she was walking, allowing the moon to reach down and guide her way until she curled away from the forest and found herself in a small gorge. Ahead of her was a mound. She sat down on its summit, felt the damp chill of the grass through her skirts, began to consider starting a fire to keep warm.

"Ask," said a voice.

Bergdis shot to her feet, looking around to see its source before realising it came from beneath her. She walked carefully down the side of the mound until she was back on level ground and circled the tump. There was no one there.

"Ask," repeated the voice. "We talked once, girl of the caul, when you were a child. I told you, you would return when it was your time."

Her time? There had been no reference to the caul, which had covered her at birth, for many a long year. The villagers had deemed it a sign of good fortune, that she would be able to charm their lives for them, but when she had shown herself to be as any other girl, and an often clumsy one at that, they had dismissed it from their minds. Her life had become one littered with insults and cruelty as the village blamed her for not being what they had hoped.

"Gudrid will no longer be able to find me," continued the voice. "With her betrayal of her gift, she has lost it, and now it is for you alone to walk this path."

The memory of her first visit suddenly presented itself to her as if it was only yesterday. She had not been frightened then, and she found she was not frightened now. All her fears were for her sister's safety.

"You will return to your village," said the voice, "and you will tell Thorkel that Mimir has spoken to you and permitted you to visit. You will allow him to ask a question, and then you will return to this mound tomorrow night and I will give the answer."

Bergdis stared at the mound. "Mimir," she whispered, "Mimir that belongs to the All-Father?"

A laugh echoed around her. "He thinks he owns me but truly I belong to no one. He buries my head when he is travelling and has no need of me. Sometimes I let him find me again, other times I prefer to help the humans who suffer the whims of those who inhabit Asgard."

Fright claimed Bergdis and she began to shake. She had never lost her faith in the gods despite their silence during times of hardship, but this! Mimir was asking her to face Thorkel after her sister's adultery, to publicly lay claim to Mimir's confidence. He would not believe her, would think it a ploy to save Noora.

"Noora will be saved," said Mimir, as if reading her mind, "provided you do as I say. Now go."

Bergdis set her feet homeward, walking in a daze but never stumbling, never hearing the wolves who padded behind her, the howl of the wind as it moaned through the trees. Too soon she found herself back in Jelling, making straight for Thorkel's dwelling before she could talk herself out of it. One of his new slaves stood outside the door and barred her way.

"Tell Thorkel I have come from Mimir," she said.

The name caused the slave to dart inside, and the door opened to her, as Mimir had told her it would. She found Thorkel and Gudrid sat before the fire in the centre of his home, Noora was seated opposite, apparently unharmed—a surprise considering what had happened.

"We've been expecting you," said Gudrid.

"You knew I would come?"

She laughed. It was a bitter sound. "Of course I did. It was the last thing Mimir told me."

"Yet you did not warn me?"

Gudrid's eyes glittered in the firelight, hard and cruel. "You expect me to help you? The one who is to take all I have from me? No. It is for you to find your own way. And that, too, was foretold."

Gathering her courage, Bergdis turned to Thorkel. "Then you must have your question ready for me?"

He looked her up and down, assessing. "Such a scrawny girl. No wonder you've not found a husband yet. Perhaps I will give you to one of my household."

No! Mimir had not told her this would happen!

"I will make a study and see who will suit you best," he continued. "And as to my question, I will give it to you tomorrow. For tonight, you may bed down with your sister."

The slave who had let her in had reappeared and taken hold of her arm, pushing her roughly over to Noora's side. Then Thorkel left the hut and only Gudrid remained with the young women.

"Knowing Mimir speaks through you now, he will not harm either of you, until you have outlived your usefulness—as I have mine. I am as much a prisoner as you."

Noora had lain down, curled herself up into a ball, and allowed herself to sleep. Brigdir joined her. Their bed was a straw pallet with a blanket, it was warm and more than she thought he would have offered. Bergdis sensed no fear from her sister, nor from Gudrid, whose span of life had shrunk to almost a breath.

"Was it truly to save me and my sister?" She could not believe they were the sole reason Gudrid had acted as she had.

SEERS AND SIBYLS – *Norse*

The *spakonur* leaned towards the fire, poking it with a sturdy branch before dropping the wood into its midst. Sparks shot up and the flames danced, seeming to hypnotise her. Gudrid ignored Bergdis's question. "If you watch the fire carefully enough, you will see the battles of man, the deeds of gods. All you have to do is open your inner eye." She took another piece of wood and tossed it in, unconcerned about the possibility of the spluttering kindling setting fire to their surroundings. "I will be given to the wolves," said Gudrid, "but they will not kill me. Mimir has promised me a kinder death. You would have done the same. Everything I have done has been preordained. Everything you will do, likewise."

Bergdis had seen such deaths, punishment meted out on the orders of Thorkel. A body ripped apart by beasts or split open by man, there was little to choose between either ending. She lay down beside her sister, curling up against her and pulling the blanket over them both. Noora stirred slightly and then settled again. Bergdis closed her eyes and allowed herself to drift off to sleep. In her dreams, the wolves howled and a longboat burned against the night sky.

The morning came round quicker than she would have liked. Food was sent into them, but no one came to speak with the women. Bergdis waited impatiently for Thorkel to ask his question. She wanted to be gone, back to Mimir and his promises of freedom, his reassurances. The sound of the village going about its business filtered through the dwelling's walls, calls for water, curses at children getting underfoot, metal on metal, weapons being sharpened. The three did not speak, even though she wanted nothing more than to ask Noora what had been said before her arrival. Noora herself remained huddled on the pallet, whilst Gudrid stared into the ashen remains of the night's fire. Eventually, Bergdis was taken outside by Thorkel's slave, discovering much of the day had passed in the process.

Thorkel had summoned the villagers and stood before them. "We have no *spakonur*, friends, but it seems our Bergdis has aspirations! She claims to have Mimir's ear—although she does not have his head!" He paused to allow the crowd to laugh at his little joke. A few obliged. "I have been allowed to ask a question, it seems, and so I *will* test her because her presumptions amuse me." He glared at Bergdis who had been placed in the centre of the gathering. Unused to such attention, she kept her gaze on the ground.

"Look at me, girl," ordered Thorkel.

She obeyed, noting the same sly expression on his face his brother had often shown.

"A visitor is to come to Jelling. I wish you to ask Mimir on what terms I have allowed him to travel to us. And will he return to his ship safely?"

A visitor? Rarely did anyone seek out their people. Unless it was the Jarl raising men to go on his raids, or a messenger summoning them to the Thing. Thorkel repeated his questions, and then she was dismissed.

One of the women walked with her to the boundary of the village and passed over a small parcel of food on their parting. Nothing had been said as they walked and Bergdis had to admit, the silence to which she was being subjected was more unnerving than the usual curses and abuse she received. She pushed back her thoughts and emptied her mind and again allowed instinct to guide her to Mimir. The journey felt quicker than the day before, as if the mound had moved closer to the village.

"Ask," said Mimir.

She spoke the question and waited.

"The visitor is a priest. A monk who wishes to convert Thorkel to Christianity. He has been given safe passage, not by Thorkel, but by Harald, who is considering the conversion of his people. The man will not return. There will be a fire and he will rescue a child, Siv, whilst he will perish."

"And myself, Noora? What will become of us?"

"That is a question for another time," said Mimir and fell silent.

Bergdis sat on the mound and ate the food she had been given.

She was in no hurry to go back, preferring to sit and gaze at the stars for a while longer. But she had to return, give the answer. She thought of Siv, five years old, blonde haired and blue-eyed, Thorkel's daughter from his first marriage.

Again the wolves accompanied her return journey, and again she was allowed to re-enter her village unmolested. The villagers gathered when they saw her walking towards Thorkel's hut. He emerged as if by magic.

"Give your answer here. In front of all," he ordered.

She repeated Mimir's words, heard the murmuring ripple through the group. Then from behind Thorkel appeared another man, dressed in a long brown robe, bound by a rope at the waist, and with a shaven head.

"A lucky guess," sneered one man. "Monks are popping up everywhere."

"Where's Siv?" asked another.

No sooner had he spoken than a shriek reached their ears. It came from Bergdis's home, not Thorkel's. She'd got it wrong!

"Mother!" She made to run towards the house, arms held her back.

"You will not save her?" asked the monk, astounded.

Thorkel gestured towards the hut. "If you wish, there is nothing to stop you."

The man sprinted towards her home. She could see flickers of orange lick at the wood.

"Not exactly what you prophesied," said Thorkel, watching as the monk pulled the door open.

Bergdis continued to struggle against her captor without success, registering for the first time, those who watched on, too frightened to act. Amongst them was her mother! But if she was there, who was inside their home? Who was screaming?

"Mother!"

"Let's hope the priest can save her," said Thorkel, returning his attention to her, thinking her cries were aimed at the burning building.

Then he followed her gaze, took in the presence of Bergdis's mother. "Who—"

He jerked his attention back to the hut, just as the priest appeared at its entrance with the child in his arms. The roof groaned above him, and he only had time to throw the child out and away from the building before its timbers crashed down on top of him. His screams were short-lived.

Bergdis's mother had come to her side and both looked at the burning remnants of what had been their home.

Thorkel scooped his daughter up and looked at Bergdis. "Go," he said. "If you want your sister to live, if you have been chosen by the gods, then you will bring me Mimir's head."

Bergdis said nothing, could do nothing but turn away from the village and set off once again. How could she do as he asked? She doubted Mimir would give himself up. Noora was as good as dead. It was with a heavy heart that she trudged towards the wood. This time she found the gorge was barely a span away from the village. She shook her head. She had eaten little and was tired. She had travelled the route without taking in her surroundings. An easy explanation. *And yet.*

"You have come for my head," said Mimir as soon as she stepped onto the mound. "And yes, I will let you unearth me and take me back. Although I doubt Thorkel will regard my presence as a blessing."

Bergdis couldn't believe it! "You will allow it?"

"I have a desire to see more than earthen walls," said Mimir. "At least for a while. Climb to the top of this mound. You will see a small hole in the centre. Reach in and you will find me."

She had clambered over the hillock earlier and had seen no gap. However, Bergdis retraced her path, came to the centre, and there was a hole as he had said. Kneeling down, she thrust in her hand and her fingers touched rough material. Carefully, she pulled it out, full of wonder at what she would see. About to open the bag, his voice stopped her. "No, not yet. When we are within the village bounds and have an audience."

She weighed the bag in her hands, it was bulky but not heavy. What man had this been, if a man?

Bergdis was amazed to find the return journey was no more than a few steps on this occasion. Soon, the mound would appear in the midst of Jelling itself!

Thorkel's warriors were sat outside his longhouse. When they spotted her, one opened the door in readiness and gestured her inside. Then they followed her. Bergdis allowed herself a quick look round. Noora sat in the same place as before, still seemingly unharmed but her anxiety more evident. Gudrid was nowhere to be seen. What kinder death had she been gifted?

Thorkel intruded upon her thoughts. "Open the bag, girl."

"No," said Mimir. "She will place me amongst the flames."

There was a gasp from those behind them, whispers and murmured prayers. They watched on in awe.

Bergdis stared at the fire, felt the intensity of its heat.

"She won't be able to do that without setting fire to herself," said Thorkel with a laugh. "It seems Mimir has tired of her already!"

Mimir had told her the fire would not hurt her. She had to trust him if she was to save her sister—and herself. Gently, she placed the head in its centre. The flames immediately claimed the cloth, revealing the skull at its midst. It seemed to turn, taking in all those who stood before it. The men behind Thorkel clutched their amulets and offered up prayers to Odin, backing away from their leader. He, meanwhile, could not hide his excitement.

"With the head of Mimir, I will have no need of women to guide me," he gloated, pulling out his knife and pointing it at Bergdis and then at Noora.

"You think so," said Mimir, "by all means remove me from this fire and let us see how you do without a woman's hand."

Thorkel made as if to take the head and then thought better of it, instead directing another to pick it up. The man paled, looked wildly at his companions. They refused to meet his eye.

"Do as I say, or I will gut you like a fish," snarled Thorkel.

The man gulped, no longer a brave warrior, scourge of the sea, but a trembling wreck. He hesitated at the fire's edge until a prod from Thorkel's sword sent him plunging his hands in to grasp the skull. Within seconds his arms were alight and in his panic, he stumbled and fell further into the flames to lie alongside the skull. His body twitched for a minute and then stopped, gradually dissolving in front of them.

"You." Thorkel pointed at another unfortunate. The same process was repeated.

"Keep trying, Thorkel, and you will have no men left to command and women will be all you have—if they will have you. Now listen to what I tell. The Jarl will come and find your village destroyed. The snows will bury all, and it will appear as if it never was. Nothing will be left. Your name will be forgotten."

The men were backing further away. Beyond the doors which had remained open, there was muttering.

"Stay!" Thorkel shouted at them, but they continued to retreat. His sword still drawn, he advanced on his men, but they merely drew theirs in return. Their fear of the magic of the gods was greater than their fear of their leader.

At last, Bergdis reached into the fire and lifted out Mimir's head. It gave off no heat. She returned it to its cloth bag, by which time, Noora had risen from her seat and come to her side.

"We need to go," she whispered. "If we stay, Harald will kill us, my baby …"

Bergdis nodded, and the women skirted around Thorkel and his men who were too intent on each other to notice them slip away. Outside, they found their mother waiting for them.

"Where do we go?" she asked, handing each a bundle containing their few belongings. Noticing her daughters' surprise at her readiness, she smiled. "I have been prepared for this since the day you were born."

"We go wherever Mimir tells us," said Bergdis, offering her arm to

Noora in support.

Angry voices erupted behind them, followed by the clash of steel. The remaining men who had stayed outside drew their weapons and charged inside to join the melee.

The three women turned their backs on the village and walked away, ignored by all in the confusion. This time, the wolves did not follow, instead crept further into the settlement, sensing a feast in the offing. Behind them, the snow began to fall.

DUET OF THE HERO AND THE SEER

A Tale from the World

By Bettina Theissen

M INE THE POWER,
Mine the pain.

Mine the darkness,
Mine the sign.

Mine the freedom,
Mine the choice.

Mine the knowledge,
Mine the voice.

DIWONA

A Tale from Ancient Britain

By Misty Urban

I F ANY OF US had actually been a seeress, we would have seen him coming.

But life on our island was quiet. The priests kept to the south end, with their high white cliffs and their sun god and the waves that scooped out the shore. Every so often we heard one had tested himself by leaping off the high white precipice, trusting in Hawelios to catch him. The god never did.

Our Lady asked only that we tend her shrine on the hill, ferry her waters to the holy baths, leave grain and oil on the offering stone. We waited for seekers who no longer came. We watched ships pass as we splashed in our lagoons, soaked in the long, slow days that were the gift of Our Lady, like the shush of the eternal waves.

In the before times, one could walk the shallows to our sister islands, carrying fish and news. Once the ships sailed to great palaces made of painted stone and brought back glazed jars with fantastical carvings, pithoi overflowing with oil and wine, robes of dyed purple, bronze dishes, and jeweled pins. Now we crushed our small bitter grapes for wine, pressed our own olives for oil, ground our mollusks for their color and bartered pins for brooches. We carved pipes for the sacred grove and then, because no one came to consult Our Lady, we took the pipes apart and fashioned new ones.

Once, Mother said, travelers came from all over to hear the words of our Lady. We were almost as important as Dodona. Girls swelled the House of Maidens and offerings to our Lady overflowed our jars, our stores, our jeweled caskets. But that was in the before times, the time of great kings and mighty palaces, of great wars and the heroes who fought them.

We lived in the twilight of such times, the heroes already myth. It was as if the cataclysms that brought down the palaces—quake of earth and roar of sea, drought and famine and plague, invaders on swift ships—marked the gods' exit from our realm.

If the gods had withdrawn, we had only Our Lady to protect us.

And Theia, the mother of our temple house, watched. If a priestess did not show the skills, she would be set to housekeeping duties, weaving wool and flax for cloth, pounding grain or beans into flour, washing and polishing our wooden plates and cups after meals. She would be sent to tend the goats, scrub the stones of the temple, or empty the chamber pots into the pits.

I would rather leap off a cliff.

Then one afternoon, Rhea came pounding up the hill, golden hair flying, thighs flashing beneath the slit skirt of her peplos.

"Ship!" She burst into the Hall of Maidens where we sheltered from the summer sun. "Ship from the north," she panted. "Heading for our bay."

Phoebe knocked over the polished board and the bone dice she'd been using to pretend to tell our fortunes. "Dorians," she cried.

Daphnis grabbed her spindle to halt its twirl. "Phoenicians."

For many of the younger priestesses, Phoenicians had brought us from our far-flung lands, and there was always the chance Phoenicians would take us back. Rahel came from Canaan. Neferu came from Egypt. Sava was kidnapped from the Illyrians, Mira came from Arzawa, and Synnada from the Phrygians, or so she said.

I was the mystery. I came from a land so far away it had no name. An island beyond the setting sun, beyond even the realms that Hawelios owned. A land of giants and mist.

Tethys went on stuffing her mattress with grasses. "Sea Peoples," she guessed.

We bolted for the overlook and stood with Theia watching the long ship nosing through the azure shallows, the oars moving in a steady rhythm, the hide sail unmarked by any sign.

As they drew near, we saw it: the flash of light on bronze-tipped spears and swords.

"Warriors. Achaeans." Theia spun, her peplos flaring. "Daphnis, Tethys. Run to the village and bid them hide in the caves. Goods, women, everything. Rhea, Phoebe, bring in our flocks. They may not take our food."

She narrowed her eyes at me. "Alba. Light the lamps and scrub the steps of the temple. Perhaps they have come to consult the Lady."

The household tasks. I might as well go to the village and become a fisherman's wife. I held back tears when I burned my hand on one of the oil lamps placed around the feet of the olive wood statue. The water from the holy well did not soothe as I scrubbed. I had not pretended like the others to see signs and portents. Mother might send me with the warship as a concubine to the soldiers. Or a slave. I lit the sage in its clam shell, and then I prayed.

Diwona. Lead me. Show me the way.

The others stood beneath the plane tree, watching the warriors rove the lowlands with their bows and spears. They cast nets at the shore and scooped clams and limpets. They snared pigeons and partridge. Men with short swords at their belts combed the brush for hares and weasel, while the archers lay in wait for the red and fallow deer that walked the thin bridge that connected us to the mainland. A small group followed the tracks of Kapros, our crafty old boar. To the warriors, the island would appear deserted. But would they leave?

Near twilight came the tramp of feet up our high hill. I lifted my head like one of the otters on the shore.

"The leader," I whispered. I saw him in my mind's eyes, the powerful moira that shimmered around him like a faint mist. "A second man, a priest. And twelve warriors. They saw the temple and are coming to make an offering."

Mother looked at me strangely and fluttered her hands at the other girls. "Hide in the storerooms. Go."

They fled like crickets into the shadows. Mother picked a cluster of pale cyclamen and held her hand out to me. "Come."

She led me to the bath house with its warm spring and crushed blossoms of almond and pear into the pool. She scraped my skin with oil of olive and brushed oil of lemon into my hair, then braided the crown of a senior priestess, though I had never learned those rites. She crushed the tuber of the cyclamen into a cup and tucked the flower into my hair. Then she gave me the cup of wine to drink.

I had watched others pass into the waking sleep. But they were ones whom Our Lady called.

She cupped her hands over my shoulders, pressing slightly. Then she draped the temple veil over my head. The delicate fabric fluttered around my feet. No mortal could touch me now.

"Alba. Whatever comes to you, it is the will of Diwona. All that will pass through you is hers," she said quietly.

My veins felt strange, my blood thick like honey. The veil floated over my skin.

"That it should be you." She shook her head as she led me to the temple. There she left me.

I poured more oil in the lamps, tamped out the burning sage and waved the smoke away. Our Lady's statue stared at me, polished, ageless, barred with shadows. Around us in the sacred grove the pipes in their oak trees twirled and sang their low music. A shiver slid down my spine, like a finger tracing my body, an awakening. The very air was alive.

They had put aside their armor and wore belted chitons and woven cloaks. The shadow around his head was stronger but his features were bold, strength flashing from his eyes and brow and firm, arrogant mouth. He was not young, nor old, but a man in his prime. At the entrance to the grove, they took off their sandals. When he stepped onto the porch, I sucked in my breath.

I had seen this face before. In dreams.

His moira cloaked him with danger and secrets. His arm was

stronger than most men's, and his fame would be everlasting. He was made for war, his body fit and hewn, power sculpted into his shoulders, his legs. Many, many threads of life had been snapped by his sword.

He looked around, and I drew back into an alcove, into the soft shadows. Two men threw a dark shape on the floor I had polished. The old boar Kapros, a gash in his side, his head lolling. I put a hand to my nose to stop the smell. Blood painted the hero's hands. He drew a hide cloak from his shoulders, then tied a thin fillet of leather around his brow. I had only known royals to do that. He washed his hands in the basin of holy water, scented with rosemary and lemon.

In the lingering time between sun and moon they took the large bronze bowl and mixed the blood of the boar with wine while the priest read the entrails. Men always seem to think sacrifice requires blood. For women who shed blood with each moon, we trade life without killing. One reason, I suppose, we are feared.

The hero took the bowl, faced east, and poured a libation to Hawelios, who drives his chariot across the daytime sky. He turned west and poured to Hermahas, god of flocks and woodlands, the traveler between worlds. The god of divination and magic.

This voyager was calling on all the Great Ones.

At last, he poured to Diwona, Our Lady, filling the small hollows of her offering stone with blood-red wine. He walked around her altar nine times, then knelt and held out his hands. His gold armlets winked with the blue glass that comes from Egypt. Someone had heaped treasure upon this man.

"Most powerful goddess." His voice shivered through me like a note from the pipes. "Terror of the forest glade, queen of the woodlands, you who traverse the airy heavens and the dark halls of the underworld. Tell me which land you wish us to inhabit. Show me to a safe dwelling-place where I may worship you down the ages. I will dedicate temples to you filled with chanting maidens. Only tell me, great goddess, where I might live."

He bowed his head to the floor and repeated the request, pouring out fresh wine and then walking again the nine-fold pattern, a ritual strange to me, though his request was clear. He was an exile, he and the souls upon his boat. He had conquered, but he had no home to welcome him. He must find and make his own.

He stretched the hide on the patterned floor before the statue, between the burning lamps. His men bowed and left him, taking the carcass of the boar. Nyx, daughter of Chaos, drew down her dark cloak, embroidered with stars. The man lay, head on his folded arms, cloak over his legs, and slept without fear of man or beast.

I breathed the smoke, the scent of blood. The pipes in the trees hummed and murmured, the Lady's voice in my ears. In the third hour of the night, I rose.

My veil whispered across the floor, and my blood hummed. The top of my head buzzed as if I wore a crown of bees. Perhaps the sacred wine had poisoned me, as it had others.

"Bruteis." So his men had addressed him.

He woke at once, his eyes a deep amber color. The eyes of a wolf.

My voice sounded like Theia's when she entered the trance and became the mouthpiece of Diwona. I knew not whence the words came, but they hung in the air like tongues of fire.

"There is an island in the sea, beyond the setting of the sun. The place where they pull metal from the ground, the silvery metal that weeps. A land once roamed by giants. There are fields and woodlands, rivers and lakes, food in abundance. Down the years it will prove an abode suited to you and your people. You will build a second Troy and the line of kings born from your stock will one day hold the round circle of the whole earth in subject to them."

He sat up, and I realized too late I stood close to him. That powerful hand snaked out and bound my wrist.

The pipes hummed an eerie harmony, growing louder.

"What do you know of Troy?" he demanded.

I sweated beneath the veil. "A king sailed through here many years ago, returning to his palace. He had been traveling for years, but he fought in the war where great Ilios was burned by the Achaeans."

"Where it fell by his treachery, in the story I heard." His hand was a lash of fire about my wrist. "The men with me. They are descendants of that city. I am to rebuild it, in a new homeland? And found a line of kings. In the land where the silvery metal is mined. The one that weeps when bent in the hand, but which makes our weapons strong."

My throat was dry with smoke and the bitter taste of the wine. "Our Lady has spoken."

His eyes glittered, and he rose to his feet. I was so small beside him. He smelled of sea air and leather and the wild musk of a beast that would never be tamed.

"Does the goddess have anything else for me?" His low voice raised every fine hair on my body, a sign of great danger. Or great holiness.

My heart skipped and stuttered as he drew off the veil, the fabric a soft whisper against my skin. His touch on my cheek, the bones beneath my throat, was as soft as the blue waves that enfold us when we bathe in the sea. I tried not to think what else those hands had done. Rivers of fire raced through me, tracing paths I had never known existed, as if I were the wax mold waiting for the rush of molten ore.

Diwona no longer asked these rites, but I knew it was an old way the goddess confers her blessing. And binds her chosen mortal to her.

I let him draw me down onto the hide and I followed him to the portal beyond the earth and stars. For a while I hung suspended in the place where Diwona herself dwells, and from which she can see all.

Theia did not try to keep me. The next morn she helped me fold my second peplos into my leather bag along with my blue woolen cloak. I gathered my few bronze hair pins and the bracelet of twisted bronze that had come with me as a girl when the traders brought me to the wine-dark sea. The girls wove flowers into my hair and made me sachets of precious herbs, sol and yperikon, bay for the sacred trance and origanon to ward off sickness. Theia gave me terebinth, seeds and leaves and the just-turning purple fruit, and a small cloth pouch, sewn shut, filled with what felt like pebbles.

"Acorns from the sacred grove," she said. "Sew them into your cloak. Thus Diwona will go with you."

In my mind I saw it, a humped and hilled land veiled with mist. Seas more grey than blue. Cliffs of white, rivers bleeding silver. Another island, like this one, but with spirits of earth and water, older and darker than those of sun and sky. Bruteis would take me there.

The warriors grumbled when I came to the shore, my sandals sifting the white sand for the last time. I would miss living under Hawelios, his bright warm sun. We were going beyond his realm. The air felt bright on my skin.

There was another woman on the ship.

Bruteis drew me aboard, his hand firm on mine. He had an omen with him now, the living blessing of the Lady. And he had a wife, hair of gold, eyes as blue as his Egyptian beads.

She was a princess sold by her father to buy peace, part of the treasure and goods sent with Bruteis from a conquered king. Her name was Innogen, and she told me the story as we stood at the bow while the sail swallowed air and the warriors rowed to their ceaseless chant.

Her father, king of the Dorians, lived in Epirus to the north, in the place where the holy river Acheron runs to the Underworld. This Bruteis had come along, exiled from his own land, and heard of the slaves who called themselves Hellenes, sons and daughters of Helenus, prince of fabled Troy. A rich city in a high place that commanded the seas, one of the mighty palaces that ruled the before times, much contested between the fierce Hattusa to the east and the Achaeans with their bronze swords. Towered Troy fell in flames before the Achaeans, and Hattusa fell to the Phrygians, and then the Achaean palaces were in turn overcome by warriors from land and sea, the Dorians, the Sea Peoples, the trembling rage of the earth itself.

Innogen's father, the Pandoris, had never believed that this Bruteis, too, was a son of Troy. His story changed with each telling. He was the son of Ascanius. He was a son of the forest. He had killed his father and been cast out of Latium, where great Aeneas had gone to dwell. But whatever his history or his past crimes, this Bruteis had besieged the Pandoris in his castle and the king gave up his daughter, and the Hellenes, to make the warrior go away.

Now they sailed the sea looking for a place to found their own great city, a place not charred with the ashes of what fell before. And Innogen, though it is the fate of a princess to leave her palace and travel to a new home, wept. She did not cheer when the delphis leapt beside us, singing to the great hum in my head, though I told her it was a great blessing that they led us, for the delphis had once been humans who turned into sacred fish after their island kingdom sank beneath the waves of our Great Sea.

He shared his cloak with me, not her, during the many nights that the ship ploughed the waves, fighting the winds to touch the southern shores of the Great Sea. One night we lay on deck, watching the sky, and I showed him the great archer pursuing the bear in his endless hunt. Someone had taught me this tale. Someone, though I could not recall who, had brought me to Leucadia. A place of refuge, for the Lady and for me.

He drew me to the side of the ship and showed me the dark shape of the land passing to the north. We were nearing the straits guarded by the Sirens, where the goddess took the shape of a bird, whose call mortal men could still hear. He pointed to the land, the mountains.

"That is Brettion. The land of the Bretti. The people of the deer."

"Your people," I guessed.

"I was hunting one day," he said. "I had passed fifteen summers, almost a man. My father drove a herd toward me, and I shot without seeing that—" He fell silent, drawing his cloak about the both of us, though the air still held the warmth of late summer.

"The chief accused me of murder," he said. "It is hard to explain an arrow in the throat."

"Did your family not protect you?"

"My mother died when I was born. A priest foretold that I would kill both my parents, that I would wander with no dwelling place. No home. His prophecy became my curse."

A cool breeze teased my ankles, the hint of the harvest months to come. I shivered. The northern channel might be closed in the winter. We could not delay.

"You could have been king of the Dorians," I said.

He shrugged. "And fight for every hide of land, scanning the horizon each day for hint of siege. I am weary of war. I wish to build something."

We were both searching for home.

We passed the salt flats where sailors prepare fish and took on stores in the port city of Russicada, in the kingdom of the Nomades. In the shadow of the mountains of Azariea, home of the Sicani, the warriors repelled an attack of pirates at our flank, and I saw the deadly swords in action. We took their plunder and sank their boat, pirates and all, beneath the blue waters.

That night he came to me with blood beneath his fingernails and the battle lust still in his eyes, and I fed on it. I was growing a secret, and it strengthened with each new place we passed, each new name I savored on my tongue. For once we passed the land of the Italic tribes, and the coast that led up to Latium, Bruteis was in new territory, and so were his men.

Except they were not new places. I knew their names. Bruteis consulted me, gleaning directions from my dreams. Past the Pillars of Hercules, when the Great Sea opened to something even greater and incomprehensible, I told him to turn north, to follow the shore. Here the sea-paths led to the place where the tin was mined.

We found one place not far north, in the land of the Counei, the people of the dog. But it was not an island. Bruteis met a warrior, Corineus, a killer of giants, a leader of his own war band and hungry for fame. They told stories over many cups of their strong native brew, which smelled of honey and yeast.

"Why, we too are descended from princes of Troy, and we will go where the goddess leads us," this Corineus said. "Which prince would you say sired us?"

"Antenor," Bruteis said, and so they joined us.

More men meant more provisions, and we put ashore in another place where the metal was found. It was the land of the Aquitani, it was not an island, and their king, Goffar, did not want to share his deer.

Bruteis and Corineus, idle aboard ship, wanted to besiege Goffar in his castle and plunder his stores. But Innogen was sickening by the day, and none of my herbs could nourish her. What swelled and strengthened me was draining her life. I could not see what would come of sowing Trojan blood in the lands of these fierce tribes, where they grew a bitter grain and not much else.

So I had another vision. It was not hard to hear the voice of the Lady. Though the delphis had left us, the birds I knew, and they were drawing us onward: the blackbird, the thrush, the croak of wise raven. Not far. Not far.

We found the paths the traders knew and left land behind. The warriors muttered and made signs to ward off evil spirits when I drew near. I could have told them their fate was already woven and would hold if they stayed with their leader. His moira grew brighter about him as we neared, as if he'd been touched by a god.

I, too, felt myself brighten. He had been touched by me, and I carried the goddess.

When the land came into sight, I felt a deep shudder, like a shell over my being falling away. The mist lifted like a temple veil. Below the rocky crag, in the deep sound where several rivers met, there were merchant ships in the harbor already, but no men of war.

"This is the place," I said, my voice not my own.

"The island beyond the setting sun? Yet I see the same sun." Bruteis looked around, his fingers clenching his spear with eager joy. "You knew it was here."

I couldn't speak. It had not been a dream or a vision of a past life.

It was a memory. From this life.

The Lady had been calling me home.

We rode up the sandy shingle and Bruteis leapt over first, then reached back for me. When my feet hit the cool water, the hard pebbles, a bright surge ran up my body, like sap. The land was full of spirits. Alive. They spoke to me without need of pipes.

"We must make an offering," I said.

I put on my best peplos and bound the fillet over my braided hair. A white hind ran to us as if offering itself for sacrifice. The Lady was already here.

Bruteis joined the ritual, wearing a headpiece fitted with the tusks of the boar he had killed on Leucadia. The horned god. Natives came, wearing woolens and hides, leather shoes, ornaments of twisted gold. I spotted a tall woman, her hair bound in the crown of a priestess, a bracelet twined about her wrist. The knowing shook me again. A faded blue mark glowed on her brow, like a star.

Bruteis cut the throat of the hind and I held the basin for the blood. When he turned to me, I thought for a moment he would cut my throat too. The first sacrifice. But he put his bloody hands on my belly, over the swelling of my womb. As if he had created life, not I. As if man could hold dominion over the Lady.

Corineus fought a local chieftain who offered challenge. The men wanted more than blood and omens. They stripped down like the fabled bull leapers of Krete, and Innogen shielded her ears from their growled curses, from crushing bones. In the end, Corineus lifted the other in his arms and threw him from the cliff into the sea. His god did not catch him.

Bruteis laughed and pointed to the river they said was the Tamar.

"You, Corineus, shall take the lands that lie west of this river, and I shall take the part east. You may name it and rule it as you see fit."

The woman with the marked brow came to me. She had eyes that could see beyond the shape of things.

"Who are you?" she asked, and I heard a language I knew. One I was born knowing.

"They are warriors and exiles. They will tell you they come from an ancient place called Troy," I said.

"But you." Her eyes swept me, a cool, calm blue. As blue as the shoals of a place I would never see again.

"I am a servant of Diwona, Our Lady." I pressed my fingers over the pearled lumps within the pouch I had protected all this time. "They called us druades. The spirits of the oak."

"We on Albion serve in the same way," she said, and in a flash I saw her temple: the sacred grove, the veiled priestess, the seekers who came for knowledge. The women who wove the rhythm of the fated days while the men sowed and reaped, fought and died.

"What do they call you?" she asked.

"Alba," I whispered.

She smiled and touched my bracelet, the match to hers. "Then the Lady has done what She promised. I am Morwen, here to welcome you home."

Bruteis said he would return for me when he had built his New Troy, his Trinovantium. I reminded him of the shrines he had promised to build to Our Lady. Let Innogen bear him kings. I followed Morwen. So much of this land was familiar, and so much new: the oak groves with their deer and badger, the rivers leaping with fish. The chiefs built round houses atop hills and kept close their cattle, their wealth. The women ground grain on flat stones and wove with a spindle much like mine. The men scratched the earth with forked sticks and hunted with bronze-tipped arrows and spears. They lived in the shadow of what giants had wrought: great circles of carved standing stones, deep ditches they had furrowed, long barrows for their sleeping bones. What could Bruteis and his men possibly bring this place beyond boasts of blood and past glory?

Morwen brought me at last to the temple of She Who Sees, a place with healing hot springs. Here people brought their offerings, their pleas. From the sacred grove dangled the horn pipes, and I did not need the sacred wine to hear what the Lady was saying.

I was not the only one sent forth to gather the ancient wisdom, but I was the only one who returned. I was fed the best fruits and meats, the sweetest honey mead. The young girls called me Mother. I spoke beneath the veil when the seekers came. I made the offerings to Her.

Morwen and I scried in the water and saw the years to follow, the warring chieftains, the hillforts growing in great heaps, the new gray metal that would cut flesh and earth. Palaces would rise again along the Great Sea and send traders, then armies north to our shores. There would be more newcomers, again and again.

Innogen's sons would divide the isle for a time and fight to hold it. But the line of kings that would descend from Bruteis, who would subject the whole round of the earth, would not come from the body of Innogen.

They would rise from me. I came to strengthen the Lady so she might hold dominion no matter what the arms and weapons of men might do. I serve the Great Mother who is never ceasing, who brings forth all from her womb and takes back the bodies of the dead. The earth-walkers may not heed her, but she sees all. And so, from my shrine in the sacred grove, do I.

AT THE CROSSROADS OF
OLD GODS AND NEW

A Tale from Medieval Frisia

By Gerri Leen

I LOOK OUT ON the surging Frisian Sea
I feel the floods before they even show
It's time to find the higher ground and flee

There was a time when all listened to me
A Viking seeress taught me all I know
I look out on the surging Frisian Sea

The priest comes by and asks me what I see
He views my gifts as something dark and low
It's time to find the higher ground and flee

I wish that I could hold Christ close to me
To not hear wisdom in the gulls and crows
I look out on the surging Frisian Sea

I tell the priest how high the waves will be
Will he protect his flock from water's flow?
It's time to find the higher ground and flee

I know too much to end up on my knees
It breaks my heart to have to finally go
I look out on the surging Frisian Sea
It's time to find the higher ground and flee

LOVE ME NOTS

A Tale from Italy

By Kayla Whittle

LOVE WAS A TENUOUS, flighty thing for most, but it came easily to Dot. It filled her veins, clogged her pores, and plagued her at night while she begged for sleep. Some days it felt like her fingertips would split, nailbeds peeling so love could pour free. Whenever it got that bad, Dot pinned on a smile. The customers expected happiness—optimism. Her smile only faded when she delivered bad news.

"He loves you not," Dot told the man waiting in the chair opposite hers. She hated this moment when expressions fell and stomachs curdled. "I'm sorry, darling."

"But—" The man hesitated, cheeks flushed with heat and agitation. "Who does, then? Who loves me?"

The air was too close and still in the little garden shed Dot used for her appointments. Two glasses of water sweated violently on the small tabletop between them. Discarded white petals wilted on the floor by Dot's feet.

"It doesn't work that way," Dot reminded him. "I can only tell you the truth about whoever you currently have in mind. You can come back when you love someone else, alright?"

"Right." The man slumped, oozing grief.

Dot knew better than to ask any questions about him or the man he loved. The details never mattered and never affected her answers. She had no choice but to report the truth about love.

"Right," he said again, moving this time.

Dot stood, reminding her client to watch his step down into the garden. Although she wished him luck, he didn't bother leaving a tip; few of her disappointments did, unless they were particularly desperate—a regular.

Gravel crunched beneath the lovelorn customer's sullen footsteps. As he moved down the path, someone stood from the bench set under a nice copse of trees she'd planted a few decades back. Dot's next appointment twisted their hands anxiously as they approached.

"Welcome," Dot said, as warmly as she could manage at the end of a long day. "Thank you for the opportunity to assist with your love life. Please, have a seat. I'll be with you in a moment."

She let them settle into the recently vacated chair before stepping outside. The heat was slightly more bearable, a breeze sneaking through her rosebushes. Dot flexed her fingers, trying to wring out the ache as she approached her flowerbeds.

Bees buzzed, the steady hum a soothing accompaniment to the sweet scent of new blooms. Dot's skin itched, ill-fitting, too tight over her knuckles and too loose near her jaw. Allowing herself an indulgent exhale, she started her search. Her garden was well-maintained, but she allowed the flowers to do as they liked to some extent and they formed a riot of blooms. Blushing peonies mixed with lavender Laconian thyme; apple-bearing sage shrubs towered over Olympus yarrow. Dot passed over it all, searching for a flash of gold nestled in white.

Her skin warmed, tingling with an uncomfortable rush of power, when she neared the daisy. *The* daisy. Dot never grew any herself, but one always appeared whenever a client was nearby. This daisy was the same as every other she'd read over the years, with a center bright as a burning sun and eerily symmetrical petals flaring around it. Something prickled in Dot's chest when she pulled it from the dirt. The fresh flower was beautiful, perfect in an ethereal, unnatural way; in a flash of frustration, Dot wanted to crush it between her hands. Instead, she brought it into the shed.

"Are you ready to begin?" Dot asked. "Think of the one you love. Focus on them until it's over."

"I'm ready," her customer said, closing their eyes.

"Alright. Here we go."

Dot pinched a delicate petal between her fingers, erratic power thrumming through the ligule. Heat lingered on her tongue, warming to the same unnatural temperature the daisy held. Her mouth opened, magic warming her throat and guiding her words. Dot could never control the outcome of her prophecies. She could only speak the truth about love, no matter how dearly she or her customer might wish to change the outcome.

"She loves me." Plucking the petal from the central flower, Dot dropped it to join multitudes on the floor. "She loves me not. She loves me—"

***

Rolling back her aching shoulders, Dot locked her broom in a little cabinet. She'd swept heaps of discarded petals out into her garden. Next, the shed itself was locked, and the front gate too; the last customer had left elated with their daisy's positive outcome. Exhaustion weighed Dot's footsteps, heels carving furrows in her gravel pathway. She turned for home—a cottage really, slightly larger than the shed—and hesitated.

Someone had turned on the light in her living room and propped open her windows.

Dot pressed her fingertips to her forehead, attempting to smooth away her irritation. Sweat dried on the back of her neck. It'd been a long day. A long year. A long however many decades it'd been since she'd struck her deal and started her work. It felt like whenever she was most tired, most alone, Cue arrived.

"Feet off the table," Dot demanded when she'd mustered the strength needed to walk through her front door. Something thumped and clattered as Cue pulled his boots off the small table in her miniscule sitting area. The two chairs there were slightly nicer than those kept in her shed, the bigger difference being the second chair here remained empty apart from Cue's visits.

"Hello, Dot," Cue smiled. "It's nice to see you."

Dot paused, watching his dark eyes watching her from behind crooked glasses. She knew what he'd see in her appearance: faded dress, tangled hair, shoulders curved inward. Cue looked the same as always. Neat clothing, too finely made to blend in well here. Hair curling by his ears and strong jawline. The glasses. The wings folded neatly against his back. Neither of them had aged since the day they'd met. Tired of his assessment, Dot rolled her eyes and busied herself in the corner that passed for a kitchen.

"It's been a month," Cue said, shifting in his seat. "I'm sorry for the delay, Dot. I wanted to check in with you."

Her hands skimmed away from the sink, heading for the wine bottle sitting on her counter.

"I have the same report as always," Dot said. "Business is good. A few regulars dropped off, but they've been replaced by new hopefuls, as usual. Everyone is looking for love."

Her hand tightened around a wineglass, choking the stem. Dot's skin had settled, as it usually did in combination with the workday ending and having Cue nearby. Still, there was an ever-present buzz at the base of her skull, a reminder that she had been gifted with something *other*.

"You know I'd prefer to hear about you, Dot," Cue said.

It was a charade, all of it. The same conversation had over and over throughout countless years as if the outcome could differ. Dot turned to him, leaning against her counter.

"How long have we been in business together?" Dot asked.

Cue glanced down toward his boots. He knew the exact numbers, whereas time and memory blurred for Dot. Whenever she asked how long it'd been since they'd made their deal, Cue often remained vague about the timeline. Said it was for her own good.

"I'm—"

"Don't apologize, darling," Dot interrupted.

"I'm not. I wouldn't." Cue stood, wings tight against his shoulders as he adjusted his glasses. "I know it's been longer for you than it's taken for the others. I know it's been hard, but I'll never apologize for it. I made the offer because it was right for *you*. If you could have some patience—"

Dot knew the expression on her face must have been unpleasant if it was enough to silence Cue. When she'd agreed to work for Cue in exchange for finding true love, she hadn't been wary. She hadn't known she would be forced to wait so long for Cue to make good on his side of the deal. That there would be others like her, working for Cue until they finally found the love that'd been meant for them. That they would strike their deals after her and find their loves before her.

"You should leave," Dot said. "I'm busy tonight."

They both knew she rarely left her property if she could help it.

"I'll try to check in sooner next time," Cue offered.

"I know there are others out there needing a visit from you," Dot sighed.

It annoyed her, the earnest concern embedded in his gaze. Her bitterness towards him had never changed that; she was the one who looked away this time, thinking she needed to be kinder to her closest friend.

"I'll see you whenever it best fits into your schedule," Dot said before draining her glass. "Don't make promises you can't keep, Cupid."

***

Dot's client was late.

Some traveled far to reach her and encountered unexpected hiccups in their journeys; others simply had cold feet and abandoned their appointments. Rarely, a client organically received the answer they sought, for good or for bad, rendering their meeting redundant. Dot spent any unexpected free time in her garden, wrenching weeds from the earth, chopping away anything dead or useless. The chance to safely destroy something usually brought her down to a healthier heartrate.

The optimism she'd held when the deal was first struck with Cupid had disappeared. Back then, the sun had beamed beautiful warmth and brightness down on her family's land, and she'd spent her days draped in soft white fabric, turning her face up toward the sky. Long afternoons were spent walking the property or sprawled on hillsides, daydreaming. Thinking of what she wanted most in life. Craving it with the force of someone starved: love.

One lazy, wanting afternoon, she'd found a perfect daisy blooming at the edge of a meadow. She'd found herself thinking of a girl down in the valley, one with hair dark as night, a voice soft enough to coax the wildest animals closer. Dot had shivered and plucked the daisy.

"She loves me," Dot started, half-joking, half-caught in the seriousness that came to those eager to find their match. "She loves me not. She loves me."

Her overworked heart faltered and sank when she received her answer.

"She loves you not." A deep voice startled her from her sorrow. "I'm sorry, Dot."

Dot stepped away from him, this dark, winged stranger who squinted as if struggling to focus his vision. She was unsettled by his inhumanity, and the fact that he should not have known her name.

"No one will love you for a long while," the stranger said. "I'm sorry to disappoint you, but you needn't worry. It happens to many people, in many places. The love you're waiting for simply isn't ready for you yet. I would like to help, to ensure you'll find that true love when the timing is right. I would only ask a favor of you."

She'd hesitated, but the stranger's sympathy was gentle, and Dot's heart held a fragility that'd made her fear pushing on alone.

So Dot, heartbroken, had asked, "What would you need me to do?"

In her garden perhaps a century or two later, Dot sighed. Even in that first moment years ago, filled with naivety and longing, she'd known all things had a catch.

Sitting back on her heels, Dot shredded a weed between her thumbs. There was something satisfying in that small destruction as the sun shone down, striving to melt straight through to her inner cavity. A bee lazed between her flowers, hovering above the abundant flush of petals.

Her front gate squealed. The first customer had never arrived, but the second was exactly on time.

Dot stood, dirt imprinted on her knees, and went to unlock the shed.

***

It was late, sun gone and a glass of wine half-gone too, when the knock came. Dot flinched, liquid sloshing within her glass. A closed door had never kept Cue away, but Dot hadn't expected a visit from him for a long while. She snorted at the thought of him showing up, towing her true love by the hand through her dark garden.

With some regret, Dot left her glass behind to open the door. A woman waited there, mildly sweating, stress wrinkling her forehead. Her yellow skirt was rumpled, dark shirt half-tucked. Her eyes were the deep brown of the richest soil in Dot's garden.

"I'm Leigh," she said. "I had—"

"An appointment." Dot recognized the name. "You missed it."

"I'm sorry to bother you. I couldn't get away," Leigh said. "I was hoping—of course, I would be willing to compensate you—if you had the time, you could perhaps tell me if she loves me. Now."

Dot glanced past Leigh. Crickets chirped an awful crescendo out on the property. A sticky wind pulled through the Laconian thyme, the crackle of dried stalks soft and familiar. Darkness swelled in patches wherever the moonlight couldn't reach.

Dot hated working at night.

"Please." Leigh's lower lip twitched—a tremble, mixed with determination but borne from anxiety.

She'd certainly worked with clients with worse attitudes. Dot hesitated, caught on the threshold. She held tight to the doorframe, tongue heavy with wine. Power simmered in her veins, waiting for Dot to enter her garden, to search for the daisy Leigh needed. Her gift pulsed eagerly, making love feel like something burdensome and ugly. Nights were meant for Dot, a chance for her to settle back in among her bones, to feel human again.

"You'll have to reschedule," Dot said before shutting the door in Leigh's face.

***

After Dot struck her deal with Cupid, Dot assumed it would compensate like a typical job. After a certain number of hours or days or weeks, she would receive her payment: true love. Three months into the gig, she broached the subject with Cupid. Unaccustomed to the buzz of power warming her veins, Dot's skin was pockmarked with small, pink scratches.

"The bargain has no timeline," Cue told her. "Your work will end when true love finds you, but you can't force someone to fall in love. You and your partner both deserve better than that. Love is in your future. Try to remember that."

"Can't you speed things along?" Dot asked, scratching hard at her forearm. "Nudge a likely person my way?"

"I wish," Cue said. "I do wish I could. Love is all around us, Dot. I can see it, see the ways humans love one another. Romantically. Platonically. I do my best to guide it, to give lovers of all sorts advice through people like you. As much as I'd like to, I can't be everywhere at once. I chose you and all the rest because this is your best chance at finding happiness. Please, trust me."

In those first days, Cupid visited more often. He introduced her to others like her, scattered around the globe and blessed with the ability to tell hopeful romantics if they were truly loved. People who had one thing in common, all waiting for a future filled with love.

It had been nice at first, kind of Cupid to connect Dot with those most likely to understand her. Any camaraderie faded when those who'd made their deals a month or a year or a decade after her began to lose their power. They no longer worked for Cue, aging and deteriorating and sickeningly, helplessly finding themselves caught up in the true love that'd finally found them.

Dot was left waiting.

***

A few weeks after shutting the door on Leigh, a string of loves-me-nots left Dot exhausted. Tears and anger filled her shed; customers tried to bargain with *her*, begging her to find a new daisy for them, to try the reading again. Some demanded to speak to Cupid personally. It never worked out well for them; Cue only spoke with the chosen few he'd struck his deals with, and those who dared to threaten his employees lost the privilege of even that assistance with their love lives.

Amid this depressing chaos, Leigh returned. Dot, elbow-deep in a rosebush, glanced up to see her waiting on the pathway.

"You're here," Dot said, gently pulling herself free.

"I rescheduled," Leigh said, the ghost of a smile lurking in the corners of her mouth.

Leigh was safely deposited in the shed before Dot returned to her garden. She poked through the ever-present weeds, the bushes, the peonies. Circled the fir trees shading her bench. Nothing stirred apart from the birds flitting between branches and the bees, hard at work, circling the unremarkable flowers filling her garden.

Nausea built in Dot's stomach. She picked at the skin beneath one of her fingernails. The day, the *week*, had drained her, and little was worse than explaining to a customer that no daisy existed for Dot to read.

Dot checked the property again, digging into the depths of her shrubbery.

Empty-handed, she returned to the shed. Leigh watched her; no impression of a smile lingered, smothered by sharp anxiety.

"You have no daisy," Dot said.

"But—that's impossible," Leigh protested. "I rescheduled. I came back. It's what I'm going to pay you for, the daisy and the reading."

Dot pressed a hand to her temple, cradling the side of her head. A headache steadily approached. "I can't read what doesn't exist. Whoever you're thinking of, you don't love them. Not really."

"That's impossible," Leigh repeated. She stood but held herself like she wasn't certain if she wanted to run or take her frustration out on the floorboards.

"You can't trick Cupid," Dot said, glancing away from those tilled-earth eyes. "Not even if you've deceived yourself. Come back when you're in love."

***

When Dot's first year of work after the deal stretched into two, Cupid's attention wavered. There were new workers taking up his time. An old friend who'd accepted a deal a few months after Dot came to visit. They talked over tea and Dot noticed new lines in her friend's face when he laughed.

"It'll happen for you too," he promised when he said goodbye, in a final sort of way that allowed both to acknowledge he'd begun aging while Dot remained the same.

When Cue returned, he sported a new pair of eyeglasses.

"Another of your followers found love this year," Dot greeted him petulantly.

"The love that's right for them," he agreed. "You have your own, Dot, I promise—"

180

"They struck their deal after I did," Dot snapped. "It should have been me first!"

"We know it doesn't work like that." Cue cleared his throat, tugging at his collar. "Love doesn't adhere to any deadline."

Dot knew she was acting like *them*, her bereaved and disappointed customers. The ones who refused to believe what the daisies said was true. Slumping into a chair, she sensed more than saw Cue seat himself beside her.

"I'm tired," she admitted, some of the unrest spiraling within her settling when he tucked an arm around her shoulders.

"I know," Cue assured her. "The right path might take a while longer. You won't have to walk it alone, Dot. I'll always be here for you."

***

Leigh returned a week after her appointment. The day had ended; Dot had gone to lock up the front gate when she'd noticed the woman waiting there.

"I know I don't have an appointment," Leigh admitted, pulling her hands from where she'd wrung at the hem of her striped shirt. "I hoped you could spare a minute to look again. Then if you found a daisy, you could read it for me later. Whenever works best for your schedule. I can wait for that answer, I promise. I just—I just want to know."

Lifting a hand, Dot smoothed it over her forehead. She was surprised to find a lack of tension there; it was probably buried beneath her weariness.

"Fine," she agreed, and allowed Leigh to follow her to the garden.

As the woman hovered, Dot searched. Leaves scattered on the ground; the summer heat had finally tapered off, and the plants were starting to dull.

There were no daisies in her garden.

SEERS AND SIBYLS – *Italy*

When Dot turned to Leigh empty-handed, she saw her own bleary dissatisfaction reflected in Leigh's expression.

"I'm sure you know you can't force anyone to love you," Dot said. "You can't force yourself to love someone either."

"I had just hoped." Leigh's voice had gone quiet, small in a way that filled Dot with prickling discomfort.

Dot itched at her wrist. Years of heartbreak and devastation had allowed her some resistance to sympathy. Not immunity though; it had been a long while since Dot had felt so sorry for someone.

"I have wine," Dot offered, and Leigh cracked a smile.

***

After she struck her deal with Cupid, Dot fell in and out of love as easily as the seasons changed. Sometimes love was subtle, a slowly unfurling bloom. Sometimes it felt like a storm, tearing and threatening all that stood in her wake. She fell for a woman at the market, a man traveling for work, a tailor in town. People who charmed her, drew her in close, leaving her emotions wrung and stale and longing.

Dot read her own daisies. She screamed her loves-me-nots out onto her empty property with only the magpies and ants and bees to hear her. When her power felt wrong, tense and coiled enough to choke her, she locked up her cottage and traveled. But it was as if Cue had shot her through with an arrow tied to a string any lover could follow; those seeking answers to love always found her. She fell into the world, tried to embrace it, tried not to fall for strangers she met beside tidepools or on cliffsides, tucked into cafes or running through fields.

"I can't," Cue admitted when, a few decades in, she asked him to take the power away. "The deal is struck. Now we see it through."

It burned through her, the sense of love filling her to the brim and leaving nothing of Dot untouched. Incensed, she screamed and shouted until Cue fumblingly made his way out her door. His glasses slid from the bridge of his nose, and in his haste, a boot trod too hard on one of the arms, bending it.

***

After so long, it was nice to have a friend outside of Cupid's orbit. The realization annoyed Dot, who might have preferred to brood alone for the next century or so.

Leigh arrived weekly no matter the weather, sometimes bearing wrapped plates of food after she'd properly processed the abyssal emptiness of Dot's kitchen. They shared cheap wine and gossiped about clients who asked for extra time and daisies, particularly the ones who never tipped. Leigh mentioned her nice, boring job occupying a nice, boring desk; her nice, large family and nice, practical dreams. They never discussed the woman Leigh hoped to see a daisy for. They never mentioned Dot's horrifically empty love life.

"I guarantee the man I work for is worse than Cupid," Leigh declared one night when they were each sprawled in one of Dot's chairs.

"If you could meet him, you'd think otherwise," Dot grumbled, though felt a little guilty for it. All things considered, Cue could have been much worse. "I don't want to talk about that."

"Alright," Leigh agreed easily, standing to fill their glasses. "Tell me how you've managed to make your yarrow blossom this deep into autumn."

There was never a daisy for Leigh, but she continued to visit despite that. It was wonderful, and surprising, and more than Dot could bear.

Sometimes they met in town, whenever the client list eased and the gaps in their schedules matched. Leigh introduced Dot to a few friends, a few siblings.

Dot taught Leigh a few gardening tricks.

"Hold tight." Dot slipped her fingers through Leigh's, guiding them through the dirt. It'd embedded itself beneath their nails, in the lines of their palms; it tumbled against their skin as Dot moved Leigh's hands. "I think the flowers like it when you care for them with confidence."

"I think they just like you," Leigh laughed, shaking her head as she leaned into Dot.

They took time on a long weekend to overhaul the shed into something slightly bigger, slightly brighter, and potentially, more encouraging. A few wayward bees hummed their approval, small bodies smacking against the new wood settled into their old flightpath.

"Even the worst news can be delivered in a nice space," Leigh declared.

Dot agreed, but it was only after Leigh walked home that she realized she hadn't searched the garden for Leigh's daisy in weeks.

***

"I have company." Dot leaned against the doorway, filling it to keep Cue out. She'd barely managed to catch the door when he'd opened it without bothering to knock.

He blinked twice before his eyes crinkled with something close enough to satisfaction to annoy Dot. She decided she was offended by the surprise lingering in his lifted eyebrows.

"Ah," Cue said, and laughed when she flicked him on the arm. The sound of his laughter was familiar in the way of old stories.

Perhaps Dot had felt bitter toward him for too long, but she would never apologize for her frustration.

"Not company like that," Dot said.

"I know." Cue caught her hand before she could flick him again. "I know."

His glasses no longer sat crooked. In the shadowed night, Cue's wings shifted, feathers fluttering against his shoulders. For once, he seemed at a loss for words.

"Thank you, Dot." Cue squeezed her hand. "Thank you for all you've done. You've helped so many."

Dot knew how hard she worked and that she was very good at her job, but still held some suspicion when that was suddenly acknowledged.

Cue patted her hand carefully and then left, darkness tucking in around him, moonlight glinting within his lenses.

"Are you alright?" Leigh asked when Dot shut the door.

"I'm not sure," Dot admitted after a long moment. She sat, and Leigh sat with her.

***

"What about you, though?"

A few years into their deal, Dot asked Cue about himself. He'd startled, wings flexing with what she'd come to recognize as discomfort.

"There will never be anyone for me," Cue said. "I can see that as clearly as I can see how love will work for someone else. There are so many happy endings I have the chance to oversee. I've had the privilege of witnessing the unlikeliest stories ending in the best ways."

"And that's enough for you?" Dot asked. She couldn't imagine feeling the burn and pull of love flowing through her and knowing there was no one waiting for her at the finish, no end to her deal. For Cue, there was no exchange; it was simply his life.

"It's more than enough for me." Cue joined her on the front step of her cottage. They were tired, and the day had been long, but back then, Dot hadn't yet realized how tiring life truly could be.

Leaning her side against Cue's, they watched the sunset together.

***

Rubbing a hand against her collarbone, Dot watched her last client of the day wander down the path. In the opposite direction, a light had already turned on in the cottage—Leigh, waiting.

A chill wind pulled through the shrubbery, rustling dry branches. Cold stung Dot's exposed skin. Locking the shed, her hands lingered on the new wood. The path through the garden was the same as it had ever been. Dot walked slowly, searching out the supplies she'd left behind earlier in the day. Leigh had surprised her with lunch and a new bottle of wine for the night, pulling Dot away from her attempts to ensure her flowers would return in the spring.

Halfway to the cottage, Dot stooped for her basket. She paused, heart racing.

Two daisies bloomed there, poking up beside the wicker, nestled beside one another. Two, when she'd only ever found one at a time.

Settling a hand over her collarbone, Dot glanced toward the cottage and the woman waiting inside. Hope felt so foreign she couldn't recognize the insubstantial thing wrapped tight around her heart. Thinking of Leigh, the smile that no longer hid but broke free whenever her eyes met Dot's, the way she pulled Dot from her circling thoughts, the electric pang that flickered through Dot whenever their skin accidentally touched—it felt familiar. It felt like something more. Dot's breath quickened, but her impatience dragged her fingertips forward, brushing against the underside of a petal. That smooth, silky softness she'd come to dread.

The tension beneath Dot's skin, sharp and demanding as a bee sting, eased. The blur of power that had accompanied her for so long abandoned her, rushing hot through her veins for one last moment before it disappeared. Her hand touching the daisy began to chill in the night air. Her heartbeat remained frantic.

It was impossible and wonderful. Cupid's gift had disappeared; the deal fulfilled.

Dot stood, abandoning the daisies. Swallowing hard, she glanced over her shoulder. On the edge of her property, a shadowed figure lingered with silver gleaming in his lenses. He raised a hand, and it felt like goodbye.

78

A Tale from the World

By Ivy L. James

SIGRID SHUFFLES HER TAROT cards
like the rush of a river,
cool and calming.

(Seventy-eight cards
cleansed by smoke and sound,
the mouthpiece of her goddesses.)

She grew up in soaring cathedrals,
but now she sets up the altar alone—
no priest, no choir,
no scripture save what she creates herself.
She was taught to laugh at the old myths—
The so-called gods were made up by their worshipers. No different, no better than humans. Not like our *God—*
but now she extends both hands to them,
reaching for solace
for solidarity
for a deity she can see herself in.

(Do you believe in the gods?)

The presence of her goddesses is an embrace,
a warmth in the air,
a reassurance she's not alone.
It's less about worship, she'll say if you ask,
and more about working with them.

IVY L. JAMES

Three of pentacles energy.

It always comes back to the cards.

The goddesses speak to her through each card's unique meaning,
and sometimes she'll hear them too
in a thought that's not her own,
a mental image out of nowhere,
an unexplained knowing.

(Do you believe in the gods?)

Sigrid keeps a pack in her purse
(worn, well-loved, worthy of her trust),
the way she used to keep a pocket Bible there.
Its weight is a comfort.

An anxious stranger sits across from her in the back of a coffee shop,
asking about his hopes, his dreams.
That's what everyone asks about, one way or another.
Who's here? Who has something to say? Sigrid feels a heavy aura, a
playfulness.
She closes her eyes and welcomes
sister
mentor
huntress
goddess
Lady Artemis
into the space.
"Lady Artemis, please show me what he needs to know,"
she murmurs as she shuffles the cards,
all seventy-eight cascading into each other,
and she repeats the prayer silently until Artemis says,

SEERS AND SIBYLS – *World*

Stop here. Cut the deck.
Sigrid obeys and glances at the bottom of the deck:
the Moon gleams there,
Artemis's signifier. She's here.
Sigrid smiles slightly, sets the deck on the table, and draws the first
card from the top.

She takes ten dollars at the end of the reading
only because the crying man presses the bill into her hand,
and she drops it into the baristas' tip jar on her way out.

(Do you believe in the gods?)

"Psychics are just in it for the money";
she's heard the accusations, some right to her face.
She doesn't want money.
Her chest aches, her ears ring when something needs to be said,
the shouts of the goddesses.
The discomfort goes away when she pulls out a deck.

Seventy-eight seeds.
Seventy-eight flashlights in the dark.
Seventy-eight letters of the alphabet, spelling out infinite messages,
if you're willing to listen.
Seventy-eight opportunities to hear the voice of whatever gods you
listen for.

(Do the gods believe in you?)

MINGXI

A Tale from China

By Matthew Yap

WHENEVER TOURISTS VISIT MY neighbourhood, they're always disappointed that Seer Street seems like any Shanghai neighbourhood. They come here with romanticised notions, expecting clanging bells, prayer chants, and incense. In their minds, these elements mark the mystic. Instead, they find laundry hanging across alleyways, silver-haired gentlemen playing chess outdoors, while teens with coloured hair carry smartphones and coffee cups.

During my childhood, mother and Aunty Pretty would bring my older cousin Yuanjian, my baby sister Gaibian, and myself for afternoon strolls. In my memories, Yuanjian is about thirteen, I around seven, and Gaibian just beginning to toddle. Our age differences didn't matter then. We girls were like points on a compass—bound by the magnetism of family.

We would meander along Seer Street, its laneways and inhabitants as familiar to us as the lifelines on our palms or the contours of our faces. These stone-walled houses are particularly permeable—each family's successes, secrets, and shame become common knowledge almost by psychic power.

Mother and Aunty Pretty would tell us each family's heritage, history, and the specialised services they offer. In the Xiao family, the men are palmists and the women face readers. The Bai family can see auras—their children manifest the gift early and are particularly prized by many professions as judges of good character.

The Xihe are astrologers; their daughter, Mei-Xing, is my childhood girlfriend. Our other friend, Lai Yicheng, comes from a family of mediums. The taboo surrounding death means their services

191

are not much in demand. So, Yicheng's brothers left to practice in the West, where they make a living connecting the bereaved with the departed.

The Ding family is the wealthiest on Seer Street. Their gift allows them to see the concealed or lost. The Dings make their fortune by divining locations with hidden pockets of prosperity. They have major contracts with construction and mining companies. Mother says their son Ku-Wei likes me, and she dreams of matchmaking us, but she's delusional.

Then there's our family, the Rui. Grandmother says we serve the nation directly because family is society's foundation, and our gift ensures the happiness of future families.

But lately, the Rui haven't been a happy family ourselves. Not since Aunty Pretty died during the first outbreak. Or since the family disowned Gaibian—who's called Shuang now and isn't quite my sister anymore.

Our family has too many wounds to be whole again. Whenever I think of all that's changed, I long for childhood's simplicity, when the future seemed so clear.

***

The Rui are Shanghai's premier matchmakers and family-planning consultants. We offer comprehensive readings about matters of the heart, matrimony, childbirth, and parenthood. Our clientele is diverse; singles looking for love; parents vetting potential sons– and daughters-in-law; married couples hoping to start perfect families.

The Rui inner-eye runs exclusively through the female line, so we always time conceptions exactly to produce daughters, never sons. Our gift is especially strong because it is intergenerational; it requires a triad of Rui women at different life stages working in unison to attain the clearest readings.

The maiden foresees a couple's emotional, mental, even sexual compatibility to determine if a pair make good partners and prospective parents. The mother divines the most auspicious day, time, even positions for a couple to conceive a child with their desired characteristics. The matriarch, with her long perspective of life, can glimpse a family's future prosperity.

Since the range of our inner-eye changes depending on whether we are virgins, have given birth, or passed menopause, each life stage is carefully maintained. Rui girls begin serving the family business at 18. In order to maintain the purity of her vision, the maiden must remain chaste until the next younger girl can assume the maiden role. Then she is free to marry and have children. To live her life.

That's how it's always been—except for me. Ever since Gaibian transitioned, there's nobody to replace me. I'm 30 now and still my family's sole maiden. My virginity is guarded like a precious commodity. I've never dated, never been with anyone intimately. Worse, nothing will change until Yuanjian's daughter, who's only six, is old enough to succeed me. That's 12 years more, a whole Zodiac cycle of waiting.

Sometimes, I feel suffocated that my entire life is already foreknown. That I'm expected to sacrifice my happiness and become a loveless old-maid. For in my family, there is no 'me'—only 'we'. Still, I can't abandon them. Without a maiden, the readings would be diminished, and the business too.

But I mustn't think these thoughts now; my mind must be clear for tonight. My friend Mei-Xing, her fiancé, and their parents are attending a reading to set her wedding date. I'm thrilled for her—really. But it's hard seeing friends reaching milestones denied to me.

When Mei-Xing's entourage arrives, there are squeals and hugs before we settle down for the reading. It's tricky business, unveiling a couple's shared future. Grandmother, mother, and I start by asking the couple personal questions.

Our readings involve *bazi*, which requires dynamically calculating the exact hour, day, Zodiacs, and dominant stars present when Mei-

Xing and her fiancé were born. Since these aspects of a person's past can never change, they allow us to predict the course of their future, including a couple's "major fortunes" in decades.

The fiancé's family watches sombrely, but Mei-Xing and I grin furtively at each other. I already know all this about her.

Grandmother, mother, and I then lock hands. As our inner-eyes interconnect and unlock, there's the familiar surging sensation of expanding, like the universe at its birth. The strands of time and destiny for Mei-Xing and her beaux become briefly visible.

Grandmother favours them a rare smile and declares, "It is a fine match". The reading's clear—they're to have a long fairy-tale life of wedded bliss, personal success, beautiful children. Mei-Xing gushes excitedly and her boyfriend fist-pumps. There are handshakes, hugs, hearty congratulations. Mr Xihe present grandmother a red packet with our payment of 55, 000 yuan, and a porcelain jar of exclusive oolong.

Later, as we're clearing up, mother sighs contentedly. "How wonderful for Mei-Xing. To know that she's destined to have everything."

I don't answer.

Am I a bad daughter and friend for wanting the same?

***

Seer Street kids always stuck together in school. Mei-Xing, Yicheng, and I were inseparable. Mei-Xing always enjoyed attention, and Yicheng was wise and knowing, even then. We held hands everywhere.

We accepted Ding Ku-Wei into our group. His quiet and shy affections made him an unimposing presence. Admittedly, his maleness and family fascinated us girls.

For when Ku-Wei turned 15, we knew he would pop his cherry. When Ding boys celebrate their 15th birthday, fathers traditionally bring their sons to high-end brothels to become men. The Ding power to divine lost things or hidden prosperity is connected to virility. Their ability is activated when a boy first makes love. Ding boys lose their virginity early so they can enter the family business.

Ironically, the power's potency reduces sharply if a Ding male impregnates a woman. So, like all the males before him, Ku-Wei swore to remain celibate until he turned 30. Ding boys give 15 years of service to their family, then are free to take a woman and start making heirs.

I find it parochial. But my family's no different.

After his 15th birthday, we peppered Ku-Wei with questions. He was the first person our age we knew who had sex. Mei-Xing's curiosity was almost unseemly. Ku-Wei blushed throughout the interrogation.

"So now you've had a taste, how will you survive waiting 15 more years without doing it again, even once?" Mei-Xing asked.

"You'll practically be a monk," Yicheng added, and we giggled at the image.

"Well, father says to think of it like competitive athletes. They abstain from sex so they can stay focused and win," Ku-Wei sounded unconvinced.

"You'll be celibate until you're 30. That's old!" I said.

Mei-Xing grinned. "All for Ding glory. But why not keep your ding-dong sheathed and keep getting laid?"

"She's got a fair point," Yicheng admits.

"Can't risk it," he said dejectedly. "We have to commit to the family business. You know how it is."

We did. I still do.

***

I haven't seen Ku-Wei in ages, even after the governments lifted restrictions. So, the next morning, I visit the Ding family apothecary. When I enter, he looks up from the counter and seems genuinely delighted to see me.

"Mingxi!" he says warmly.

We hug and I take him in. He's grown an attractive beard that doesn't hide his still-shy eyes.

"How've you been, my friend?" I ask.

We spend the morning catching up, oblivious to the customers who enter to buy herbal remedies, joss sticks, and tortoise shells. All of Seer Street gets its divination supplies from the Ding apothecary.

Ku-Wei and I talk about everything: the outbreaks, how business has suffered. We skirt around what happened with Gaibian. Then we turn to happier things, including Mei-Xing's impending nuptials.

"I hear she got a stellar reading last night," he nods.

"Yes, I always knew she'd be the first to marry," I say. "Speaking of, you're 30 now! You're free to get hitched! Settling down soon?"

His eyes grow intent. "That's something I want to talk about with you, actually," he says.

"Oh? You've found someone special?"

He looks steadily at me. "Mingxi, do you wish you could start a family?"

I'm thrown because he should know how hurtful asking that is. "You know my situation, Ku-Wei. Since my sister became…ineligible…I'm stuck as maiden. By the time I'm free, I'll be 42. Dating's out of the question, let alone marriage. Nobody will wait for me that long." I hope I don't sound bitter.

"I would."

I feel momentarily blindsided. This conversation is entering weird territory.

"Don't joke," I warn.

"I'm serious. I would wait for you. I know what waiting's like. To give yourself completely to your family, to suppress all your desires for years." His voice is loaded with longing. "I have feelings for you. Haven't you felt it?"

Honestly, I haven't, and as someone who predicts people's love compatibility, that doesn't bode well. I avoid meeting his gaze. "The day I'll be free is too far away to think about."

"The time will pass," Ku-Wei says. "And, if you're willing, I'll be there, waiting for you. We could have a life together."

As I rise to leave, he takes my hands gently. "You've got 12 years to think it over. Maybe you'll love me by then?"

***

Aunty Pretty was the family's storyteller. She especially enjoyed re-telling how we were named.

"When Yuanjian was born, we sensed that her inner-eye was long, so I named her 'farsighted'. The palmist said Yuanjian had the straightest head, heart, and fate lines he'd ever seen. Her life's path would run straight and true."

At this, Gaibian and I would roll our inner-eyes. We privately agreed that Yuanjian was straight-laced as hell. She hit every life milestone perfectly; after she passed her tenure as maiden to me, she married an accountant and dutifully birthed a daughter.

"Now Mingxi, even from birth, you've had the clearest perception in our family in generations. You can see forever, deep into anyone's soul. So, your mother named you 'clarity'." I'd smile with a touch of pride at this description.

"Madame Xiao, our face reader then, said your facial features have strong water elements. Clear like clean water, you can assume the shape of anything you're poured into and become anyone you want in this life.

"But naming Gaibian was hard. She was a difficult birth for your mother. And we all saw it inside her, even as an infant—that unmistakable duality." Aunty Pretty's eyes would cloud.

"Gaibian's palm lifeline splits sharply, showing that her fate would change around her 18th year. Your mom was very troubled. She consulted the other families. Madame Xiao said Gaibian's face showed strong *yang* energy that would harden with age.

"So, your mom tried everything to change her daughter's faith. She painted the nursery pink, took Gaibian to ballet, anything to alter her tomboyish nature…" I remembered the epic battles of shouting and sobbing between mother and Gaibian.

"Your mom even considered sending Gaibian for plastic surgery, hoping that altering her facial structure would change her destiny," Aunty Pretty sighed sadly.

Well, Gaibian did eventually go for surgery—just not the kind that mother wanted.

***

The vantage from Shanghai's Skybar is spectacular. Above the clouds, you feel like you can see into infinity. Below us, the Huangpu river curves along the Bund. The city's lights glow attractively, diffused by the smog.

Yicheng and I are hosting a girls' night to celebrate Mei-Xing's impending nuptials.

Ganbei!" Our cocktail glasses clink cheerfully.

"To the happy couple!" Yicheng says.

"May marriage make you an honest woman," I add.

"I can't believe I'll have to give you crones red packets next Lunar New Year," Mei-Xing complains.

Yicheng groans. "This New Year was horrible."

"Why?" I'm surprised. "After three years of lockdowns, everyone finally got to have reunion dinners and see their families again."

"That's exactly the problem," Yicheng huffs. "I'd actually forgotten how annoying relatives can be. The entire night, the aunties ganged up to demand if I'm seeing anyone. 'Don't wait so long, you're thirty, so old already, nearly expired. Don't be selfish, give your parents grandchildren,'" she mimes. "They actually offered to find me a husband."

"That's appalling," I shake my head.

"Did they mention getting productive for the Rabbit Year?" Mei-

Xing teases.

"Don't joke. They'll expect you to make babies immediately," Yicheng warns.

"Already started!" Mei-Xing giggles.

"Why can't my accomplishments be enough for them? Why must my life be defined by being with a man?" Yicheng demands.

"Hey, at least you've got a chance at love, Yicheng. No oldies ever ask me anything. They know I'm in lockdown mode, love-wise."

The girls know me well enough not to feel sorry for me, but the levity grows heavy. To break it, I share the latest gossip about Ku-Wei's unexpected proposal.

"Oh god! Ku-Wei's a hopeless romantic. Pining for someone unattainable," Mei-Xing says.

"Do you love him?" Yicheng asks quietly.

"No. But I might feel differently when I'm older. He may well be my only chance at marriage, post-40."

Yicheng doesn't respond, but I notice her looking meaningfully at me throughout the evening.

After drinks, Mei-Xing's beaux picks her up. Once we're alone, Yicheng takes my hand. "Hey, don't go home yet. Come to my place." Yicheng recently moved downtown to gain some distance from her family, although she still commutes to Seer Street to perform séances.

I've never visited her apartment, so I'm intrigued. We walk hand-in-hand to her new home. She's made it a place that's entirely her own, free from her family identity. While she changes clothes, I look around.

Yicheng emerges from her bedroom in a nightgown. She plays soft music, and we sit side-by-side.

"I'm sorry about earlier. It was thoughtless to complain about my aunts trying to matchmake me," she blurts.

"Don't worry."

"I can't stand how our society pressures women to get married. But I also feel it's wrong for your family to obligate you to be alone, Mingxi. To deny you happiness."

I silence her with a finger on her lips. "Don't say such things." For she is voicing my worst thoughts. "I've accepted my fate. Besides, I'm not alone. I've got my family."

"You have me."

"I know I do."

"You can have me in every way."

My finger, still on her lips, grows warm. Maybe it's the unfamiliar setting, but Yicheng appears different somehow. The curves of her face, the thoughtful tilt of her chin, are so familiar that they've become obscured to me, but now appear anew.

I'm seeing her clearly for the first time.

I glance away, afraid to look too long and longingly. She takes my hand. Like everything else, this familiar gesture feels electrifyingly new. My heart thumps and I swallow.

"Want to stay with me tonight?"

I don't need to be clairvoyant to see that however I answer, my fate will change. Irrevocably.

***

Grandmother has always been a slightly intimidating and opaque figure all my life. Bony and smelling of talcum, she cuts a sternly taciturn figure. Still, grandmother can be loquacious, especially about our abilities.

"Chinese divination traces its roots to the I-Ching, the Book of Changes," grandmother would hold court with us all listening attentively. "Gifted people like us can glimpse through time and detect patterns in destiny.

"The truly wise know how to use this information to ride the flow of fate and act at the right time to optimise their destiny. Our family shares these insights to help others. We advise our clients how best to live their lives in harmony with their past and in balance with their future.

"Females have always struggled and suffered in this country. But throughout history, the inner-eye has empowered women with access to foreknowledge. This makes us powerful.

"Remember, girls, your gift comes from our family, and family is your gift. Never abandon either."

***

The next morning feels full of promise as I leave Yicheng's place. But once I return home, my happiness falters at the mere sight of the family's ancestral altar.

My cousin Yuanjian is the first to greet me. "Morning, Mingxi! Did you have fun with Yicheng last night?"

"What? Oh, yes! Lots," I blanch slightly at her question.

Yuanjian looks curiously at me. "What'd you two get up to?"

"Same old things," I mumble before excusing myself to shower. I scrub myself vigorously as if it'll remove guilt. I emerge clean but still uneasy, so I approach the altar, light some joss sticks, and fervently pray for forgiveness.

The day passes in a daze. Mother chides me for spacing out. We need to be sharp for tonight's reading. Yuanjian has secured a new client—an influential chairman. His eldest son's getting married, and mother hopes to impress the chairman so we can gain more elite clients.

My phone buzzes–it's Yicheng, her WeChat messages bubbling with happiness. I don't respond. I can't think about this now, and try to forget what happened.

Soon, her messages grow concern—she asks how I'm doing, is everything ok? Am I angry at her?

I delete her messages.

Mother and Yuanjian make a performance when the chairman's entourage arrives. There's lots of air-kisses and ass-kissing. Since Yuanjian secured this client, she assumes the mother role for tonight's reading. Grandmother, Yuanjian, and I proceed with the usual steps, and everything progresses smoothly.

It's only when we three clasp hands that I feel something is different. For the first time ever, our inner-eyes are not intersecting normally. My vision, always so sharp, seems to conflate and conflict with Yuanjian's. It's as though we're both trying to see through the same peephole. That's impossible–I should be viewing this couple's compatibility while Yuanjian sees any future children. Instead, I see swift snatches of many years of miscarriages and misery lying ahead of them.

Grandmother senses the discordance and she immediately releases our hands, breaking the connection. Yuanjian cries out.

"What's wrong?" mother asks worriedly.

"It's nothing," Grandmother answers. She addresses the chairman. "I apologise for the interruption. I need to confer with my family. Privately."

The chairman's unused to being dismissed, but his entourage rises and leaves the parlour.

"Something interfered with the reading. Somehow, we couldn't connect properly," Yuanjian tells mother.

"The problem's source originated from Mingxi. Her vision has shifted," Grandmother says gravely.

"Yes, I felt that," Yuanjian accuses. "It's like she was competing with me, crowding me out."

"How do you mean?" mother twists her hands anxiously.

"It felt almost like Mingxi assumed the mother role."

"That's impossible. That can only happen if she…if she…"

"It seems Mingxi's no longer a virgin anymore, aunty."

"But she's a maiden. Our maiden," mother insists.

They've been talking like I'm not present, but now they turn to me. My insides twist. I force myself to look calm.

Mother gasps. "Mingxi! Did you have sex with a man? Tell the truth!"

I choose my words carefully. "No, mother. I did not have sex…with a man." That's an honest answer.

"There's one way to know for sure. A virginity test," Yuanjian says grimly.

Sanctimonious bitch, I think.

"Yes, good idea. Our family's future depends on it," mother says almost too eagerly.

Grandmother raises her hand. "Only I will conduct the examination. Leave us."

Once we are alone, Grandmother indicates for me to disrobe and lie down. Reluctantly, inevitably, I do so. She parts my thighs. I close my eye throughout and try not to compare Grandmother's cool, papery hands to Yicheng's warm ones.

The entire procedure passes in silence. Finally, it's over. The others are summoned back. "Mingxi remains intact," Grandmother announces.

Mother collapses with relief. "Praise the ancestors! She's still a virgin."

"Then why has her maiden's eye changed?" Yuanjian demands.

"We'll cancel tonight's reading. Tomorrow, we'll consult the other seers to determine the problem's root," Grandmother instructs.

I already know the problem. Once I'm alone, I finally text Yicheng back. *My life's ruined. You've killed me.*

***

I've spent the entire morning being poked, probed, and prodded with fingers, acupuncture needles and talismans. The other seers agree that while physically I'm the same, something's definitely changed. They just can't tell what. Mother's growing increasingly tense with the mysterious issue ailing me.

I'm sent to the Ding apothecary to buy herbs for a brew to 'cleanse' my inner-eye. I'm glad because I desperately need Ku-Wei. The moment I see him, I collapse into his arms. He holds me and makes shushing sounds.

Finally, I pull away. "Ku-Wei, I need your help."

He brushes my hair. "Anything you want."

"I'm afraid I've lost something precious. I need you to do a reading for me. See if it's been lost for good."

Ku-Wei agrees and holds my hands for the first time. I've never experienced a Ding reading before. The sensation's peculiar, like déjà vu.

He shakes his head. "I don't know what to tell you, Mingxi. I can't find anything missing. It doesn't seem that you've lost anything."

I shake my head forcefully. "No, this can't be. I must have. I can't see clearly."

Ku-Wei, who expected me to be relieved, is surprised as I begin shaking. "Oh Ku-Wei, I've lost my family's trust. I've lost my self-respect, my purity." Breaking into sobs, I confess everything.

Ku-Wei stands stock-still. "You and Yicheng?" he asks, his voice oddly colourless.

I nod, snuffling tears.

"That's why your vision's changed."

"Yes."

"Does your family know?"

"No. Grandmother examined me and found nothing…amiss. But I can't see like a maiden anymore."

"Then your family's business will be affected."

"I know. They're getting desperate," I sigh.

"I can help you with that."

"How?"

Ku-Wei grows business-like. "My proposal still stands, Mingxi. I'll overlook this…incident…with Yicheng. Call it a temporary oversight. And I won't tell your family. You don't need the shame."

"How will this help me?" I ask cautiously.

"If you can't see clearly anymore, your family has no maiden to perform readings. They'll need help financially. My family can support yours. If we marry, you'd be part of the Ding family fortune."

I draw back. "How can you pressure me right now? When I'm having a personal crisis?"

"I'm offering to help save you from this mess you've made, Mingxi. You'll have a good life as my wife."

All my tears evaporate. "You know, Ku-Wei, I'm beginning to see you clearly for the first time. And I don't like what I see."

***

On her 18th birthday, my baby sister became the man he was meant to be. Gaibian left the family with a letter bearing his new name, Shuang.

The letter explained Shuang's desire to live an authentic life. He hoped to be accepted by our family, but knew it was beyond mother's capacity. To prevent further sorrow, he was moving out.

The household was rocked by mother's rage. Aunty Pretty said the betrayal nearly killed her. The entire neighbourhood gossiped that the Rui family never saw this coming. But I always knew. I was happy that the misery Shuang endured as Gaibian was over. But I also mourned my own loss. For Shuang's freedom meant my continued incarceration.

***

Shuang's the only person who escaped the dense gravity of our family, so we arrange to meet in his stylish FFC neighbourhood, where lots of expatriates live. I recognise Shuang instantly—a beautiful young man, sleek hair in a man-bun. We embrace, and the years of separation melt.

We sit in a trendy cafe where nobody from Seer Street's likely to patronise. Shuang tells me all about his life. His work as a fitness consultant, his friends, his sugar daddy Olivier. I squirm at that—it's more than I want to know. He grins at my reaction. Then he gets serious.

"*Jiejie*," he says, meaning 'older sister'. "I'm sorry for all the trouble I caused you when I left."

"Oh, I never blamed you! You only wanted to be free to be yourself. I understand that."

"Well, you can be free too. Now that your maiden's eye has changed, nothing's keeping you."

"How did you know about that? Who told you?"

Shuang laughs. "Nobody. I can see it for myself."

"That's impossible. You're a guy now. Men don't have the Rui gift."

"I didn't lose my inner-eye after I transitioned. In fact, since the surgery, I see lots of interesting things that I didn't before. Maybe the testosterone is tweaking my sight," he explains.

"If that's true, that's major news. Our family could have boys!"

Shuang's expression darkens. "I believe the family actually prevents having sons."

"Why?"

"Because girls are easier to police. How would anyone check for male virginity? They tie your power to your 'purity' to control you. They put the family's honour between your legs. Now you've lost it, they're scrambling…"

"I haven't lost my virginity," I protest.

"Your inner-eye says otherwise."

"No! I'm still intact. What happened with Yicheng, that wasn't real."

"Why not? Because she's a woman?" he challenges. "*Jiejie*, losing your virginity doesn't come solely from hot beef injection."

"Gross!"

"I just mean, it's more than the physical. It's about the connection you share with someone, regardless of their gender. And you and

Yicheng clearly have a connection."

Shuang looks at his smartphone. "Listen, if you decide to leave the family, come stay with me. Olivier and I have a spare room."

Our conversation gives me lots to consider on the walk home. But as I approach the house, I sense a seismic shift. Tension is emanating from the building. Something's terribly wrong inside. Just then, the door opens and Ku-Wei emerges.

***

I've cried myself to sleep. The air still rings with mother's outraged screams that I've defiled myself and ruined the family. My heart is as shattered as the broken plates mother flung in fury.

I dream of that night with Yicheng. Soft lights, silken sheets, scented hair, sighs. Warm hands everywhere. I feel a rush of release.

The dream's quality changes and I realise Yicheng is dream-walking into mine. As girls, we sometimes entered one another's dreams to chat. There's no awkwardness over how we left things, since in dreams, only truths surface.

"Mingxi, I'm sorry for the trouble I've caused."

"I should be the one apologising for how I treated you. And I should thank you. I think you've freed me, Yicheng."

"How?"

"You let me experience something precious."

"What will you do now?"

"I don't know. The family may disown me."

"Want to stay with me for good?"

A knocking at the door awakens me before I can answer. But knowing that our friendship hasn't changed, that she still cares, fills me with peace.

I'm stunned to see Grandmother outside and brace for another onslaught. Instead, she surprises me.

"I can't agree with what you did, child. Young people these days…your values are different. But I know things change. I've seen enough to accept how fluid the world is. Old people cannot remain immovable, for even a stone will be washed away by time's currents.

"I know you never meant to hurt us. You wanted to experience something long denied to you. You've sacrificed your youth to serve our family. We should be thanking you.

"So, don't let us hold you back. You've helped so many people find love and happiness. Now it's your turn to have a future. May this gift help you on your new path, darling Mingxi."

Grandmother presses a thick red packet into my hands. Then she kisses me. I'll treasure both gifts forever.

***

The house is silent. Besides grandmother, everyone else is still asleep, emotionally exhausted from yesterday's revelations. Even though I'm about to sever forever the bonds with my family, the morning feels full of promise. All is not lost. There are still people who love me.

Shuang and Yicheng have both offered me a place to live. But I don't want to intrude upon the life Shuang and Olivier have built. To become an unbearable third-wheel that disrupts their dynamic. And as much as I care for Yicheng, she still lives too close to my family for comfort. The last thing I want is to remain within their odious orbit.

Perhaps I can go abroad and start my life anew in a different land where I can be anyone I want? Away not just from my family, but from my community and culture too.

My suitcase is packed, but I don't know where to go. I find this uncertainty thrilling. For the first time, my future's unclear. I savour this liberating indecision. Maybe the writer of my story can see what lies ahead. For now, I'm a woman just like anyone else, heading into the great unknown.

PORTRAIT OF A MAN IN
BROKEN GLASS

A Tale from the World

By Cormack Baldwin

OW IT ALL BEGAN didn't matter. Perhaps the Weber family had angered a god, or run afoul some witch, or simply tumbled headlong into a fate that they could not yet see. The exact history had long crumbled to stone and dust, and the Webers had little time for history regardless.

What mattered was that Horatio Weber-Banks woke up one morning to watch the day reach the same nonsensical point over and over again. Half-formed futures swarmed and danced and—

Tip tap tip tap water on the drain, wear away wear away—

Look and wait, hello who's that, coming, coming, coming break bone break skin—

—generally did nothing useful. He dug the heels of his palms into his eyes, letting the pressure scrub away some of the defunct futures as they got tied up in other people's morning routines. His own present was slow to start as he tried to decipher foggy hints among the gnat cloud of possibilities. A man in a suit; that seemed consistent. A beige room. The leer of a predatory gaze.

As if any of that helped. The College of St. James on the Thames had no shortage of men in suits, nor beige rooms, nor predatory gazes. If he didn't get going though, it would have a shortage of bookkeepers. After Harry, they were in a bad enough spot as it was. Reluctantly, he pushed back the covers. He didn't want to think about it.

Those who had observed Horatio's morning ritual tended to assume it was out of some militant need for uniformity. In reality, it was a practical matter of surviving the day. If the heat of roaring housefires grew around him as he lit the stove, it died just as quickly as he shut it off when the kettle whistled. If he only had one kind of tea, the universe couldn't flood him with the potential moral endpoints of choosing Darjeeling over Ceylon. Walking took longer than the trolley but kept the fractals of interactions at bay. Past the shuttered bar, past the gray-stone church, past the statue of an angel holding a book with the name of the college on her pedestal. By the time he settled at his desk, he could be certain of two things: one, that his choices up until that point had been airtight; two, that at some point that day, a white man in a suit and a greasy smile would make him an offer that would split his world in—

Clock in clock out one day down. Say hello yes hello you are the good one yes you are the good one, you will always be—

You are the secret; you are the key. The man in the suit at the front of an empty board, possibilities hovering in his chalk. The vinegar sting of ozone, the dust and musk of old books—

—well, infinity, but twice the infinities he was used to. Or the same amount of infinities, now clearer as the date approached. Maybe he had seen it all long ago, as he had with Harry, and his mind had simply purged the information to keep it all straight until it was too soon to fix. Maybe he'd tried to ignore it when he thought it was unlikely, until it became omnipresent. He preferred not to think of the math of it. There was no algebra, no calculus to get around the fact that he didn't know what answer he was supposed to give to lead to one or the other. And until he gave that answer, he wouldn't.

"Horatio."

The force of the voice startled him into realizing that it wasn't one of the many babbled voices of things that might never happen. He looked up from his ledger (mostly full, though he didn't remember grabbing a pencil) to see his supervisor, a portly white man who usually had a policy of benign negligence towards his employees. Horatio attempted a smile, which Mr. Abbott didn't return.

"I called your name five times," Mr. Abbott started. Then as an afterthought, "You're an odd one, aren't you?"

Was he supposed to respond to that? If so, confirm it or deny it? Perhaps apologize for not noticing Mr. Abbott among the background noise? Or just grimace and nod? By the time he came to a semblance of an answer, the moment had passed, and Mr. Abbott was talking again.

"Mr. Montserrat wants to speak with you. Something about Harry, bless his soul." The last part came out even more pointed than the first, an accusation without a crime.

"Alright." It was the wrong response, but he didn't have a better one. "Er, where is he? Montserrat, I mean." A flash of paper in his mind's eye, remembered or yet to be seen, drew a dotted line between the name Montserrat and 'Dean of Studies', but that made even less sense than letting it lurk in the unknown.

"Presumably in his office. Next building over. Punch out on your way over." With that, Mr. Abbott waved him away and disappeared back into his cloistered station.

Guilt chewed holes in Horatio's stomach over the short walk from his brick building to the pillared administrative center. Those holes poured acid and dread as he entered the tiled reception and the cacophony of shoes on marble, burbling voices, and flickering, buzzing lights shook apart any coherent whole. People, real, current, imagined, he didn't know, but there were people everywhere, speaking, yelling, demanding—

"Who the bloody hell are you? I'll call the police! Get out, I'll call the police! I'll—"

Five lights on one off three lights off one on one left six lights on two lights off burst and hiss, smell of sulfur and burning, shower us with sparks—

"Hello? Can you hear me? Hello?"

"What are you doing here? Where are you from? Get—"

"Hello are you alright hello are you alright hello are you are hello are you—"

"—alright?" And like a rainbow entering a prism, there was a near-singular woman in front of him. Her face did not flicker among possibilities. It was dark, and kind, and watching him with an expression he couldn't read.

He wanted to lie and say that yes, he was fine, or possibly confess his mind was being pounded full of nails. Instead, the line between his brain and his mouth seemed to be severed, a blown fuse refusing to let anything through until it was repaired. He tried to smile and managed a twitch. *You're an odd one, aren't you?*

A voice behind him both startled him and saved him from trying to rewire his mind on short notice. "No worries, Helen. He's here for me. I'm sure I don't need me to tell you that it can get rather overwhelming here." The man chuckled kindly before stepping from the haze of possible entrances and into proper view. Montserrat, pale and wiry in his deep gray suit, smiled the half inch down at him. "Come along, Horatio, there's a quieter way up." With that, he turned and waved for him to follow. Helen pursed her lips but returned to her desk without comment.

Luckily, his legs behaved where his throat wouldn't. He followed Montserrat like he used to follow his older sisters, waiting for them to break the crowds of people so he could slip by unnoticed. The man led him up an austere staircase, where the only futures were near-impossible flickers of its collapse, to a nondescript hallway of nondescript doors.

Remembered futures and new branches clicked into place at the sight of the room when Montserrat opened the closest door. The office was monochrome and minimal, an illustration in tans and grays, dipping only so far as bronze and reaching only as high as a creamy off-white. The bookshelves that flanked the desk held few items and fewer books. A silver owl figurine watched them from a shelf as Horatio folded himself into the chair. From this height, out the window taking up the side wall, Horatio could see his entire commute tilted at an angle. Children in the alley behind the bar. The back of the church, covered by a stained-glass image of Jesus, not crucified but still with a spear through his chest. He hadn't been aware that either existed except from feverish flashes as he took his well-worn route.

Montserrat's voice startled him to attention. "I'd like to ask you a couple of questions about Harry."

This was the part Horatio didn't want to be there for. Guilt squirmed back to life, and he pressed a hand onto his knee to keep from kicking the desk absentmindedly. Knowing that he wasn't going to be fired didn't stop the fractal of smiles and deals and—

Outstretched hand break the—

Not right now. There would be time for panic after work. He swallowed the lead in his throat. "Alright."

Montserrat took a seat and folded his hands into a temple. Echoes of his fingers twitched and shifted, spider-like. "Tell me, on his last day, what did you say to him?"

Too much. Not enough. He didn't know. Did it matter now?

He ordered the words with care, each feeling like a puzzle piece he had to slot into place. "Er, I tried to convince him not to drive home. A couple of times. He told me not to bother him." *Called me insane, wished aloud that I would go back to being "the quiet one" as blood and bone filled every corner of my vision,* he didn't add, because he needed to prove that he *wasn't* insane, that he *could* be the quiet one. He would pretend that he didn't hear the pop of lungs and rush of dead air past shredded metal, nor the crystalline tinkle of glass against the road. He was nearing thirty with his eyes and his mind intact, something not promised to minor seers. He wasn't losing that now.

Montserrat's tone was gentle but insistent, like a teacher asking after a bad report card. "Why?"

Horatio took in a breath, let it hiss between his barely-parted lips before he answered. "It was… dangerous. There was traffic." Even with all his willpower poured into keeping together, he couldn't suppress the urge to twist around and look at something that wasn't watching him with what felt like far too many eyes. The owl stared him down in response. When he spoke again, it came out in almost a child-like whisper. "I just wanted to help."

"And what did you see?"

His racing mind stopped as if it had hit a wall. He turned to Montserrat, whose smile had become sly, triumphant. Horatio missed the dead eyes of the silver owl. "I… what do you mean?" It took a moment for the question to process enough for him to even deny it. "I didn't see anything. What would I have seen?"

"Horatio Weber, isn't it?" Montserrat asked.

And with that, he knew he had lost. He just wasn't sure what it was he was losing. "Weber-Banks," Horatio corrected. As if his father's name would protect him from whatever was about to happen.

Montserrat waved off the relation. "You know, I always did want a palm reading from Madam Penelope Ruby Weber."

The sound of his sister's real name, even with the kitschy "Madam" appended to the front, shook what little resolve he had left away. "She—she goes by Penelope Cassandra. What—"

He wasn't looking, but he could feel Montserrat's smile like a coating on his tongue. "But there already was a Cassandra Weber, wasn't there? And you hate the fact that she uses your mother's name, don't you?"

He did. He hated the fact that she had known her beyond a vague impression of a smile or a lullaby. Hated that her memories were real, not wistful thoughts doubtless planted long after the fact, like a weed in a field of wheat. He bit his bottom lip, hoping the thin skin would break and bleed. At least the taste of metal would be something to hold onto.

"So, Mr. Weber, what did you see?"

Horatio closed his eyes, letting the aftereffects of visions play over his lids, and breathed in. "I kept seeing Harry's car crash. Over and over again. I don't know if it was inevitable or if I just kept my focus on those. I thought if he just walked, or took the Tube, or *anything*, he might survive. So, I tried to convince him, but he wouldn't listen to me. And—I did everything I could, didn't I? I can't make people listen to me. I couldn't tell him what I knew. Was I supposed to?" The thought of his coworkers knowing what he saw felt like a knife to his throat. Then again—*you're an odd one, aren't you?*—not as if his ruse was working that well.

When he looked up again, he found Montserrat standing not behind his desk, but so close Horatio could feel the pressure of his presence. The future twitched around him like a dying spider, half-real hands extending and retracting at random. He flinched as ghostly fingers grazed his neck. "I can't imagine you were keen to risk your employment by claiming awesome foreknowledge. But wasn't Harry worth that?"

Horatio turned, tried to find something, anything other than those eyes to focus on. He couldn't do this. He needed air. He needed an escape.

Instead, the nails of dry fingers pressed into his chin, pulling him to look up at Montserrat's placid, empty smile. Every ounce of his body urged him to pull away, but a wandering thumb ran a line from the bottom to the top of his throat, pausing over his windpipe. "Ah, ah, Horatio, I asked a question."

He swallowed, feeling his Adam's apple press against the touch. "Sir, I don't think you understand. The Webers—we don't last long. My mother passed soon after my brother was born. That brother nearly bled to death after cutting out his own eyes so he wouldn't see what was to come. I've made it to twenty-six without being jailed or hospitalized for a public breakdown—"

Yet click click click go the orderly's heels, sterile sweet of alcohol and chloral hydrate white linoleum glare will reflect the world and the world and the world back at—

"There must be twenty of us, cousins and all, and we're lucky that we're all free citizens for the moment. For all I know, that will change before the sun turns down—"

Wail of sirens, siren song, come along, five four three—

"I have a normal job, a *good* job. I need to keep that. For my sake. For my family's sake." No, not an abstract family. Not the Webers, lineage of prophets. For his niece and nephew, left alone when his sister had been sequestered in a ward somewhere. For his uncle, whose house Horatio stayed in so someone could pay the rent while he was in jail for having the gall to collapse under the weight of it all in public. For his own future, or futures, which could only exist if he made it. So he didn't become part of someone else's liturgy of trauma.

With that final confession, Montserrat let go, though echoes of his fingers crawled up and down Horatio's throat, cascaded down his spine in a shiver. "I think I understand completely, Mr. Weber. You have a secret. I consider myself a connoisseur of such matters. Really, your situation is better than I'd expected. I feared you would deny it wholesale. I'd have to pull everything out from between your teeth." He chuckled, but the warmth had run out. "I should have trusted you more. I apologize for that. Twenty-six, you said? And tell me, do you think your family is alone?"

Pressure built and threated to break in his mind. "We're the only ones I know of."

Knew of. Futures, suppressed, forgotten, or never to be realized until now, swirled around him in half-understood snippets. Women with the eyes of wolves and the smiles of tigers, auroras of green over realities that flickered like a dying light, lightning cracking through a silent sky.

It was beautiful. His throat tasted of blood and bile.

Montserrat's hand found a place on Horatio's shoulder. His words were comfort and dread at once. "But you're not the only ones. Not in the slightest. You have a unique gift perhaps, but you're not the only ones. Powerful objects, twists of fate, it doesn't really matter how one gets them." He shook his head, and his tone turned from self-satisfaction to something bordering on nostalgic. "In my case, the Montserrats spent quite some time trying to cultivate a vessel for the esoteric. My purview is unfortunately limited to a general swath of the unknown present, but that was enough to find you, wasn't it? A perfect counterpart. A living omen."

Others like him, but not like him. A universe of the known that had always danced just out of reach, until he learned to avoid it without even noticing. And suddenly the world stung with want. "I still don't know why you want to know all this," Horatio admitted. But he did. There would be an offer, a deal. But whether that was a promise or a purpose, a cure or a curse or both or—

Fox sly man licks his lips and grins. Secrets and truths play on his tongue.

"To teach you, dear Horatio. To be what you

> *Want to be*

>> *Were supposed to be*

>> *Need to be*

>>> *Are."*

Outstretched hand repeated again and again, a wheel of propositions punctuated by watching, watching eyes. Shattered mirror reflecting in on itself. Knowledge for the predator, wisdom for the prey just one question only one question—

"Do we have a deal?"

DESTINY BEGINS

A Tale from the World

By Shannon Connor Winward

D ESTINY BEGINS

with a cigarette.
She takes her smoke break at moonrise,
        throws a coat over her bright bosom,
          hikes up her skirts to straddle
    her perch in the corner.

     Go on.
     Give her a light.

She'll tell you
what you want to know.

That's how it starts,
    and how it ends too,
        the measure of a life
to ash,
    so,
    best have your question ready

hold it
in your mind   and don't

let go. See,
    the show must go on and

Destiny

(*inhale,*

       exhale)

… takes
her own sweet time.

STRIKE ME, SOLEMNITY

A Tale from North America

By Jacqueline Kate Goldblatt

THE PYROMANCER LIVED JUST off the corner of Verdigris Street and above Mr. O'Malley's drug store in a small, shabby apartment that stank of tobacco and ennui. He'd had a name once. Carl told me that his mother knew it at one point, that it started with an M. Michael, maybe? Mitchell? It didn't really matter. By that point, we'd all just started calling him The Pyromancer, and his real moniker had been swept under the rug like the crap that came off the ends of his cancer sticks. The crap that he didn't use in his readings, that is.

Y'see, a name like that isn't just given to those who have fiery tempers or red hair. You had to have a certain skill set. In the case of Pyro, his gig was telling the future using the element that had elevated the cavemen from ugly mugs who trekked barefoot for miles to get food into ugly mugs who wore saddle shoes and went to Woolworth's for Tulip Sundaes. That element, of course, was fire. Now, the man didn't go out there committing acts of arson or doing anything like that. His approach to divination was a practical one: cigarettes.

Every day, just after four-o-clock, The Pyromancer would lean out the window of his dingy grey windowsill and smoke. Whether it was rain or shine, special occasions or average days, his routine never changed. Ours didn't either. Richie, Babs, some of the other neighborhood kids, and I would camp out at O'Malley's, stuffing ourselves on candy and dishing out dimes on comic books to pass the time. Babs, our lookout, would whistle as soon as she caught sight of our man, and all of us would rush into the street. We'd stand under the window and watch The Pyromancer blow out a thundercloud of smoke, his eyes observing its shape, the way it dissipated with keen interest. Once the last trace of vespers faded, he'd look down at us from his perch and tell us what he'd seen in the haze.

They tended to be relatively general things, like "The Yankees will win the World Series!" or "Expect a pop quiz sometime this week!" Babs, despite being our watchman, regarded everything he said as a real crock of bull. Still, to my friend Richie and I, these were prophecies that we lived by. Richie did, especially. The kid had always been indecisive. Ever since we were toddlers, Rich couldn't make up his mind worth a damn. At the diner, he'd hem and haw over whether to get a burger or chicken strips. He'd drive himself crazy trying to decide what game to join at recess. When I asked him if he wanted to trade baseball cards, he'd look at me like I'd asked him to decide which one of his parents to murder. "Life," he once told me, "is one giant series of decisions, and there's just too many for me to handle!" As such, the little prophecies The Pyromancer told us were the bits of guidance he needed to function. I guess I never realized just how deep that dependence ran. If I had, I never would have suggested Richie and I see the Pyromancer for a personal reading.

Pyro had always offered to give sessions that went into specifics, kind of like what those carnival psychics at the county fair offered every year. Problem was, his prices weren't exactly cheap. It would cost us twenty-five cents each, and back in the 50s, that was a fair amount of money. So far, none of our ragtag group had had the patience, means, or courage to save up for it. Richie was determined to though. He wanted to know the future, and he wanted to know BAD. Now that we were "on the cusp of manhood," as he called it, we would have to decide what we wanted to do with our lives soon. I always told him he was overthinking things, that there was still time. The message never seemed to get through that thick, blond skull of his though. He'd just look at me with those fevered green eyes of his and say, "I need to figure it out for sure, Charlie. I just gotta make sure I'm on the right track."

JACQUELINE GOLDBLATT

The two of us had been saving up our respective allowances for a few weeks in order to get the amount we needed. I took extra stops on my paper route, and Rich mowed lawns on the weekends. It was slow going, but after a particularly generous tip from old Mrs. Lahey down the block, we finally had enough. Part of me wanted to take my share of the money and run. I mean, I could buy a new copy of *The Hobbit* or two comic books and a nice bottle of Coke. I could invest in something solid, that I could be certain of. Something that wasn't shrouded in smoke. Unfortunately, my conscience has always been a bit of a goody-two shoes loudmouth. In the end, I couldn't just leave my friend. I had promised I'd be there alongside him, that I too would participate in this peek into the future. So, that Saturday, we met at O'Malley's and steeled our courage before ascending the creaky stair to The Pyromancer's door.

Richie had knocked on the door before I had even made it up off the top step. I snorted.

"Jeez Richie, you couldn't have waited five seconds?"

"The future waits for no one, Chuck."

"Oh, go suck on a lemon!"

Our spirited banter was interrupted by the door swinging open and slamming into the wall with a loud *wham!* The Pyromancer, amber eyes rapidly fading in and out of focus beneath a wash of greasy black hair, stood before us in a worn leather bomber jacket. His face was all sharp angles, and he looked as though he hadn't slept in a month.

Rubbing what appeared to be apricot jam from the corner of his mouth, he sighed out a muddled "Whaddayawant?" compressing three words into a single smeared sound. Richie, who was expecting a warmer welcome than the one we had gotten, froze in place.

Quickly, I grabbed the change out of Richie's back pocket and held it up for Pyro to see. "We'd like a reading, if you'd please." The Pyromancer looked between the money and us, gaze darting back and forth. Finally, he slid the change out of my palm and turned to walk back into the apartment, gesturing with his left hand for us to follow.

SEERS AND SIBYLS – *North America*

The inside of the apartment was as dingy looking as the outside. A ratty green sofa sat in the corner of the living room. The coffee table was covered in old newspapers and ashtrays. A lone daffodil wilted in a dented tomato soup can. *This,* I thought to myself as we followed the man leading us, *is The Pyromancer's home? What an absolute dump!* A very strong part of me wanted to get out of there right then. This was no place for me to be. It was cramped, ugly, and made my inner hypochondriac scream. However, an even larger part of me wanted to stay. My entire life I'd been surrounded by sterile, saccharine suburbia. This place was *different.* It was an adventure. Besides, we'd gotten this far, and the money was out of our hands. There was no real point in leaving now.

The Pyromancer stopped before a small plywood desk that lay off to the side of everything, empty save for a box of matches and a small dish of water. He fished around in his pocket before pulling out a cigarette, which he deftly placed into the corner of his mouth. "So," he said, peering down at the two of us, "Which one of you wants to go first?"

Having been the one to give him the money, I volunteered.

He handed me the box of matches. "OK. Give me light."

I struck one and lifted its fiery surface to the cig, watching as the tip caught on fire just enough so that it would light. He breathed in with a happy sigh and leaned over the dish. The ashes fell from the blackening tip and hissed softly as they hit the water. A trail of smoke blew out of The Pyromancers nose as he tilted the dish gently from side to side like he was panning for gold until, finally satisfied, he set it down and peered at it for a few minutes. Then he looked at me.

"Good news, kid. Looks like you've got a long, happy life ahead of you. That love of stories you have and your special way with words? Try using it to your advantage. Pick up a pen and it'll take you far."

My eyebrows shot up in surprise, and my stomach fluttered with happy butterflies. Not once had I mentioned my love of reading and my dreams of becoming a writer, and yet the Pyromancer had picked up on it somehow. The man didn't know me from Adam, but he had spotted my ambitions from a mile away and validated them in an instant. I was about to ask him another question when Richie, excited as anything, practically jumped forward.

"Me next! Me next!"

The Pyromancer smiled and stubbed out the cigarette before fishing out a new one. "Alright, alright. You know the drill, kid. Light me up."

With trembling hands, Richie scraped the match against the strip. But it wouldn't light. Again, he tried, but to no avail. Frowning, he picked up another and set to work. But that one wouldn't catch either. Nor did the next. Or the one after that. Six matches later, and the cigarette wasn't lit. Richie stared at his hands, then the matches, and up at The Pyromancer. His mouth opened and closed like a fish gasping for air and sweat dripped down his face. "I... I..." he croaked, the matchbox falling from his hands. "I have no future!"

Before either of us could blink, Richie was running down the stairs at full tilt.

"Shit!" cursed The Pyromancer as he ran after him, me trailing close behind.

"Richie, it's just a pack of matches! They're probably defective or something!" I screamed as we raced past O'Malley's counter and into the street after him.

But Richie couldn't hear me.

He didn't hear the milk truck coming down the road either. The coroner said that he was gone before he'd even realized he was hit.

After the accident, The Pyromancer skipped town. I guess he didn't want to be surrounded by reminders of what happened. I couldn't really blame him. I'd have left too, if I could. Speaking of left, Pyro did give me one more thing other than his prophecy. A few days after the funeral, I found an envelope containing fifty cents and a ballpoint pen on my front stoop. Both of them ended up in the sewer grate next to O'Malley's, along with an entire box of my dad's cigarettes.

THE OCEANOGRAPHER WAITS

A Warning for the World

By Devan Barlow

WHEN THE OCEANOGRAPHER WARNED,
She was ignored
Numbers mocked, science swept aside,
Yet she felt the waters coursing through the world
Linked by channels fresh and salt
All at risk
She returned to the shore that had sculpted her,
The place where her love for water began

In those tides gathered
Deities of waters:
Ocean, puddle, river, pond,
Trusting her to listen
They came to her, desperate,
Offering time.
The oceanographer let their waters encase her

So she waits, paused in ice
At the shore which shaped her,
A frozen pillar
Though so much has already melted,
And seas have risen
The waters hold her fast
Until one who will listen,
One who will make sure she is heard
Comes to fetch her

The ice will melt,
And she will emerge
To do the waters' work.

JUNIEL AND THE MOON

A Tale from Ancient Egypt

By Jay McKenzie

ALL GODS ARE *NOT* created equal.

There was a time where they praised us in simpatic harmony, eyes gazing our way for guidance to maintain Ma'at, repel Isfet.

But that was then.

"Khonsa, friend. It is in their nature to seek the gold and the light."

That is what he said to me when the last Khonsation temple was razed, the lector priests banished to Napata, the practice of moon-worship outlawed.

He appeared to me then as a boy: a dusting of gold on the apples of his cheeks, well-deep rivets cupping his smile. A benevolent smile, but it could not mask the triumph beneath

Sometimes he appears as a ball of light, an elegant dog, a broad-beaked eagle.

I could shapeshift too once. When I had followers willing to make offerings or lend their voices to the celebration of my power. I could slither across the sands like a cobra, howl for their attention as a majestic wolf, soar across their skies as an owl. Or I could appear as a young, beautiful maiden bathing in the Nile. How I loved to feel the water trickling across my skin.

But that was then.

I am trapped now, a silvery wisp, light as air, inconsequential: a mere fog in the plane of the Gods.

Now it is I who prays to my errant followers.

Love me, I implore to their sleeping heads. But they shake me from their minds, a strange dream, a daylight yearning soured.

SEERS AND SIBYLS – *Ancient Egypt*

***

Mehmet waits until the sun slips behind the dunes. Silhouettes of prostrating figures rise and fall against the golden stripe it leaves as he closes the door behind him. He pulls his hood low so that his face is hidden, leans heavily on his staff, and begins the long walk to the Eastern Quarter of Napata.

He carries no torch, seeks not the light burning in the windows of dwellings on the main stretch. Instead, he presses himself into the shadows, glancing up only occasionally for guidance by the early evening stars.

To those heading home from their sun encomium, he appears as nothing more than a wretched old man. Or worse: a vagabond. Men with their thoughts turned to the emmer bread and beer awaiting them pay little heed to limping bearded men of the shadows.

I was important once, thinks Mehmet, two boatmen passing by within a whisper. *I am invisible now.*

Once, he wore the pleated linens encrusted with lapis lazuli of his lector brethren, a gorgerine hanging across his chest. He misses the cool metal on his skin.

It is longer of late, his journey to the small dwelling of Kharum-Tu, where the tiny, outlawed Khonsan faction meets. He will feast with the men before heading into the courtyard to teach their boys under an opalescent moon. The boys, suspended somewhere in time between babies at their mothers' breast and their fathers' talk of arrows and art, will snigger each time he bends to scratch a symbol in the sand, knees creaking like the hinges of the door. They will stretch their eyes and contort their mouths when he gazes up into the wash of gleaming stars overhead, returning to abrupt normality when he looks back at them. And they will nudge one another with their pointed elbows when he invariably drifts off thinking about his old temple at Abydos.

JAY MCKENZIE

***

It was I who taught them to feel. It was I who showed them the beauty of the dark, the shadows, the hidden. Because of me, they can trust themselves to know what they cannot see.

But they are forgetting.

I dance through the Nile Valley and see only eyes seeking light. In the corners not illuminated by the sun's rays, they burn torches, hang white canvas and metal to reflect yet more light.

Remember, I implore. *Remember the way you used to sit in the darkness after the torches were extinguished? Remember the way that in just a few patient blinks, your eyes would gently be able to see once more?*

But with their eyes blind in the dark, so too do their ears become deaf.

***

Mizoftouti ines kou alai.

The boys chant the words mechanically. *There's no soul in it,* thinks Mehmet, *no love.* Once, the belief in Khonsa-heka—the magic of the moon—was strong enough to tear a guttural chant from the throat of a mute.

Before they were blinded by Aten-Ra.

He is about to begin this evening's sermon, when a *fsh fsh* takes his mind from his work.

"What is that sound?"

The boys snigger.

In the corner of the courtyard, a young girl rakes a tamarisk frond through the sand.

"Stop that!" yells Mehmet.

The raking stops. The girl props the frond against a wall, retreats into the shadows.

In his sermon, Mehmet speaks of the healing powers of moon

231

bathing. One boy rudely falls asleep and has to be nudged into wakefulness by the foot of his brother. In the last hour, they move onto interpretation of the skies. Mehmet peers into the sky, etches symbols into the sand with his staff, asks the boys, "what is our beloved Khonsa trying to convey here?"

The boys in turn yawn, scratch their heads, idly twist daisies between their fingers. When the first stripe of orange morning light stretches across the horizon, the boys barely wait for their dismissal before heading indoors to their welcoming beds.

Mehmet shakes his head.

"Please, Mehmet-sa." A young girl hands him an acacia cup filled with beer. He drinks it gratefully, throat parched from all of the talking.

"What are you doing?"

The girl stands amidst the scratched symbols, silently gesticulating. She stops at Mehmet's inquiry, bobs a small curtsey, turns away. She is almost inside when she looks back.

"It is about the tides," she says quietly. "The question the boys didn't answer. Khonsa is conversing with the tides."

Mehmet tilts his head slowly. "Oh? And how would a little girl know such a thing?"

The girl tucks her chin tightly to her chest. "I listen sometimes."

"I see."

"I'd like to learn."

"Girls don't learn."

"I'd like to learn."

Mehmet waves her over with his staff. "What is this?" he asks, pointing at a scored crescent with two spots pressed on either side.

"It is the Harvest Moon."

"Correct. And why is it here," he points at the symbols, "between these two?"

The girl frowns, bites her thumb. "A late harvest?"

"Early." Mehmet taps his staff on the ground. "What is your name, little girl?"

"Juniel."

"You may listen, Juniel, to my next class, then after, I will ask you three questions. Answer correctly, and I shall teach you."

Juniel nods

"Now clear this up."

Mehmet allows himself the ghost of a smile.

***

The tides are still my faithful servants. They care not for the whims and fashions of these foolish mortals, but dance instead to my song.

I skim the surface of the Ocean now, the waves rising to greet me. I twine and dive through the spindrift, alive, pulsating.

Out here, at sea, there is nothing inconsequential about a fog, nothing meaningless in a mist.

On land, I skim the heads of those who once worshipped me, whisper by their ears. They turn blindly, shout louder to drown out my voice.

But there is one. Her voice is reverent, her heart listening quietly.

***

Juniel is quick and bright. She is rested and ready for their lessons, her stick sharpened so that she may etch her own workings out into the sand alongside Mehmet's.

"Now, Juniel, when can we expect the next New Moon?"

"Twelve days from now, Mehmet-sa."

She is the daughter of Kharum-Tu, Mehmet's most promising student from Abydos before the banishments, and she has his hawkish eyes, his serious temperament.

"Tell me, Juniel. Do you pray alone?"

"All of the time, Mehmet-sa."

One night, he arrives to see her dancing under the silver strands of light, swaying from side to side, arms raised, undulating as though no bone runs through her.

"It is what she wants," Juniel says. "Her power comes from more than just thought: she needs action."

Mehmet drops his staff. "Is she…does she commune with you?"

It is a redundant question, as it is written there in the faint argentine glow of her skin and in the burning black holes of her eyes and the opalescent beams encircling her.

***

I have found a voice.

She is unsullied, untainted by mortal yearnings and material desire. She seeks me, and she listens and watches and waits. Bright as Sopdet's glow, I am drawn to her, and she absorbs all that I whisper in her ear at nightfall.

Aten-Ra scoffs. "A little girl? Pray, friend, do you really think a little girl can restore your standing with the people?"

He is half-man, half-lizard today, flicking tongue startling me with every word.

I do not respond, but instead remember the people: Pharaoh Akhenaten promised riches to all for the sole worship of the Sun God, yet the poor are still waiting for their gold. Perhaps impatience will open their ears to the words of a little girl.

And if not, I have something else on the horizon.

***

Tonight, Juniel quivers.

"Please Mehmet-sa. I need your help."

She explains that when praying alone by the river, Khonsa came to her, a silver shimmer, a wisp of a face reflected in the dark waters.

"Are you certain it was really her?" asks Mehmet quietly.

Juniel nods. "Her voice was a soft breeze at first, then I heard her. It was a song, and in it, a message that she wishes me to deliver to Pharaoh Akhenaten."

Mehmet feels his pulse quicken high in his throat.

"If Akhenaten has not granted pardon to those who worship Khonsa by the Perigee Moon, she will send forth a great wave to destroy those who seek to persecute us."

"Oh Juniel! If we deliver that message to Akhenaten, he will put us to death!"

Juniel stares with a thousand moons of wisdom burning in her eyes. "Then so be it."

She stands then, shoulders back, arms by her side. "It is my duty, Mehmet-sa. Your teaching has inspired in me great faith. I bow to her will."

Mehmet struggles to his feet. "Then I shall be at your side, Juniel-sa." And though there is a tremor in his voice, his spine finally has something to stand up straight for.

***

I did not set out to be a destroyer.

No, I sang of peace, danced in love. But I see them now: the poor, bending and breaking under the weight of greed.

They push their hands into the neighbour's purse, take food from the mouths of their own children, rip the blankets from their trembling elders.

"You are too soft for this world, Khonsa," he laughs, a roaring lion haloed with a golden mane today. "Let them fight it out amongst themselves."

But at night, the Cosmos trembles, the Ocean quakes, and the faithful weep.

Ma'at must be restored.

Whatever the cost.

SEERS AND SIBYLS – *Ancient Egypt*

***

Thebes is dusty.

It has been the driest summer in memory after the floodwaters receded, and the city wears the scars of the scorched earth.

At the wells bordering the city, people swelter in lines that snake out towards the desert, clutching pots and jugs, hoping that today they might make it to the front of the queue. Men hawking dates and figs at inflated prices stalk the line, honing in on the thirstiest eyes, prising meagre coins from desperate mothers.

Mehmet shakes his head.

"It was not always like this."

Juniel says little but sticks close to her mentor. Along the way, on their journey from Napata, Mehmet and Juniel have spread Khonsa's message to all that would listen. Some have spat at them, some sneered and laughed, their fingers dipping into someone else's goods. But many listened.

Just a few hundred metres from the steps of Akhenaten's principal palace, Amun-Pala Square thrums with city bustle. "Sulaad," yell men passing cargo from boat to land. Carters gleam with sweat under heavy sacks hoisted across their shoulders; donkeys laden with baskets of grain bray impatiently. The air is hot and heavy and thick and tangs with the excrement of the asses.

"Here is the spot."

Grain sacks piled haphazardly against a wall form a makeshift platform from where a small girl could make herself visible to the crowded square. The top stands higher than Mehmet's head.

"And these walls will help your voice to abound," he tells her. "But you must speak as clearly and plainly as you can."

Juniel's lips tremble, swallowed around a silent prayer.

"When you finish, Juniel-sa, clamber down to me as quickly as possible. We must get lost in the crowd."

Nobody pays heed to the wiry body climbing the stack, nor do they notice a small girl drawing herself to full height, closing her eyes, pressing her fingertips together to summon the courage of Khonsa-ra. Those close to the stack though, do pause when a voice rings across the square.

It is not the timbre of a girl singing out to her brothers to seek where she hides. Nor is it the pensive tones of a perfectionist student puzzling over the latest astrological equation. No. The voice that leaves Juniel's lips seems not to come from her at all. It rings with the jewel-sharp clarity of the skies themselves, the sound of a thousand stars racing one another across the sky.

"She comes," says Juniel.

Mehmet is rooted to the spot.

Around him, life pauses. Industry slows to a halt, conversations die in the stultifying air, asinine complaints are swallowed by crystalline words. The bodies of the people turn to the small girl with her arms outstretched.

Juniel continues:"and she seeks her rightful place once more."

Too ensorcelled, too completely captured by the young girl's words, none of the crowd are aware of the Aten-Guard moving silently between them. It is only when her voice is muffled, when the words become a jumble of confusing sound that they notice her swift capture.

Juniel is hauled from the stack, a length of linen stuffed into her mouth, arms wrenched hard behind her back. There are four of them, towering over the little girl. Mehmet gasps and rushes towards her, but the crowd closes in, resuming normal business.

"Juniel!" he cries.

But he catches only a glimpse of her silvered eyes, hair streaming behind her like a waterfall.

***

Captive.

237

SEERS AND SIBYLS – *Ancient Egypt*

That we may not even speak without guarded tongues in these times is why I must act.

The girl was caught, imprisoned, though my words had barely begun to flow through her. They fear, you see. They fear, because they know that Akenhetan has wronged not only me, but the entire Cosmos.

"You failed, Khonsa. Pretty words from a little mouth took you nowhere. Akenhetan is too powerful for you." Today, he is a many-headed dog. "Accept defeat, Khonsa, you little puff of air."

All of the heads laugh in unison: a terrible sound, a bark, a howl.

But when he is gone, I shift.

Flicking wings, I become a tiny firefly.

I am small, true, but look! I can shift once again.

You are wrong, Aten-Ra, I whisper, my luminescent abdomen throbbing. *The people heard.*

*****

For two days and nights, Mehmet waits outside of the jail. He eats little, talks to few, sleeps only during the relentless midday sun, seeking shade and silence where he can.

"Where is the young Khonsa-prophet?" he asks each guard who enters and leaves, but he is told nothing.

He listens though, to voices in the street. The people are talking and *Khonsa* is on their lips. She is whispered into cocked ears, murmured on quiet mouths. And he senses her growing strength in the brightened beams of starlight, in the hurry of the shooting stars.

On the third night, he espies a colony of glow worms hanging from the underside of a market awning, fireflies illuminating the acacia trees, a sleek fox slinking in the shadows. On that same night, he gasps as a prison guard takes his arm and leads him to an abandoned jetty.

"I will help you," the guard tells Mehmet. "I will release the girl."

Mehmet weeps. "How can I ever repay you?"

"There are a number of us here in Thebes: Khonsa worshippers. Secretly so. We want you to lead us to Al-Qurn."

"Al-Qurn?" Mehmet frowns. "It is dangerous, sa. Men have lost their lives making the ascent."

"Juniel-sa has communed further with Khonsa. She instructs the faithful to get to higher ground."

"Then so be it," says Mehmet. "I will be your humble guide."

The men grip one another's palms in agreement.

In the dark swell of the gathering clouds, a distant groan of thunder rumbles.

***

Akhenaten is a vain and stupid pharaoh.

I visit his rooms as a wide-tailed nightjar, wings cutting through the dry sands that are blowing through Thebes.

Sleep evades him these days. Oh, he tries, flipping beneath the thin linen sheets of his bed, soaked in sweat, but his mind cannot commit to the sweet release of sleep. Not when it is consumed by the gold and riches he thinks about day and night.

I have tried to speak to him, but his ears are closed to all but his own desires. Only Aten-Ra commands his attention, and even then, during worship, he pictures his hands sifting through trunks of amber, jasper, lapis lazuli, and his one true mistress, gold.

While there is much beauty in darkness, there also lies much danger.

Akhenaten will learn very soon what it means to turn your back on the moon.

***

Juniel has grown taller during her incarceration.

Or perhaps, Mehmet realises, she is simply carrying herself

differently.

Although there is an urgency to their escape from the prison, Juniel moves with unhurried grace. Her face breaks into a wide smile when she sees her mentor leaning on his staff beneath a date palm. Omari, the guard who has aided her escape, looks furtively from side to side.

"Juniel-sa, we must make haste."

Through the shadows, the three make their way on foot to the city walls encircling Thebes. Khonsa-moon, looming large in the sky, is almost full: only a thin sliver remains in darkness, waiting to bloom and ripen into a full sphere.

The harsh wind carries a bite, while the heat of the blustering sand which scratches their skin, stings, burns. They stick to the shadows, trusting Khonsa, trusting the pearlescent moon, trusting the great constellations that wink and beam upon them.

"Not far now," says Omari. "A small group gathers beyond the city walls, my mother amongst them."

Quicker now, they move, and the wind wails from rolling black clouds over the sea. Twitching guards wave them across the city limits and they skit down the slopes of the Wadi Al-Bakrie.

"Oh!" exclaims Juniel.

For gathered in the basin of the valley is a crowd of pilgrims, a thousand or more, faces tilted to the moon, waiting to be led to Al-Qurn.

***

I sing, and the Ocean responds.

The tiny ships floating on her dark-cast waters are tossed and tumbled, and the sailors cry my name. I soothe them then, smoothing the rippling mass, lulling them back to sleep once more.

"Go back to dry land," I urge in their dreams. "Take your ships home, kiss your wives, play with your children, for soon, I shall rip the Ocean from its bed."

I glow ever brighter, shifting, dancing, flying in all my majestic nocturnal forms.

The girl listens beautifully.

She uses the words, paints the pictures I show her in her sleep, makes the promises I whisper.

Rewards await her on the other side if she can be my voice for a little longer.

My name spreads through Thebes and far beyond. And the disk of my moon is but days away from the perigee.

***

It is a long and difficult ascent to the summit of Al-Qurn.

As the sun raises his cruel scorching head, the pilgrims press on, aiding the old and infirm, carrying the children. Though the mountain provides sparse shade in the naked trees, the pilgrims improvise: a sheet here, a goat-hide there, anything to cast shadow from the relentless morning sun.

At midday, they set up a makeshift camp. Many sleep, but more still lounge against one another, talking. There is a buzz in the air.

Just before dusk, a tremulous cloud blocks the sun. The temperature plummets, the pilgrims grip their clothes and belongings. Loose branches are plucked by the wind from the trees, swirled, thrown from the rocky slopes.

They press on under a low sun, Mehmet and Juniel at the fore, sharing juniper berries and figs, pressing down a quiver in their bellies.

And just before nightfall, they reach the summit.

***

I come to Akhenetan as a wolf: offer him one last chance at redemption.

But he does not recognise me, orders his guards to slit my throat.

I shift of course, but tonight, I become Apep the serpent, Enemy of Light. I am longer than the Nile, and my fangs gleam bright as the moon.

The songs of the faithful feed my fury and I grow and writhe, power surging with every drop of sunlight that the darkness devours.

"Khonsa, no!"

Aten-Ra, an elegant cat today, is right to be afraid.

I dive and whip my tail, gnash my beastly jaws, command my faithful servant the Ocean to rise, rise, rise and destroy.

***

Alae muza guo epipsa zotuma ne apokalýpsei ti vithýtoru.

When their song ends and the moon reaches its perigee, Juniel turns her eyes to the North.

They turn with her, a thousand pairs of eyes awaiting Khonsa's revenge.

At first, it is a distant rumble, a groan. Then it grows louder, louder. A thick tumult of black cloud rolls above the Nile, electricity rippling through their swollen belly like a painful belch, scarred with silver streaks.

Quicker it rolls, faster, and dragging behind it, a wall of black, surging water, tall as Kheops mound.

It is all they can do to watch in silence as the wave surges on, annihilating the riverbanks and everything in its path.

They press their hands to their ears to block the roar, spread their feet wide as the wave rolls by beneath them, shaking the mountain, screaming its arrival.

Some close their eyes, others cover their mouths as the wave smashes over Thebes, crushing the streets and squares, drowning everything, destroying all.

And then, a thick, acerbic silence.

Juniel exhales.

JAY MCKENZIE

The wave recedes as swiftly as it came, sucking thirstily back upriver, tossing the carcasses of disbelieving Thebeans like driftwood.

***

Aten-Ra bows low.

He is a mouse today, tiny, timid.

I am a luminescent maiden, hair billowing from my crown, beautiful, powerful, and he quakes in my presence.

"I should never have doubted you, Khonsa."

Ma'at is restored. The Cosmos is once more in balance, the people free to worship us equally.

The Pharaoh is gone.

I personally wrapped my tail around his greedy body and dragged him to the depths of the Ocean. *Then* he said my name. *Then* he pleaded for mercy.

On the throne sits Juniel, Queen of Thebes. She will be a patient and benevolent leader, bringing Egypt into its most peaceful dynasty yet. At her right hand, her faithful and wise advisor Mehmet guides and instructs, the cool metal discs of his gorgerine pressed to his chest.

One day, they will forget me again, and I will be forced to crash the Ocean back onto the heads of the disbelievers.

But for now, I moon bathe in the Nile, the sweet percussion of cicadas in my ears, fireflies illuminating my lavation.

LAGNIAPPE

During a staff meeting one gloriously stormy night, the idea of having a section titled "Lagniappe" near the end of some of the works published by Brigids Gate Press was discussed. The staff unanimously voted in favor of the idea.

Lagniappe (pronounced LAN-yap) is an old New Orleans tradition where merchants give a little something extra along with every purchase. It's a way of expressing thanks and appreciation to customers.

The Lagniappe section might contain a short story, a small handful of poems, or a non-fiction piece. It might also feature a short novella. It may or may not be connected with the theme of the work.

***

The extra offering for this anthology is "On the Wings of a Black Dove" by Sam Muller.

ON THE WINGS OF THE BLACK DOVE

A Tale from Troy

By Sam Muller

Cassandra 1: Memories of the Future

THE FUTURE IS AN open book to me.

I am fated to die at the side of a man I loathe, slain by a woman I pity. In my memories, I try to tell her that I understand her grief. She has lost a daughter, the first innocent victim of a war that should never have been waged. I struggle to get the words out, but her axe is faster. She has been waiting for this moment for ten years.

Midnight, sleepless; that is when the mind is most vagrant. I try to tether it to the present, to locate this moment in the scale of times. My marker is Hector. The Greek assault on Troy has entered the tenth year. Yet, my brother lives. Every evening he returns to the waiting arms of ebony-hued Andromache and Astyanax, the shining star of their universe.

Tonight, my mind provides me no glimpses of my murdered father, my slain brothers, my driven-insane mother, my sacrificed sister, and my violated sisters by marriage. Tonight, my mind is hooked on my future. I feel the heat of the fires engulfing this citadel of many towers, smell the smoke laced with the reek of burning flesh; I hear the screams of the vanquished and the roars of the victors.

When I feel the first hateful touch of the man who would become the master of my body, I can bear it no longer. I yank at my mind, forcing it to stop, to return. Suddenly it veers, affording me a glimpse of an unrecognizable land, trees taller and thicker than the towers of

245

SEERS AND SIBYLS – *Troy*

Ilium…

Last night I saw a lake, its waters as pink as a spring rose.

These strange visions began two months ago. They vary, from seas of trees, of golden sands, of snow. Their only commonality is their end: a black dove and a white raven, the tiny dove attacking the huge raven, sending it fleeing, saving her young…

I get out of bed, tie my hair up with my snake-shaped bronze pin—a gift from Hector—wrap myself in a woolen cloak, and exit through a side door.

There are advantages in being considered mad. I'm not bound by tradition. Unlike other royal women, eternally protected for their virginity or chastity, I can come and go as I please.

The wide cobbled streets are deserted. People stay indoors mourning the dead, tending the wounded, fearing the dawn. Several men and women, their pitiful rags no proof against the night chill, huddle by the marble walls of the temple of Athena, human detritus from some allied city turned into rubble by Greek wrath. A woman sits apart from the others, trying to warm an emaciated baby with her own thin body. I unpin my cloak and offer it to her. She stares at me with eyes that see nothing because they have seen too much.

I fold the cloak and cover the baby with it.

The mother makes a sound that could be anything, a mumble of thanks or the leftover from a bygone scream.

I exit the city through the Simoeis Gate. The guards ignore me as they usually do.

The Marshes of Simoeis is probably the safest place in all Ilium. It's redolent with the clean scents of the river Simoeis, as yet untouched by the war, unlike its counterpart the river Scamander, its banks torn, its waters polluted by blood, flesh, and gore.

I pick a well-remembered path through the mud to a mound of stones shielded by a thorny thicket. When we were children and the marshes were our playground, this little oasis was my favorite hiding place. Now it provides me with a refuge, a place to sit and think with only the stars for company.

I must bring Astyanax here.

Astyanax; I've told Andromache of her fate and that of Hector. When it comes to foretelling the fate of Astyanax, my tongue refuses to obey me.

Unspoken does not mean unremembered.

This morning, I walked to the towering oak by the Scaean Gate. The sloping gardens between the city wall and the palace compound were full of women, children, and old men, waiting for news from the battlefield. Astyanax was playing with his cousins. He saw me and came running, demanding a story. The memory of his young body breaking against the very walls we were standing on hit me like a tidal wave. I swayed, trying to stay on my feet. Astyanax took my arm, his face, dark like his mother's, full of concern. His gaze was probing, but he asked no questions, just guided me to a stone bench and sat next to me. I held him tight for a few seconds, my face bent over his black locks.

When I lifted my head, I saw Andromache standing by the jasmine arbor. Our eyes met and held for a long heartbeat. Then she turned back and fled into the palace, her maids trailing her...

A tiny sound, perhaps the crunch of a pebble by a heavy foot, intrudes into my mental meanderings. As my mind returns to the present, it veers momentarily, affording me a glimpse of the dove, darker than the night, its steady gaze daring me.

Then it's gone and I'm looking into the eyes of a man, a soldier, a Greek.

The expression on his night dark face is unthreatening. He holds up his hands, empty. "Fear not, lady," he says, his voice gentle. "I'm no enemy of yours."

Thersites 1: A World of Shame

The entire host is at assembly when the guards bring the old man to the dais where the commanders sit. He looks like a wraith from

Hades, gaunt, gray haired, and gray cloaked.

The herald shouts his name, Chryses, priest of Apollo.

He falls on to his knees before Agamemnon's high chair, telling he came to ransom a captive, describing the wealth he brought with him. He places his wrinkled forehead before Agamemnon's leather clad feet and asks for the freedom of his daughter, Chrysies. As her name leaves his lips his steady voice wavers.

Chrysies, she glittered like a star even in the extremity of her fate. And Agamemnon grabbed her for himself. Lion taking lion share.

I am seated far from the dais, as befits an ordinary soldier, useful and expendable. Even at this distance I can see the gathering anger on Agamemnon's face.

The agonized plea of a broken father: what is that to the man who slaughtered his own daughter? I've heard tell that he wept as he wielded the sacrificial knife against Iphigenia's tender throat, but tears are cheaper than blood, aren't they?

All around me, faces soften and eyes mist. I wait for a man better placed than me, a commander or a warrior, to point out that honor and custom demand the immediate acceptance of Chryses' plea. Nothing. The might of Mycenae has shackled tongues again.

Agamemnon waves an angry hand at the guards. They move towards the prostrate figure.

I spring to my feet. "My lord king, commanders, warriors, comrades," I shout, anger slurring the first words, "the bargain this priest of Apollo offers is a just one. By disregarding his plea, we risk not just the wrath of man, but the wrath of gods."

Odysseus rises, leisurely, almost lazily, pointing a contemptuous finger at me. Before he can accuse me of vile rebellion, a charge he has thrown at me with great liberality in recent years, Achilles intervenes. He shoves Odysseus aside, strides up to the priest, and raises him to his feet. Holding the weeping father by the elbow, Achilles faces the assembly, his voice winging into men's hearts like a homing bird.

"Restoration of Greek honor is supposed to be the purpose of this war. If we disregard this man's plea, we would be dishonoring our own cause." He turns to Agamemnon, his gestures as theatrical as words. "King, you claimed this man's daughter. Accept the ransom and release her. Prove that you are the highest among us, not just in might, but also in honor."

It is like a dam breaking. Men and commanders alike stamp their feet, raise their hands, shouting agreement. Only Menelaus and Odysseus remain silent.

Agamemnon holds up his right hand, the scepter clasped in meaty fingers. Voices recede. He turns to the priest, his words flowing like lava. "Hear me now, you priest of impertinence. You will never get your daughter back. She will warm my bed until Troy falls, then sail in my lion-flagged ship. She will live the rest of her life in my marble palace, bearing my children, obeying my lady-wife. Now be gone, before my mercy runs its course and my justice takes over."

He strides away, trailed by other commanders. Only Achilles remains on the dais, still holding the old priest by an elbow.

***

Shame descends over the camp like a toxic fog. A mirror has been held before each one of us, and we don't like what we see.

Soon after the fires are lit, I leave the camp driven by the need to be alone. I walk and walk on the soft-sanded beach, the gentle murmur of the sea no balm to my tortured soul.

When I volunteered to go to Troy, I left behind my aged parents and my little sister. A fast war with rich pickings had seemed a good idea.

Ten years later, Troy looks as impregnable as ever. The looting, murdering, raping spree that follows every victory against a Trojan ally had some attraction in the early months. No more. The agonized cries of the victims remind me of my aged father, my ailing mother, my sister. I ask myself what I am doing on these faraway shores, bringing sword and fire into the peaceful lives of people who have done me no harm.

At the sound of wind beats I look about. I am standing by an estuary. A black dove sits on a rock jutting out of the water regarding me.

As I return its stare, it flies away inland. Driven by a compulsion I don't understand, I set off after it.

Suddenly the ground gives beneath my foot, dragging it into a slushy depth. I snatch it back and look around. I am by a far-flung marsh. From its midst, the dove is watching me, perched on a darker shape that might be a dead branch.

I set off once again, finding a path through the sucking mud, the dove ever in my sight.

The moon vanishes behind a cloud bank. When it reappears, the dove is gone. Instead, seated on a rocky outcrop by a thicket is a woman. At first, I take her for a goddess. Then I realize she is mortal, a Trojan woman, bronze skinned, dark haired, beautiful, wild.

"Fear not, lady, I'm not your enemy." It is the truest thing I've said since I joined this accursed war. Why should I be her enemy or she mine? What have we against each other?

She peers at me, so close I can smell the subtle scent of some costly perfume. Her eyes, a deep gray, hold no fear, only surprise, then puzzlement.

"I don't remember you."

A strange way to greet a stranger!

"We have never met, lady," I respond, a sense of unreality gripping me.

She frowns. "You don't understand. What is your name?"

Her tone is peremptory. But behind the demanding words, I sense a desperate urgency. "Thersites, my lady," I reply.

Her eyes seem to be focused on something only she can see. "You are not in my memories."

"I cannot be since we've never…"

Her smile, sad and solemn, silences me. "My clearest memories are of times to come. And this meeting was never in them." She pauses and says, "My name is Cassandra."

Ah, the Trojan princess Apollo wanted for himself. Rumor has it that he gifted her with foresight to wear down her resistance and made her go mad when she continued to resist. "You are the…" I stop in a welter of confusion and shame.

"The mad prophetess of Troy," she murmurs. There is irony in her smile. "I'm not mad yet, but I should be, given the future I see."

"What is the future you see?" I ask, caught between derision and curiosity.

She stares at me thoughtfully. "Why shouldn't I tell you? You won't believe me either. Troy will burn to the ground. My family will be murdered and enslaved. Your king Agamemnon will take me to Mycenae as his slave."

Impregnable Troy, it would never be conquered. No wonder they laugh at her—

Agamemnon… enslaved by Agamemnon.

I look at this beautiful woman, sorrow etched into her delicate features. It is easy to imagine the leer on Agamemnon's lips, the lust in his eyes, his meaty fingers gripping her elegant wrist as he drags her to his tent.

She watches me, her eyes gray nooses. "What are you doing here, Thersites?"

"I was following a black dove."

Her gaze turns inwards. "A black dove…" The words lapse into silence. Then she leans close, her warm breath caressing my cheek. "Has Chryses come to your camp yet, to ransom his daughter?"

I gape.

"He obviously did. When?"

"Last evening," I manage.

She shudders. "Then the end is near." She lays a soft hand on my arm. "Take care, Thersites. Soon, Apollo's plague will infect your camp."

Cassandra 2: Destinies

I sit back on the bench by the wall, leaning against the ancient oak, musing on my strange visions. I always understood the symbolism, dove defeating raven, Aphrodite setting Apollo to fight. But until last night, I didn't know if the visions were real or delusions created by my fervid mind.

After meeting that strange Greek, I know the vision is no delusion but a message that another future is possible…

The door leading to the council chamber opens. Hector steps out. Weariness shrouds him like an invisible cloak.

I smile a welcome as he sits next to me. He does not believe my memories, but he is still kind.

"You look tired," I say.

He takes my hand, his battle-hardened fingers gentle on mine. "The council is becoming another battleground. Greeks can afford to waste ten years in battle. They are warring tribes anyway. We are a trading city. This war is destroying our present and our future. Even if we prevail, we'll be poor and weak for decades, a ready prey for some other enemy."

I know he discusses matters of state with Andromache, but he has never talked such things with me, his little sister.

"Then sue for peace," I say.

"Paris won't permit a compromise. His party has a majority in council. They think victory is inevitable. Their plan is to annihilate the Greek host, then attack Greek cities, starting with Mycenae. There's increasing talk of turning Troy into a mighty empire. Even Father finds the prospect beguiling. I and my allies are in a minority. Our voices go unheeded. Behind our backs we are called cowards, even me."

I grab his hand. "Forget my prophesies. Listen to reason. When the war began, we had a ring of allies. Their presence protected our

252

flanks. Now they are gone, turned to dust and ashes by Greek fire. We are alone. How long are we going to go on? Another ten years? Until Helen is so old, no one desires her?"

He sighs. "I sometimes think Helen is only an excuse. Agamemnon has nursed imperial dreams for too long. He thinks he is Zeus among men. Independent cities are anathema to men like him."

As he gets up to go I ask, "How did the battle go?"

"Well. The rumor is that the Greek camp is affected by Apollo's plague."

So it is here already.

"Try to stay alive, Brother," I tell him. "Your first duty is to Andromache and Astyanax. Who will protect them if you are gone? Andromache no longer has a father to care for her. Or brothers to fight for Astyanax's rights. They've all died in this pointless war."

Hector sighs. "No man can avoid his destiny. If the gods have willed that I die in this war, then I will die. We are but playthings in the hands of the immortals."

Fury warms me. "I will not be the plaything of anyone, mortal or immortal," I say through gritted teeth.

Hector smiles, sorrowfully. "Oh, my foolish one, mortals cannot contend against the will of the divine."

I watch him, thinking of the Greek the black dove led to me. In that ordinary soldier who stood up to his own commanders, I might have found a fellow rebel willing to confound Zeus and chart a different future for all of us. The question is, have I convinced him of the truth of my words? And will he survive Apollo's plague darts?

SEERS AND SIBYLS – *Troy*

Thersites 2: On Plagues and Kings

The plague comes creeping, infecting first animals, then men.

Exactly as she said it would.

Calchus, assured of protection by the commanders, divines the reason. The wrath of Apollo has come upon us for the insult and dishonor done to his priest.

We wait for the commanders to persuade or compel Agamemnon to return the priest's daughter. They mutter to each other, but none dares raise his voice against the tyrant from Mycenae.

Achilles is our only hope. Yet he stays away, holed up in his own hut. Patroclus, his cousin and inseparable companion, is stricken on the second day. Achilles, sleepless and untiring, cares for him as a mother would a child. The other stricken men die, mayhap because they lack care or cure. Only Patroclus survives thanks to Achilles' tender ministrations.

On the ninth day, I see them walking on the beach, Achilles holding Patroclus by an elbow, Patroclus leaning against Achilles.

Tonight, Achilles calls an assembly.

Achilles, as a commander, has the right to summon an assembly, just as I, as a free Greek soldier, have the right to voice my mind at such gatherings.

Such ancient freedoms do not suit Agamemnon's notions of almighty kingship. He sits in his high chair, jaws clenched, eyes darting fire.

Achilles begins the proceedings by calling on Calchus to reveal his divinations to the host. The old seer repeats his words, casting nervous glances at Agamemnon. Achilles then addresses Agamemnon directly, asking him to assuage Apollo's anger and save Greek lives by sending the priest's daughter back.

Agamemnon raises the scepter high, his standard ploy. "By the power vested in me, as the…"

Achilles strides up to him and grabs the scepter. The collective indrawn breath of the host is like the hissing of a massive serpent.

Achilles waves the scepter in the air. "Look well. Once this was a living tree. Now it's deadwood. Someday, it'll rot and die, as we do. It has no power of its own. The only power it possesses is the power we have accorded it. Do not fear this wooden rod. Ask yourself why you remain mute while this man," he jabs a finger at Agamemnon, "risks Greek lives to satisfy his lust." He pauses and shouts, "Return Chrysies to her father, now."

Suddenly the host is on its feet as one man, shouting, "Return!"

Agamemnon grips the arms of his chair, waiting for the clamor to end. When it does, he strides over to Achilles, standing so close there's not an inch between their noses. "Bear in mind I'm kinglier than you." he snarls. "If you lay a hand on my woman, I will take yours."

Achilles laughs. "I always knew this was a pointless war. Now you have turned it into a shameful one. The civilized Greeks, what a farce! Under your kingship, Greek is becoming a byword for dishonor."

Odysseus walks up to the two men, standing between them and laying a hand each on their shoulder. "Achilles, these matters must be talked not in assembly, but in council, among us commanders. And you err when you call this a pointless war. This is a war men will sing about for eons. And their most adulating words will be in praise of your glory."

"Glory!" Achilles' voice bristles with contempt. "What use is glory in the House of Hades, Odysseus?"

***

Next morning, Chrysies is returned to her father. In the evening, Agamemnon's guards invade Achilles' camp while Achilles and Patroclus are away on their now customary slow walk on the beach and take away Briseis, Chrysies' cousin who was given to him after the sacking of Moesia. A furious Achilles berates Agamemnon in public and withdraws from battle along with his Myrmidons.

All exactly as Cassandra predicted.

I think of her last words. "If Achilles leaves the battlefield and returns home, this war will end. And Thetis is the only immortal who has something to lose in this pointless war."

***

That evening, I go to Achilles' camp and tell the guards I'd like to talk to Lord Patroclus. From the hut Achilles shares with Patroclus ripples a sound as soft and sweet as a spring breeze; Achilles playing his silver-topped lyre.

Some minutes later, Patroclus comes out, walking slowly. His face is thin and drawn, but his smile is as friendly as ever. "Thersites, what may I do for you?" Unlike most of his kind, he bothers to learn the names of ordinary men. He is strong in battle, gentle away from it.

"May we talk?" I ask.

He nods, motioning the guards to move away.

"Tomorrow, or the day after, Agamemnon will summon an assembly. He will say that Zeus has sent him a dream promising victory over Ilium the very next day. But that battle will go ill for us. Our people will die like flies before the high steep walls of Troy."

Patroclus' eyes widen in horror. "You mean Agamemnon is planning a deception, misleading the men for his selfish purposes?"

"Agamemnon, for once, will be telling the truth as he knows it. Zeus will send him a false dream at the urging of Goddess Thetis. She has asked that of him on her son's behalf."

Patroclus' brown face turns a deathly gray. He leans against the wall of the hut, as if his legs can no longer bear his weight, diminished though it is due to illness. "Are you saying…" he whispers.

"I'm saying Achilles will sacrifice our own people to revenge on Agamemnon for taking Briseis. Greek lives will be lost as a sop to Achilles' ego."

"I don't believe it," Patroclus' stricken eyes and hoarse voice belie his words.

"You will know when Agamemnon summons that assembly and proclaims his dream," I say. "If you do nothing, Hector will slay you. Achilles will slaughter Hector in revenge and be killed by Paris."

He covers his face with his hands.

"Achilles is caught between his two destinies, Lord Patroclus. You can help him make the better decision. Tell him of your death. Tell him that Hector will kill you in battle and desecrate your body. He'd risk the world to keep you safe. Urge him to ask the divine Thetis about your coming death. If he does, she will answer truthfully, even at the risk of incurring Zeus' eternal ire." I smile bitterly. "She is his mother. Glory would not matter to her. She'd want him to live."

Cassandra 3: Necessary Ends

Every night since that first encounter, I have sat here waiting for him. In vain.

Tonight, he is there waiting for me. As I come close, he stands up and I notice his face, three bloodied welts creating a strange pattern of red on black.

"What happened?" I ask, surprised at my own concern.

He swallows. "The mark of Agamemnon's scepter, my lady, wielded by Odysseus as punishment for not heeding my betters. I tried to caution my fellow Greeks against going to battle tomorrow, on the basis of one man's dream. Odysseus got the guards to hold me and beat me with the scepter."

I close my eyes. "Odysseus is an evil man. He is the one who will persuade the Greeks to fling my nephew from Troy's highest tower."

Thersites sighs. "When the world is a lie, truth becomes a form of abuse. The men were distressed at the beating Odysseus gave me but did nothing to stop it. They even laughed at his witticisms which accompanied each strike." He indicates the stony outcrop he has vacated. "Sit down, Princess, my tale is long."

At the end of his recital, I lean forward and touch a bloody welt, gently. His indrawn breath is sharp. "You are a bold heart, Thersites."

A mist is rising from the marshes, wreathing the world in its noxious fumes. It bothers me a little. Is this nature or a divine trick? But my attention wavers as Thersites leans forward, peering at me searchingly. "Princess, what if Trojans attack the departing Greeks?"

I shake my head. "If Greeks leave, Trojans will not attack."

"How can you be so certain?"

"Because Hector will not permit it. I…"

Thersites vanishes into the mist. I am seized by a pair of hands. As they yank me up, I see three forms struggling below. Through the misty veil, I cannot tell Thersites apart from the other Greeks, but his voice comes clearly, warningly. "Odysseus."

I cease struggling, making myself go limp. My captor, Odysseus, eases his grip, securing me with one hand, his attention on Thersites.

"So this is how the traitor spends his nights, in the arms of a Trojan woman," he jeers. "Bind him first. He is mine. Then bind this woman, the princess of Troy, priestess of Apollo. She will be a suitable gift for Agamemnon, some recompense for losing…"

He doesn't notice my hand stealing to my hair, pulling out the poisoned pin that was Hector's gift to me.

The eye. If only I do not lose my nerve, miss my aim.

He helps me by bending over me. The rest is almost indecently easy. He utters a high keening cry and drops me to the ground before collapsing beside me.

By the time I get my breath back, sit up, and pull the pin out of his bloody eye, the mist has cleared and Thersites is done with the guards. "This one's dead," he says, pointing at a torn body with a bloodied knife. "The other one I managed to push into the mire, thanks to the distraction you caused." He stares down at Odysseus, his jaw dropping. "What? How?"

"A poison pin," I say, wiping it on a patch of fresh reeds and inserting it carefully into my hair. "Best throw them both into the marshes." I get up. "Here, I'll give you a hand."

He says, "Wait," and crouches by Odysseus' body, removing a gold bracelet and several rings. His smile mocks me. "War booty. This will provide for my sister's future and my parents' care." He pauses and adds, almost in a whisper, "If they are still alive."

When the bodies are lost in the mire, he turns to me, "What will you do if this war is stopped, Princess?"

I glimpse the dove in my mind's eye. For the first time, she looks at me, her gaze full of mystery. Then she's gone.

I smile, touching his face. "Maybe I will go see the world beyond Ilium's walls. Follow the black dove again."

He holds my wrist gently. "Keep safe, Princess."

"Cassandra, call me Cassandra."

"Cassandra." His voice is a whisper.

"Stay awhile," I say. "Dawn is still many hours away."

***

When Hector emerges from his bedchamber to head to the baths, I'm waiting for him. He blinks. "Cassandra?"

I push him gently back into the room and close the door behind me, nodding to Andromache. "We need to talk."

Thersites 4: Ships Sailing Away

I reach the camp as dawn breaks.

Everything is in an uproar. Huts and tents are being dismantled, men carrying their contents to the waiting ships.

Relief turns my world into a welcome emptiness.

"Thersites!"

Patroclus comes running. "I've been looking for you everywhere. Achilles called an assembly late in the night and announced he was leaving. He put the question of staying or going to a free vote.

Everyone voted to leave. It may have gone different had Odysseus been there with his persuasive tongue. But he's missing." His gaze turns questioning. "Did you encounter Odysseus?"

"I've had encounters enough with Odysseus to last me a lifetime," I grunt. "Where's Achilles?"

"He's waiting for me in the main ship with his mother. I didn't want to leave without talking to you." He places a hand on my shoulder. "You helped me save the one I love more than life itself. Come with us. I will make sure you lack for nothing."

"I have a family waiting for me," I say, wondering… no I must keep hope alive. "But I thank you."

"Hector sent a herald just now announcing a truce." Patroclus' gaze turns inquiring. "I'd like to know how this came to pass."

For a heartbeat, I hear her again. "I realized Aphrodite was sending me a counter-vision of a different future, one that could be mine if I knew enough and dared enough."

The memory makes me smile.

"You won't tell me." Patroclus laughs, pulling me into an embrace. "Fare well, my friend."

He vanishes into the crowd. I run to my own ship, my name, shouted in many voices, guiding me. Before embarking, I pause on the sands of Ilium, gazing at what I am leaving behind.

The morning sun has turned Troy's towers into pillars of gold. I raise my hand. And see another hand, slim and elegant, strong too, enough to contend with gods, rising in response, a black dove perched on the fingers that loved me barely an hour ago.

ABOUT THE AUTHORS

David Marino is a New York City CPA by day and a fantasy novelist by night. His fiction has been published in <u>Hex Literary</u> and the <u>Croaker</u>. He is a graduate of the 2023 Clarion Writer's Workshop and is currently attending Sarah Lawrence in pursuit of an MFA in writing with a focus on speculative fiction.

Instagram: <u>@davidmarinowrites</u>

Beth O'Brien is an English Literature BA and Creative Writing MA graduate from the University of Birmingham and the author of four adult poetry books, including *The Earth is a Bookcase* (<u>Black Pear Press</u>). Having been born visually impaired and with an upper-limb difference, Beth has a long-standing interest in the representation of disability in literature and is currently studying for a PhD in Creative Writing funded by <u>Midlands4Cities</u>, researching the (mis)representation of disability in contemporary fairy tale retellings. She is the founder and editor of <u>Disabled Tales</u>, a website dedicated to discussing disability in fairy tales and folklore. Her debut novel, *Wolf Siren,* is forthcoming with <u>HarperCollins Children's Books</u> in Spring 2025.

Facebook: <u>bethobrienwriter</u>
Instagram: <u>@bethowriter</u>
Twitter: <u>@bethowriter</u>

Victoria Brun is a writer and project manager at a national laboratory. When not bugging hardworking scientists about budget reports and service agreements, she is writing stories you can find at <u>Factor Four Magazine</u>, <u>Daily Science Fiction</u>, <u>Nature Futures</u>, and beyond.

Twitter: <u>@VictoriaLBrun</u>
Website: <u>victorialbrun.wordpress.com</u>

ABOUT THE AUTHORS

Rose Strickman is a speculative fiction author living in Seattle, Washington. Her work has appeared in anthologies such as *Sword and Sorceress 32*, *Beach Shorts*, and *Die by the Sword*, as well as online e-zines. She has also self-published several novellas on Amazon.

Amazon author page: author/rosestrickman

Zach Rosenberg is a horror and SFF writer living in Florida. By night, he crafts horrifying and fantastic days. By day, he practices law, which is even scarier. His work has appeared or is forthcoming in Dark Matter Magazine, the Deadlands, and Seize the Press. His first book *Hungers As Old As This Land* was released May 17 by Brigids Gate Press and his second, *The Long Shalom* is out from Off-Limits Press.

Instagram: @ZachRose32
Twitter: @ZachRoseWriter

Erin L. Swann is a lifelong lover of fantasy and space adventures living in Central Maryland. She's an avid home cook and works as an art teacher, feeding the imaginations of others while fueling her own creativity. Her work appears in numerous publications including Factor Four Magazine, The Colored Lens, and NewMyths.com. She is currently querying her debut Science Fantasy novel, *Awakener*.

Twitter: @swannscribbles
Website: swannscribbles.com

Nico Penaranda is a Filipino-American writer and musician from Washington D.C. He graduated from American University's MFA in Creative Writing Program in May 2022. His poetry can be found in Mistake House Publishing, Gardy Loo, The Keezel Review, and Z Publishing.

A. L. Munson is a Louisiana-born speculative fiction author and member of the Vancleave Live Oak Choctaw tribe. She now lives in Kansas where she works as an archivist while majoring in physics. Her

ABOUT THE AUTHORS

work is slated to appear in *Cosmic Horror Monthly* in late 2023.
   Twitter: @A_L_Munson
   Website: almunson.com

Nominated for the Pushcart Prize and Best of the Net, **Caroline Johnson** has two illustrated poetry chapbooks, *Where the Street Ends* and *My Mother's Artwork,* and a full-length collection, *The Caregiver* (Holy Cow! Press, 2018). She has won numerous local and national awards for her poetry in the past 15 years, including the 2012 Chicago Tribune's *Printers Row Poetry Contest.* Her work can be found in Garrison Keillor's *Writer's Almanac,* Origins Journal, Naugatuck River Review, Encore, Pink Panther Magazine, Blast Furnace, and others. A former college English teacher, she has led workshops for veterans and other poets on topics such as Poetry and Spirituality, Speculative Poetry, and Writing About Chicago. She is past president of Poets & Patrons of Chicago and is a member of the P2 Collective, a group of Chicago-area poets and photographers.
   Email: carolinejohnson.author@gmail.com
   Facebook: carolinejohnsonauthor
   Twitter: @twinkscat
   Website: caroline-johnson.com

Marshall J. Moore is an award-winning short story author and fantasy novelist. His debut novel, *The Pale City*, takes place in a society where the dead are recycled into unliving servants, until a wounded soldier-necromancer uncovers a plot to use these Attendants to overthrow the Republic he has dedicated his life to protecting.

N.R. Lambert is a speculative fiction author from New York City. Her stories have appeared or are forthcoming in several publications and anthologies, including *Lightspeed, Vastarien, The Modern Deity's Guide to Surviving Humanity,* and *Don't Turn Out the Lights.* She's also written articles and essays for TIME, LIFE, and Entertainment Weekly. She

ABOUT THE AUTHORS

was a U.S. National Park Service Artist-in-Residence at Fire Island National Seashore. In addition to her work as a writer, pop culture author, and freelance copywriter, she teaches creative writing workshops at conferences, libraries, and the Center for Fiction in Brooklyn.

Facebook: nancyrlambert
Instagram: @nanbits
Twitter: @nanbits
Website: NRLambert.com

Susan Jordan (born 1947) edited The Empty Closet, an LGBTQ newspaper, in Rochester, NY, for 28 years (1989-2017). She self-published a chapbook, *Crystal Spirit*, in the 1970s, and has been published in magazines including Sailing the Road Clear, and more recently in OutWrite, the literary journal of ImageOut Film Festival in Rochester. In 1972, she assisted George Butterick in cataloguing the "Charles Olson Papers" at U. of Connecticut.

Jeremy Megargee has always loved dark fiction. He cut his teeth on R.L Stine's *Goosebumps* series as a child and a fascination with Stephen King, Jack London, Algernon Blackwood, and many others followed later in life. Jeremy weaves his tales of personal horror from Martinsburg, West Virginia with his cat Lazarus acting as his muse/familiar. He is a member of the West Virginia chapter of the Horror Writer's Association and you can often find him peddling his dark words in various mountain hollers deep within the Appalachians.

Instagram: @xbadmoonrising
TikTok: @jmhorrorfiction

Nwejesu Ekpenisi is a Nigerian writer whose works delve into the intricacies of family dynamics, mental health, abuse, and self-discovery. He was the third prize winner in the 2023 Alika Ogorchukwu nternational Poetry Competition. He was also shortlisted for the 2023

ABOUT THE AUTHORS

April Centaur Short Story Prize. His works have been featured or forthcoming in Poemify Publishers, Wingless Dreamers Publishers, PoeticAfrica and elsewhere.

Facebook: E.Nwajesu
Instagram: @e_nwajesu
Twitter @E_Nwajesu

Jennifer Bushroe once swore on a statue of Peter Pan that she'd never grow up. She fulfills this oath by dancing like nobody's watching, eating dessert before dinner, and writing stories and poems for all ages. You can find her work in On Spec, DreamForge Magazine, Mermaids Monthly, and more.

Twitter: @JenniferBushroe
Goodreads: Jennifer Bushroe

Laura Marden (she/her) is a sci-fi and weird fiction writer. She lives in Maryland with her family and their two dogs and finds that the best time to write is when they're all asleep.

Instagram: @lauramardenauthor
Twitter: @LauraJMarden

Joseph Mathias got into the English Romantic poets in high school, and started reading Homer after college, first in Pope's translation, then in the original. After reading *Beowulf*, he started turning his mythical daydreams into verse. He is currently working on an epic poem based on the ancient Jewish *Book of Enoch*. He lives in Lansing, Michigan.

Stephanie Ellis writes dark speculative prose and poetry and has been published in a variety of magazines and anthologies. Her longer work includes the novels, *The Five Turns of the Wheel,* and *Reborn,* and the novellas, *Bottled* and *Paused,* whilst her short stories can be found in the collections, *The Reckoning,* and *Devil Kin.* She is a Rhysling and Elgin

ABOUT THE AUTHORS

Award nominated poet, and her dark poetry has been published in her collections *Foundlings* (co-authored with Cindy O'Quinn), *Lilith Rising* (co-authored with Shane Douglas Keene) and *Metallurgy*, as well as the HWA *Poetry Showcase Volumes VI, VII, VIII* and *IX*. She can be found supporting indie authors at HorrorTree.com via the weekly Indie Bookshelf Releases. She is an active member of the HWA.

Facebook: stephanie.ellis.353
Instagram: @stephanieellis7963
Twitter: @el_stevie
Website: stephanieellis.org

Bettina Theissen is an avid reader and occasional poet and writer who lives with her two kids in Germany. She is the author of *A Sacred World: Divine Encounters* and has contributed to several editions of Eternal Haunted Summer and to *Bearing Torches: A devotional anthology to Hekate* published by the Bibliotheca Alexandrina.

Misty Urban is a fiction writer, medieval scholar, freelance editor, and college professor. In addition to writing about medieval romance and monstrous women, she writes historical and contemporary romance, fantasy, creative nonfiction, and lots and lots of book reviews. She lives in a small town on a big river in eastern Iowa with a handsome park ranger and two budding authors who like to critique her work.

Instagram: @authormistyurban
LinkedIn: Misty Urban
Website: mistyurban.com

In addition to being an avid reader, **Gerri Leen's** passionate about horse racing, tea, and collecting encaustic art and raku pottery. She has stories and poems in The Magazine of Fantasy & Science Fiction, Nature, Strange Horizons, Dark Matter and others, and has a poetry collection coming out from Trouble Department. She's a member of SFWA and HWA.

Instagram: @leengerri

ABOUT THE AUTHORS

Twitter: @gerrileen
Website: gerrileen.com

Kayla Whittle works in acquisitions at a medical publisher. She has published stories in <u>Luna Station Quarterly</u> and <u>The Colored Lens</u>. She also has stories in the anthologies *Beyond the Veil* (<u>Ghost Orchid Press</u>), *Eros & Thanatos* (<u>Quill & Crow Publishing House</u>), *Of Fate & Fury* (<u>Silver Wheel Press</u>), *Of Ink and Paper* (<u>Nightshade Publishing</u>) and *Exquisite Poison* (<u>Phantom House Press</u>), and has pieces included in *Dangerous Waters: Deadly Women of the Sea* and *Daughter of Sarpedon: A Tempered Tales Collection*, both out by <u>Brigids Gate Press</u>. Her work has also been featured on <u>Flash Fiction Podcast</u>. Much of her writing features queer representation, often including ace or sapphic characters. When not writing, she's usually busy reading or planning her next Disney vacation. She currently resides in New Jersey.

Instagram: @caughtbetweenthepages
Twitter: @kaylawhitwrites
Website: kaylawhittle.wordpress.com

Ivy L. James wrote her first story on Post-it notes as a child. Since then, she has graduated to regular paper and enjoys writing inclusive romance, short fiction, and poetry. She lives in Maryland with her wife and their corgi, cat, and two snakes.

Facebook: authorivyljames
Instagram: @authorivyljames
Twitter: @AuthorIvyLJames
Website: authorivyljames.com
YouTube: @authorivyljames

Matthew Yap is a Malaysian writer, editor and educator. He graduated from Monash University with a PhD in Literature. Matthew has taught Film Studies and writes a weekly newspaper column where he shares his love for books, films and TV. At 19, he published the academic

ABOUT THE AUTHORS

book *Answering is An Art for Australian Matriculation students.* In 2020, Matthew's short story "MARI" won first prize in a national writing competition. "MARI" explores Malaysia's pandemic experience told from the perspective of a data-tracking app. Matthew is interested in writing stories from a Southeast Asian perspective that resonate with readers
worldwide.

    Column: New Straits Times
    Facebook: matthew.yap.98

Cormack Baldwin has had two prophetic dreams in his life, neither of which led to much. However, he still writes about the slippery nature of fate and causality, as well as curates documents skimmed from the multiverse, in the form of the magazine Archive of the Odd.

    Twitter: @cormackbaldwin
    Website: cmbaldwin.carrd.co

Shannon Connor Winward collapsed from a congenital curse and now speaks of herself in the past tense, regretting all those times she said, "I wish I never had to leave my bed." In other lives, she authored the Elgin Award-winning *Undoing Winter* (Finishing Line Press, 2014) and *The Year of the Witch* (Sycorax Press, 2018); served as Secretary for the Science Fiction & Fantasy Poetry Association and a Delaware Division of the Arts Fellow in Fiction; and founded Riddled with Arrows Literary Journal. Shannon's relics can be found (or are forthcoming) in eclectic places from Analog Science Fiction & Fact to Zetetic, including The Magazine of Fantasy & Science Fiction, Strange Horizons, Flash Fiction Online, Pseudopod, Literary Mama, Native Skin, Deaf Poet's Society, SageWoman, Poetry Ireland Review and Rattle, and a feature in Poets & Writers. For now, her ghost lingers in the broken down tower of her body in a blue room, where she writes madly against the gods and the clock.

    Facebook: shannon.connorwinward

ABOUT THE AUTHORS

Websites: shannonconnorwinward.com & riddledwitharrows.com

Jacqueline Kate Goldblatt is an alumnus of Rutgers University, having graduated Summa Cum Laude with a B.A. in Journalism and Comparative Literature. She has had a love affair with language since she was very young and expects it to continue for some time. Her work has been published by <u>PCMag</u>, <u>Coffin Bell Journal</u>, and the <u>Rutgers Review: Arts and Culture Magazine</u>. When not working her job as an Assistant Social Media Editor or writing, you can find her reading, listening to video essays, playing tabletop RPGs with her amazing friends, taking walks at unreasonable hours of the night, and baking.

Instagram: @jacquelinegoldblatt
Twitter: @JackieGold514
Website: shadowrunner514.wixsite.com/website

Devan Barlow is the author of *An Uncommon Curse,* a novel of fairy tales and musical theatre. Her short fiction and poetry have appeared in several anthologies and magazines including <u>Solarpunk Magazine</u> and <u>Diabolical Plots</u>. When not writing, she reads voraciously, drinks tea, and thinks about fairy tales and sea monsters.

Twitter: @Devan_Barlow
Website: devanbarlow.com

British writer **Jay McKenzie** lives on Australia's Gold Coast with her fiancé, daughter, and a dog called Duck. She is a prize winning short story writer whose micro, flash, and short stories have been published in numerous publications and anthologies, including <u>Unleash Lit Magazine</u>, <u>Cerasus Magazine</u>, <u>Leicester Writes</u>, and <u>Fabula Nivalis</u>. She won the 2022 <u>Exeter Short Story Prize</u>, <u>Fabula Aestas 2023</u>, the fifth <u>Writers Playground challenge,</u> and is a two time winner of <u>AWC's Furious Fiction</u>. She was shortlisted for the <u>2022 Exeter Novel Prize</u> and the <u>2023 Commonwealth Short Story Prize</u>. Her debut novel *Mim and Wiggy's Grand Adventure* will be published in September 2023 with

ABOUT THE AUTHORS

<u>Serenade Publishing</u>.
    Facebook: <u>profile.php?id=100090564052820</u>
    Instagram: <u>@jay_writes_books</u>
    Website: <u>jaymckenzieauthor.com</u>

Sam Muller loves dogs and books and spends much time trying to save one from the other. Her first novel, *I will Paint the Night*, a YA/fantasy murder mystery, was published by <u>Fractured Mirror Publishing</u> in August.
    Book Link: <u>https://www.amazon.com/dp/B0CCPS2CT5</u>

ABOUT THE EDITOR

MJ Pankey is an author, editor, host of the <u>Augusta Writer's Critique Group</u>, and co-host of the <u>Buzzed British Book Club podcast</u> (code name "Kit"). She has been writing fiction since she was 12 and has published several short stories. Her muse is most inspired by ancient mythology and the intricacies of human psychology and behavior, which she fueled by majoring in Psychology at the University of Mississippi and minoring in Classical History for her undergraduate degree. She went on to obtain an MS in Information Technology Management from Western Governor's University, and also has a partial MA in History from the University of Nebraska Kearney.

She lives in Augusta, Georgia with her husband, Eric; three children, Dante, Athena, and Artemis; and furry writing companion, Petey.

Her debut novel, *Epic of Helinthia,* publishes in October. It is the first in a series of three (possibly four) novels. Learn more about her at the following social sites:

Facebook: <u>mjpankeyauthor</u>
Instagram: <u>@authormjpankey</u>
TikTok: <u>@mjpankey</u>
Twitter: <u>@mjpankey1</u>
Websites: <u>mjpankey.com</u> & <u>museandquill.com</u>

ABOUT THE ILLUSTRATOR

Elizabeth Leggett is a Hugo award-winning illustrator whose work focuses on soulful, human moments-in-time that combine ambiguous interpretation and curiosity with realism.

Much to her mother's dismay, she viewed her mother's white washed walls as perfectly good canvasses so she believes it is safe to say that she has been an artist her whole life! Her first published work was in the Halifax County Arts Council poetry and illustration collection. If she remembers correctly, she was not yet in double digits yet, but she might be wrong about that. Her first paying gig was painting other students' tennis shoes in high school.

In 2012, she ended a long fallow period by creating a full seventy-eight card tarot in a single year. From there, she transitioned into freelance illustration. Her clients represent a broad range of outlets, from multiple Hugo award winning Lightspeed Magazine to multiple Lambda Literary winner, Lethe Press. She was honored to be chosen to art direct both Women Destroy Fantasy and Queers Destroy Science Fiction, both under the Lightspeed banner.

Elizabeth, her husband, and their typically atypical cats, live in New Mexico. She suggests if you ever visit the state, look up. The skies are absolutely spectacular!

Website: archwayportico.com

CONTENT WARNINGS

Violence
Death (including child death)
Gaslighting
Snakes
Graphic Sex **(CW)**
Human sacrifice **(CW)**
Child sacrifice **(CW)**
Rape **(CW)**

MORE FROM BRIGIDS GATE PRESS

A Quaint and Curious Volume of Gothic Tales; 23 stories of madness, pain, ghosts, curses, unspoken secrets, greed, murder, and one of the creepiest collections of dolls ever. Ranging from traditional gothic themes to more modern tropes, this anthology is sure to please the reader…and send a cold shiver or two down their spine.

So, come on in; enter the parlor, find a place by the fire, and experience the beautiful, dark, and occasionally heartbreaking stories told by the authors. The editor, Alex Woodroe, has passionately and carefully curated a powerful volume of stories, written by an amazing and diverse group of contemporary women writers.

MORE FROM BRIGIDS GATE PRESS

Sing O Muse, of the rage of Medusa, cursed by gods and feared by men…

From the mists of time, and ages past,
The muses have gathered; hear now their songs.

A web of revenge spun 'neath the moon;
A poet's wife who breaks her bonds;
A warrior woman on a quest of honor;
A painful lesson for a treacherous heart;
A goddess and a mortal, bound together by the travails of motherhood.
And more.

Listen to the muses, as they sing aloud… HER story.

Musings of the Muses is an anthology of 65 stories and poems based on Greek myths. The stories and poems, like the myths themselves, cast long shadows of horror, fantasy, love, betrayal, vengeance, and redemption. This anthology revisits those old tales and presents them anew, from her point of view.

MORE FROM BRIGIDS GATE PRESS

Medusa.
Cursed by the gods.
Slain by Perseus.
A monster.
So the poets sang.

The poets got it wrong.

Daughter of Sarpedon: A Tempered Tales Collection is an anthology of short stories, poems, and drabbles, ranging from retellings to completely new stories, from ancient to modern day.

Featuring the talents of Eva Papasoulioti, Laura G. Kaschak, Linda D. Addison, SJ Townend, Christina Sng, Ann Wuehler, Amanda Steel, Ellie Detzler, Elizabeth Davis, Katherine Silva, Megan Baffoe, Rachel Horak Dempsey, Romy Tara Wenzel, Stephanie M. Wytovich, Die Booth, Rachel Rixen, Federica Santini, Thomas Joyce, L. Minton, Catherine McCarthy, Ai Jiang, Katie Young, Lyndsey Croal, Elyse Russell, Deborah Markus, April Yates, Theresa Derwin, Jason P. Burnham, Claire McNerney, Marisca Pichette, Gordon Linzner,

MORE FROM BRIGIDS GATE PRESS

Patricia Gomes, Stephen Frame, Sharmon Gazaway, Kayla Whittle, Alexis DuBon, Sam Muller, Avra Margariti, Christina Bagni, Kristin Cleaveland, Eric J. Guignard, Marshall J. Moore, Owl Goingback, Renée Meloche, Cindy O'Quinn, Eugene Johnson, Alyson Faye, Jeanne Bush, and Agatha Andrews.